Catalina

'Then I will tell you how you may be cured. The son of Juan Suarez de Valero who has best served God has it in his power to heal you. He will lay his hands upon you in the name of the Father, the Son and the Holy Ghost, bid you throw away your crutch and walk. You will throw down your crutch and you will walk.'

This was not at all what Catalina expected. What the lady said was surprising, but she spoke with such calm assurance that the girl was impressed. At once doubtful and hopeful, she stared at the mysterious stranger. She wanted a moment to collect her wits before she asked the questions that were already forming themselves in her mind. And then Catalina's eyes nearly started out of her head and her mouth dropped open, for where the lady had been there was nothing. She couldn't have gone into the church, for Catalina had had her eyes fixed on her, she couldn't have moved, she had quite simply vanished into thin air. The girl gave a great cry, and more tears, but tears of a different kind, coursed down her cheeks.

'It was the Blessed Virgin,' she cried.

Also by W. Somerset Maugham
available from Mandarin Paperbacks

W. Somerset Maugham

Catalina

Mandarin

A Mandarin Paperback

CATALINA

First published in Great Britain 1948
by William Heinemann Ltd
This edition published 1991
by Mandarin Paperbacks
Michelin House, 81 Fulham Road, London sw3 6rb

Mandarin is an imprint of the Octopus Publishing Group,
a division of Reed International Books Limited

Copyright © by the Royal Literary Fund

A CIP catalogue record for this title
is available from the British Library

ISBN 0 7493 0429 4

Phototypeset by Input Typesetting Ltd, London
Printed and bound in Great Britain
by Cox & Wyman Ltd, Reading, Berks

1

It was a great day for the city of Castel Rodriguez. The inhabitants, wearing their best clothes, were up by dawn. On the balconies of the grim old palaces of the nobles rich draperies were spread and their banners flapped lazily against the flagpoles. It was the Feast of the Assumption, August the fifteenth, and the sun beat down from an unclouded sky. There was a feeling of excitement in the air. For on this day two eminent persons, natives of the city, were arriving after an absence of many years, and great doings had been arranged in their honour. One was Friar Blasco de Valero, Bishop of Segovia, and the other his brother Don Manuel, a captain of renown in the King's armies. there was to be a *Te Deum* in the Collegiate Church, a banquet at the Town Hall, a bull-fight and when night fell fireworks. As the morning wore on more and more people made their way to the Plaza Mayor. Here the procession was formed to go out and meet the distinguished visitors at a certain distance from the city. It was headed by the civil authorities, then came the dignitaries of the Church, and finally a string of gentlemen of rank. The throng lined the streets to watch it pass and then composed themselves to wait until the two brothers, followed by these important personages, should enter the city, when the bells of all the churches would ring out their welcome.

In the Lady Chapel of the church attached to the Convent of the Carmelite nuns a crippled girl was praying. She prayed with passionate devotion before the image of the Blessed Virgin. When at last she rose from her knees she fixed her crutch more comfortably under her arm and hobbled out of the church. It had been cool and dark there, but when she came out into the hot breathless day the sudden glare for a moment blinded her. She stood and looked down at the empty square. The shutters of the houses round it were closed to keep out the heat. It was very silent. Everyone had gone to see the festivities, and there was not even a mongrel dog to bark. You would have thought the city was dead. She glanced at her own home, a small house of two storeys wedged between its neighbours, and sighed despondently. Her mother and her uncle Domingo, who lived with them, had gone with all the rest and would not be back till after the bull-fight. She felt very lonely and very unhappy. She had not the heart to go home, so she sat down at the top of the steps that led from the church door to the plaza and put down her crutch. She began to cry. Then suddenly she was overcome with grief and with an abrupt gesture fell back on the stone platform and burying her face in her arms sobbed as though her heart would break. The movement had given the crutch a push, the steps were narrow and steep, and it clattered down to the bottom of them. That was the last misfortune; now she would have to crawl or slither down to fetch her crutch, for with her right leg paralysed she could not walk without it. She wept disconsolately.

Suddenly she heard a voice.

'Why do you weep, child?'

She looked up, startled, for she had heard no one approach. She saw a woman standing behind her and it looked as though she had just come out of the church, but she had just done that herself and there had been no one there. The woman wore a long blue cloak that came down to her feet, and now she pushed back the hood that had covered her head. It looked as though she had indeed come out of the church, since it was a sin for women to enter the house of God with uncovered heads. She was fairly tall for a Spanish woman and she was young, for there were no lines under her dark eyes, and her skin was smooth and soft. Her hair was very simply done with a parting in the middle and tied in a loose knot on the nape of her neck. She had small delicate features and a kindly look. The girl could not decide whether she was a peasant, wife perhaps of a farmer in the neighbourhood, or a lady. There was in her air a sort of homeliness and at the same time a dignity that was somehow intimidating. The long cloak concealed the garment underneath, but as she withdrew her hood the girl caught a brief glimpse of white and guessed that that must be the colour of her dress.

'Dry your tears, child, and tell me your name.'

'Catalina.'

'Why do you sit here alone and cry when all the world has gone forth to see the reception of the Bishop and his brother the captain?'

'I am a cripple, I cannot walk far, Señora. And what have I to do with all those people who are well and happy?'

The lady stood behind her and Catalina had to turn round to speak to her. She gave a glance at the church door.

'Where have you come from, Señora? I did not see you in the church.'

The lady smiled, and it was a smile of such sweetness that the bitterness seemed to fade from the girl's heart.

'I saw you, child. You were praying.'

'I was praying as I have prayed night and day since my infirmity fell upon me to the Blessed Virgin to free me of it.'

'And do you think she has the power to do that?'

'If so she wills.'

There was something so benign and so friendly in the lady's manner that Catalina felt impelled to tell her sad story. It had happened when they were bringing in the young bulls for the bull-fight on Easter Day and everyone in the town had collected to see them being driven in under the safe conduct of the oxen. Ahead of them on

3

their prancing horses rode a group of young nobles. Suddenly one of the bulls escaped and charged down a side street. There was a panic and the crowd scattered to right and left. One man was tossed and the bull rushed on. Catalina running as fast as her legs would carry her slipped and fell just as the beast was reaching her. She screamed and fainted. When she came to they told her that the bull in his mad charge had trampled over her, but had run wildly on. She was bruised, but not wounded; they said that in a little while she would be none the worse, but in a day or two she complained that she could not move her leg. The doctors examined it and found it was paralyzed; they pricked it with needles, but she could feel nothing; they bled her and purged her and gave her draughts of nauseous medicine, but nothing helped. The leg was like a dead thing.

'But you still have the use of your hands,' said the lady.

'Thanks be to God, for otherwise we should starve. You asked me why I cry. I cry because when I lost the use of my leg I lost the love of my lover.'

'He could not have loved you very much if he abandoned you when you were stricken with an infirmity.'

'He loved me with all his heart and I love him better than my soul. But we are poor people, Señora. He is Diego Martinez, the son of the tailor, and he follows his father's trade. We were to be married when he was finished with his apprenticeship, but a poor man cannot afford to marry a wife who cannot struggle with the other women at the market place or run up and down stairs to do all the things that need to be done in a house. And men are but men. A man does not want a wife on crutches, and now Pedro Alvarez has offered him his daughter Francisca. She is as ugly as sin, but Pedro Alvarez is rich, so how can he refuse?'

Once more Catalina began to cry. The lady looked at her with a compassionate smile. On a sudden in the dis-

4

tance were heard the beating of drums and the blare of trumpets, and then all the bells began to ring.

'They have entered the city, the Bishop and his brother the captain,' said Catalina. 'How is it that you are here when you might be watching them pass, Señora?'

'I did not care to go.'

This seemed so strange to Catalina that she looked at the lady with suspicion.

'You do not live in the city, Señora?'

'No.'

'I thought it strange that I had not seen you before. I thought there was no one here that I did not know at least by sight.'

The lady did not answer. Catalina was puzzled and under her eyelashes looked at her more closely. She could hardly be a Moor, for her complexion was not dark enough, but it was quite possible that she was one of the New Christians, that is to say, one of those Jews who had accepted baptism rather than be expelled from the country, but who, as everyone knew, still in secret practised Jewish rites, washed their hands before and after meals, fasted on Yom Kippur and ate meat on Fridays. The Inquisition was vigilant and, whether they were baptised Moors or New Christians, it was unsafe to have any communications with them; you could never know when they would fall into the hands of the Holy Office and under torture incriminate the innocent. Catalina asked herself anxiously whether she had said anything that could give rise to a charge, for at that time in Spain everyone went in terror of the Inquisition, and a careless word, a pleasantry, might be a sufficient reason for arrest, and then weeks, months, years even might go by before you could prove your innocence. Catalina thought it better to get away as quickly as possible.

'It is time for me to go home, Señora,' she said, and then, with the politeness that was natural to her, added: 'So if you will excuse me I will leave you.'

She cast a glance at the crutch that was lying at the bottom of the steps and wondered if she dared ask the lady to fetch it for her. But the lady paid no attention to her remark.

'Would you like to recover the use of your legs, child, so that you can walk and run as though you had never had anything the matter with you?'

Catalina went white. That question revealed the truth. She was no New Christian, the lady, she was a Moor, for it was well known that the Moors, Christian only in name, were in league with the devil and by magic arts could do evil things of all kinds. It was not so long ago that a pestilence had ravaged the city, and the Moors, accused of having caused it, confessed on the rack that they had done so. They perished at the stake. For a moment Catalina was too frightened to speak.

'Well, child?'

'I would give all I have in the world, and that is nothing, to be free of my infirmity, but even to regain the love of my Diego I would do nothing to imperil my immortal soul, for that is an offence to our Holy Church.'

Still looking at the lady she crossed herself as she spoke.

'Then I will tell you how you may be cured. The son of Juan Suarez de Valero who has best served God has it in his power to heal you. He will lay his hands upon you in the name of the Father, the Son and the Holy Ghost, bid you throw away your crutch and walk. You will throw down your crutch and you will walk.'

This was not at all what Catalina expected. What the lady said was surprising, but she spoke with such calm assurance that the girl was impressed. At once doubtful and hopeful, she stared at the mysterious stranger. She wanted a moment to collect her wits before she asked the questions that were already forming themselves in her mind. And then Catalina's eyes nearly started out of her head and her mouth dropped open, for where the lady had been there was nothing. She couldn't have gone into the church, for Catalina had had her eyes fixed on her, she couldn't have moved, she had quite simply vanished into thin air. The girl gave a great cry, and more tears, but tears of a different kind, coursed down her cheeks.

'It was the Blessed Virgin,' she cried. 'It was the Queen of Heaven, and I talked with her as I might have with my mother. Maria Santissima, and I took her for a Moor or a New Christian!'

She was so excited that she felt she must tell somebody at once, and without thinking she slithered down the stairs on her backside, helping herself with her hands, till she got her crutch. Then she hobbled back to her home. It was not till she got to the door that she remembered there was nobody there. But she let herself in, and discovering she was hungry, got herself a bit of bread and some olives and drank a glass of wine. It made her drowsy, but she sat up determined to keep awake till her mother and her uncle Domingo came back. She couldn't think how she could wait to tell them her wonderful story. Her eyelids drooped and in a little while she was fast asleep.

2

Catalina was a very beautiful girl. She was sixteen, tall for her age, with breasts already well developed, very small hands and feet, and before she was crippled walked with a sinuous grace that charmed all beholders. She had eyes that were large and dark, shining with the glow of youth, black hair naturally curling, and so long that she could sit on it, a brown soft skin, cheeks of a warm rose and a red moist mouth; and when she smiled or laughed, which before her accident she did often, she showed very white even small teeth. Her full name was Maria de los Dolores Catalina Orta y Perez. Her father, Pedro Orta, had sailed for the Americas to make his fortune soon after she was born and since then no news had been heard of him. His wife, Maria Perez by birth, did not know if he was dead or alive, but she still hoped that one day he would return with a coffer full of gold and make them all rich. She was a pious woman and every morning at Mass said a prayer for his safety. She grew angry with her brother Domingo when he said that if Pedro was not long since dead he was living with a native woman, or perhaps two or three, and had no intention of leaving the half-caste family he had undoubtedly produced to come back to a wife who had by now lost her youth and beauty.

Uncle Domingo was a sore trial to his virtuous sister, but she loved him, partly because it was her Christian duty, but also because notwithstanding his grave faults he was lovable and she could not help it. She remembered him too in her prayers, and she liked to think that it was due to their efficacy and not only to the fact that he was getting on in years that he had abandoned at least the worst of his wild ways. Domingo Perez had been destined to the priesthood, and at the seminary of Alcalá de Henares, whither his father sent him, took minor orders and received the tonsure. One of his fellow pupils was Blasco Suarez de Valero, the Bishop of Segovia, whose arrival in the city that day the inhabitants were celebrating. Maria Perez sighed when she thought how different the careers of the two had been. Domingo was a bad boy. He got into trouble at the seminary from the very beginning, for he was headstrong, turbulent and dissipated, and neither admonition, penance nor beating served to tame him. Even then he was fond of the bottle and when he had had too much to drink would sing lewd songs that were an offence to his fellow seminarists and to the masters whose business it was to instill into their young minds decency and decorum. Before he was twenty he had got a Moorish slave with child, and when it appeared that his misbehaviour must be exposed ran away and joined a troupe of strolling players. With them he wandered about

8

the country for two years and then suddenly turned up at his father's house.

He professed repentance for his sins and promised to amend his ways. He was evidently not meant by Providence to enter the priesthood, and he told his father that if he would give him enough money to keep him from starving he would go to a university and study law. His father was eager to believe that his only son had sown his wild oats, and indeed he had come back mere skin and bone, so it did not look as though the life he had led had been an easy one, and he let himself be persuaded. Domingo went to Salamanca and stayed there for eight years, but he pursued his studies in a very desultory fashion. The pittance he received from his father obliged him to live in a boardinghouse with a group of other students and the food was only just sufficient to keep them from dying of hunger. In after years he used to regale his boon companions at the taverns he frequented with stories of the horrors of that establishment and of the cunning shifts they were put to to supplement their meagre fare. But poverty did not prevent Domingo from enjoying life. He had a glib tongue and charm of manner, and he could sing a good song, so that he was welcome at any entertainment. It may be that the two years he had spent with the strolling players had not taught him to be a good actor, but they had taught him other things that now came in useful. They had taught him how to win at cards and dice, and when a young man of fortune came up to the University it did not take him long to scrape acquaintance with him. He constituted himself his guide and tutor in the ways of the town, and it was seldom that the newcomer was not a good deal poorer for the experience he acquired. Domingo at that time was a personable fellow and now and then was lucky enough to excite the passions of women addicted to venery. They were not in their first youth, but in comfortable circumstances, and Domingo thought it only just that they should relieve his necessities in return for the service he rendered them.

The period he had spent as a strolling player had inspired him with the desire to write plays, and every hour he could spare from his amusements he devoted to this occupation. He had considerable facility, and besides writing a number of comedies, would often indite a sonnet to the object of his profitable attentions or write a set of verses in honour of a person of note which he would then present in the hope of receiving in return a present in cash. It was this knack he had for stringing rhymes together that finally led to his undoing. The Rector of the University by some ordinance he had passed had aroused the anger of the students, and when a set of indecent and scurrilous verses at his expense was found on a tavern table it was hailed with delight. In a very short time copies were passed from hand to hand. It was bruited abroad that the author was Domingo Perez, and though he denied it, it was with such complacency that he might just as well have admitted it. Kind friends brought the verses to the attention of the Rector and at the same time told him who had written them. The original copy had disappeared, so that Domingo could not be convicted by his handwriting, but the Rector made discreet inquiries which convinced him that this bad and dissolute student was responsible for the insult. He was too astute to bring a charge that might be hard to prove, but, determined on revenge, took a more subtle course. It was not difficult to discover the scandal Domingo had caused as a seminarist at Alcalá, and the life he had led during the eight years he had spent at the University was notoriously profligate; Domingo was a gambler and it was well known that gambling was a common source of profanity; witnesses came forward who were prepared to swear that they had heard Domingo utter the most horrid blasphemies, and there were two who had heard him say that to believe in the Articles of Faith was first and foremost a matter of good breeding. This in itself was enough to make him a proper subject for inquiry by the Holy Office, and the Rector put the information he had received into the hands of the Inquisitors. The Holy Office never acted in haste. It collected evidence with secrecy and care and until the blow fell the victim seldom knew that he was suspect.

Late one night, when Domingo was in bed and asleep, the alguazil knocked on his door and when he opened it arrested him. He gave him just time to dress and pack his scanty baggage and his bedding roll, and conducted him, not to prison because he was in minor orders and the Inquisition took pains to avoid scandal to the Church, but to a monastery where he was incarcerated in a disciplinary cell. There under lock and key, allowed to see no one, allowed to read nothing, without even a candle to light the darkness, he remained for some weeks. Then he was brought up for trial before the Tribunal. It would have gone hard with him but for one fortunate circumstance. Not long before, the Rector, a vain and irascible man, had quarrelled violently with the Inquisitors over a question of precedence. They read Domingo's verses and laughed with malicious delight. His misdeeds were evident and could not be passed over, but they perceived that by tempering mercy with justice they could put an affront on the indignant Rector that he would resent but would have to bear. Domingo admitted his guilt and professed repentance; he was then sentenced to hear Mass in the audience chamber and to be exiled from Salamanca and the immediate neighbourhood. He had had a fright. He thought it well to absent himself from Spain for a while, so he went soldiering in Italy and spent some years there gambling, cursing when the dice or the cards played him false, fornicating and drinking. He was forty when he returned to his birthplace, as penniless as when he left, with a scar or two which he had got in drunken brawls, but with many recollections to entertain his idle hours.

His father and mother were dead and his only kin were his sister Maria, abandoned by her husband, and his niece Catalina, then a pretty child of nine. Maria's husband had dissipated the dowry she brought him on marriage and she had nothing but the little house in which she lived. She supported herself and her daughter by doing the difficult and skilful needlework in gold and silver thread which decorated the velvet cloaks of the images, images of Jesus Christ, the Blessed Virgin and patron saints, that were carried in the processions of Holy Week, and the copes, chasubles and stoles that were used in the ceremonies of the Church. Domingo had reached an age when he was ready to exchange the adventurous life he had led for twenty years for a settled one, and his sister, wanting the protection of a man in the house, offered him a home. When this story opens he had been living with her for seven years. He was not a financial burden on her since he earned money by writing letters for the illiterate, sermons for priests who were too lazy or too ignorant to write them for themselves, and affidavits for suitors before the law. He was ingenious also at making out the genealogies of persons who wanted declarations of purity of blood, by which was meant that for at least a hundred years their ancestors had not been tainted with Jewish or Moorish blood. The little family would thus have not been so badly off if Domingo had been able to break himself of his bad habits of drinking and gambling. He also spent good money on books, chiefly volumes of verse and plays, for on his return from Italy he had taken once more to writing for the stage, and though he never succeeded in getting anything produced he found adequate satisfaction in reading his compositions to fellow topers in his favourite tavern. Having become respectable he resumed the tonsure, which was a safeguard amid the perils of life in Spain at that time, and dressed in the sober habiliments which became a scholar in minor orders.

He grew very fond of Catalina, so gay, so vivacious and so pretty, and watched her grow into a beautiful girl with a satisfaction in which there was nothing of desire. He took her education upon himself and taught her to read and write. He taught her the Articles of Religion and attended her first communion with all the pride of a father; but for the rest he confined his teaching to reading verse to her, and when she was old enough to appreciate them the plays of the dramatists who were just then getting themselves so much talked about in Spain. Above all he admired Lope de Vega, who he declared was the greatest genius the world had ever seen, and before the accident that crippled her he and Catalina used to play the scenes they most admired. She had a quick memory and in course of time knew long passages by heart. Domingo had not forgotten that he was once an actor and he taught her how to say her lines, when to be temperate and when to tear a passion to tatters. He was by this time a skinny, loose-limbed man, with grey hair and a lined yellow face, but there was still fire in his eyes and resonance in his voice; and when he and Catalina, with Maria their only audience, acted a striking scene, he was no longer a withered, drunken, elderly ne'er-do-well, but a gallant youth, a prince of the blood, a lover, a hero or what you will. But all this ceased when Catalina was trampled by a bull. The shock kept her in bed for some weeks, during which the surgeons of the town did what their poor science suggested to bring life back to her paralyzed limb. At last they admitted that they could do nothing. It was an act of God. Her lover Diego no longer came to the window at night to make love to her through the iron grille, and it was not long before her mother brought home the rumour that he was going to marry the daughter of Pedro Alvarez. Domingo, to divert her, still read plays to her, but the love scenes made her cry so bitterly that he had to stop.

3

Catalina slept for some hours and was awakened at last by the sound of her mother bustling about in the kitchen. She seized her crutch and hobbled in.

'Where is Uncle Domingo?' she asked, for she wanted him to listen to what she so urgently wanted to say.

'Where do you suppose? At the tavern. But if I know him he'll be back for supper.'

As a rule, like everyone else, they had their only hot meal of the day at noon, but they had eaten nothing since morning except a hunk of bread spread with garlic that Maria had taken with her, and she knew Domingo would be hungry; so she lit the fire and set about making the soup. Catalina could not wait a minute longer.

'Mother, the Blessed Virgin has appeared to me.'

'Yes, dear?' Maria answered. 'Clean the carrots for me, will you, and cut them up.'

'But, mother, listen. The Blessed Virgin appeared to me. She spoke to me.'

'Don't be silly, child. I saw you were asleep when I came in and I thought I'd let you sleep on. If you had a nice dream all the better. But now you're awake you can help me to get the supper ready.'

'But I wasn't dreaming. It was before I went to sleep.'

Then she related the extraordinary thing that had happened to her.

Maria Perez had been good-looking in her youth, but now in middle age she had grown stout as do many Spanish women with advancing years. She had known a lot of trouble, two children she had had before Catalina had died, but she had accepted this, as well as her husband's desertion, as a mortification sent to try her, for she was extremely pious; and being a practical woman, not accustomed to cry over spilt milk, had found solace in hard work, the offices of the church, and the care of her daughter and of her wilful brother Domingo. She listened to Catalina's story with dismay. It was so circumstantial, with such precise detail, that she would not have been unwilling to credit it if only it hadn't been incredible. The only possible explanation was that the poor girl's illness and the loss of her lover had turned her brain. She had been praying in the church and then had sat in the hot sun; it was only too probable that something had gone awry in her head and she had imagined the whole thing with such force that she was convinced of its reality.

'The son of Don Juan de Valero who has served God best is the Bishop,' said Catalina when she finished.

'That is certain,' said her mother. 'He is a saint.'

'Uncle Domingo knew him well when they were both young. He can take me to him.'

'Be quiet, child, and let me think.'

The Church did not look with favour on persons who claimed to have had communication with Jesus Christ or His Mother, and discouraged these pretensions with all its authority. Some years before a Franciscan friar had caused a great to-do by healing the sick by supernatural means, and so many people had resorted to him that the Holy Office had been obliged to intervene. He was arrested and never heard of again. And through the gossip of the Carmelite Convent for which she did work now and again Maria Perez knew of a nun who asserted that Elias, the founder of the order, appeared to her in her cell and conferred singular favours upon her. The Lady Prioress had forthwith had her whipped until she confessed that she had invented the story to make herself important. If then friars and nuns suffered for making such claims it was only too likely that the Church would take a serious view of Catalina's story. Maria was frightened.

'Say nothing to anybody,' she told Catalina, 'not even to Uncle Domingo. I will talk to him after supper and he will decide what had better be done. Now in heaven's name clean the carrots or we shall have no soup to eat.'

Catalina was not satisfied with this, but her mother bade her be quiet and do as she was told.

Presently Domingo came in. He was not drunk, but neither was he sober, and he was in high spirits. He was a man who liked to hear himself talk and, while they had supper, for Catalina's benefit he held forth loquaciously on the events of the day. This affords a suitable opportunity to tell the reader how it came about that the city was in a turmoil of excitement.

4

Don Juan Suarez de Valero was an Old Christian, and unlike many of the most noble families in Spain whose sons, before Ferdinand and Isabella united the kingdoms of Castile and Aragon, had married daughters of rich and powerful Jews, he could trace an ancestry unspotted by misalliance. But his ancestry was his only wealth. He owned a few poor acres a mile from the city near a hamlet called Valero, and it was to distinguish themselves from other persons called Suarez rather than to give themselves importance that he and his immediate forebears used the hamlet's name as part of their own. He was very poor, and his marriage with the daughter of a gentleman of Castel Rodriguez brought him little to enlarge his circumstances. Doña Violante bore her lord a child every year for ten years, but of these only three, all sons, survived to adolescence. They were named respectively Blasco, Manuel and Martin.

Blasco, the eldest, from his infancy showed signs of

unusual intelligence and fortunately of piety as well, and so was destined to the priesthood. He was sent at a suitable age to the seminary of Alcalá de Henares and in due course attended the University. He took his degrees of Master of Arts and Doctor of Theology at so early an age that it was evident he could look forward to high distinction in the secular clergy. Promise of high preferment was made him. But on a sudden, saying that he wished to live out of the world so that he might devote himself entirely to study, prayer and meditation, he announced his intention of entering the monastic order of the Dominicans. His friends sought to dissuade him, since the rule was austere, with a midnight office, perpetual abstinence from meat, frequent disciplines, prolonged fasting and silence; but nothing served and Blasco de Valero became a friar. His gifts were too great to be ignored by his superiors, and when it was discovered that besides a fine presence and great learning he had a voice both powerful and melodious, and a fiery eloquence, he was sent here and there to preach; for St. Dominic had been ordered by Pope Innocent III to preach to the heretics and ever since the Dominicans had been noted as missionaries and preachers. On one occasion he was sent to his old University of Alcalá de Henares. He had by then a considerable reputation and the whole city flocked to hear him. His sermon was sensational. He put forth all his resources to convince the vast congregation of the importance of preserving the faith in its purity and of utterly exterminating the heretics. In tones of thunder he commanded the laity, as they valued their souls and dreaded the rigour of the Holy Office, to report whatever came to their notice that might savour of the sin and crime of heresy, and he impressed upon them in menacing words that it was the religious duty of each one of them to inform against his neighbour, the son against his father, the wife against her husband, for no ties of natural affection could absolve a son of the Church from conniving at an evil which was a danger to the State and an offence to God. The result of the sermon was satisfactory. There were numerous delations and in the end three New Christians, convicted of having cut the fat off their meat and changing their linen on the Sabbath, were burnt; a goodly number were sentenced to perpetual imprisonment, with confiscation of their possessions, and many more were scourged or subjected to penalties pecuniary or otherwise.

The friar's forcible eloquence had made so deep an impression on the authorities of the University that he was shortly afterwards appointed Professor of Theology. He protested his unworthiness and wished to be excused from accepting this responsible position, but his superiors in the order commanded him to undertake it and he was obliged to obey. He acquitted himself of his duties with credit, and his lectures were so popular that though he lectured in the largest hall at the disposal of the University, there was not enough room for all who wanted to listen to him. His reputation grew to great heights and after some years, being then seven and thirty years of age, he was made Inquisitor of the Holy Office in Valencia.

Though still sincerely conscious of his unworthiness he accepted the post without demur. Valencia was a seaport where foreign ships, English, Dutch and French, often put in. Their crews were not seldom Protestants and so were proper objects for the Inquisition to deal with. Moreover they frequently attempted to smuggle in prohibited books, such as translations into Spanish of the Bible and the heretical works of Erasmus. Blasco de Valero saw that he could do much useful work there. But besides this, there were great numbers of Moriscos at Valencia and in the surrounding country; they had been forcibly converted to Christianity, but it was common knowledge that with the great majority their conversion was but skin deep, and they adhered to many of their Moorish customs. They would not eat pork, they wore in their homes clothes which they were forbidden to wear, and they refused to eat animals that had died a natural death. The Inquisition, supported by royal authority, had succeeded in stamping out Judaism, and though the New Christians might still be regarded with suspicion it was becoming more and more rare for the Holy Office to find occasion to prosecute them. But the Moriscos were a different matter. They were industrious, and not only was the agriculture of the country in their hands, but all the trading; for the Spaniards were too idle, too proud and too dissipated to engage in menial pursuits. The consequence was that the Moriscos were growing richer and richer, and since they were exceedingly prolific were increasing in numbers. Many thoughtful persons foresaw the time when the whole wealth of the country would be in their hands and they would outnumber the native population. It was natural to fear that then they would seize power and reduce the shiftless Spaniards to servitude. Somehow it was necessary to get rid of them at all costs and several plans were devised to effect this. One was to turn them over to the Holy Office and bring them to trial for their notorious heresies and then burn so many at the stake that the remainder would be harmless. Another, and less troublesome one, was to deport them; but the government had no wish to increase the power of the Moors across the Straits of Gibraltar by adding several hundred thousand hardy and industrious men to their population; and so the ingenious suggestion was made to send them to sea in unseaworthy ships under the pretence of landing them in Africa and then scuttle the ships so that all would be drowned.

No one was more concerned with this problem than Friar Blasco de Valero, and perhaps the most famous sermon he preached during his sojourn in Alcalá de Henares was that in which he proposed that the Moors should be transported *en masse* to Newfoundland, the males young and old having been previously castrated, so that in no long time they would all perish. It may be that it was this sermon which caused him to be given the high and honourable post of Inquisitor at the important city of Valencia.

Friar Blasco undertook his new duties with confidence, fortified by fervent prayer, that there was before him the opportunity to do great work to the honour of the Holy Office and the glory of God. He knew that he would have to contend against vested interests. The Moriscos were vassals of the nobles, to whom they paid tribute in money, kind or service, and it was to their advantage to protect them; but the friar was no respecter of persons and he decided that he would allow no one, however great, to interfere with his duties. Before he had been many weeks in Valencia it was reported to him that a powerful nobleman, Don Hernando de Belmonte, Duke of Terranova, had prevented the officials of the Holy Office from arresting some wealthy vassals who contrary to the law wore Moorish dress and used baths, so he sent his armed familiars to seize the Duke, fined him two thousand ducats and sentenced him to perpetual seclusion in a convent. It was a bold stroke to attack at once one so highly placed, and it terrified the most stout-hearted. When, however, it became evident that the Inquisitor was determined to exterminate the Moriscos the authorities of the city went in a body to remonstrate. They pointed out to him that the prosperity of the province depended upon them and it would be ruined if he continued in his course. But he berated them sharply, threatened them with excommunication, and so forced them to submission and humble apology. He succeeded before long by punishment and confiscation in reducing the Moriscos to misery and destitution. His spies were everywhere and it went ill with any Spaniard, lay or ecclesiastic, who laid himself open to suspicion. Since in his sermons he continued to impress upon the people of Valencia the obligation to denounce anyone who in jest or anger, ignorance or carelessness uttered a thoughtless expression, it was not long before everyone in the city lived in fear.

But the Inquisitor was just a man. He was careful to fit the punishment to the crime. For example, though as a theologian he condemned fornication between the unmarried as a mortal sin, it was only if people declared it was not a mortal sin that it concerned him as an inquisitor, and then he sentenced them to a hundred lashes. On the other hand he punished the assertion, equally heretical, that the married state was as good as celibacy with no more than a fine. He was also a merciful man. It was not the death of the heretic that he desired, but the salvation of his soul. On one occasion an Englishman, master of a ship, was arrested and confessed that he was a member of the reformed faith, whereupon his ship was seized and the cargo confiscated; he was tortured till his strength failed, and then consented to become a Catholic; it was with heartfelt satisfaction that the Inquisitor thus was able to condemn him to no more than ten years in the galleys and perpetual imprisonment. Two or three further instances may be given of his merciful disposition. Ever since the death of a penitent as the result of two hundred lashes, he had insisted on the scourging being limited to one hundred. When torture was to be applied on a pregnant woman he postponed its infliction till after her confinement, and it was his tender heart, rather than regard for the law, that made him take the utmost care that torture should cause neither permanent crippling nor broken bones, and if occasionally an accident happened and someone died as the result of its application no one could have more bitterly regretted it.

Friar Blasco's term of office was highly successful. In the course of ten years he celebrated thirty-seven *Autos de Fé* at which some six hundred persons were penanced and over seventy burnt either alive or in effigy, thus not only rendering a service to God, but also edifying the people. A less humble man than he might have looked upon the last of these celebrations as the crowning glory of his career, for it was held in honour of Prince Philip, the King's son. The various ceremonies were conducted so properly and provided the royal prince with so much entertainment that he sent Friar Blasco a present of two hundred ducats with a letter in which he congratulated him on the improving spectacle and exhorted him to continue thus to serve God to the glory of the Holy Office and the advantage of the State. The zeal and piety of the Inquisitor had evidently made a deep impression on him, for when shortly afterwards Philip the Second died and he ascended the throne he lost no time in appointing Blasco de Valero to the bishopric of Segovia.

He accepted this new dignity only after spending a whole night on his knees wrestling with the Lord, and left Valencia amid the lamentation of great and small. He had won the admiration of the highly placed by his zeal, the austerity of his life and his scrupulous honesty; and he was worshipped by the poor for his charity. He received a handsome salary as inquisitor, and the canonry at Malaga to which he had been appointed was accompanied by a considerable income; but he spent every penny on relieving the necessities of the needy. The confiscations of the wealth of convicted heretics and the fines inflicted on penitents brought large sums into the treasury of the Holy Office, and these moneys served to pay the great expenses of the organization, but it was not unusual for the inquisitors to keep considerable amounts for themselves. Even the saintly Torquemada thus accumulated an immense fortune, which he spent on building the monastery of St. Thomas Aquinas at Avila and enlarging that of Santa Cruz at Segovia. But Blasco de Valero never countenanced this practice and left Valencia as poor as when he arrived.

He never wore anything but the humble habit of his order, he never tasted flesh, nor wore linen or used it on his bed, and regularly disciplined himself, on occasion so severely that blood was splashed on the wall. His reputation for sanctity was such that when his habit became so worn that he was obliged to provide himself with a new one people paid his servants money to be given fragments of that which he had discarded so that they could wear them as a charm against the pox great and small. Before his departure several influential persons made so bold as to try to extract from him a promise that when at length the Almighty called him to Himself they should have the privilege of burying his body in the city where he had laboured so fruitfully. They were assured that they could bring enough influence to bear on Rome to obtain if not his canonization at least his beatification, and to have his bones in the Cathedral would be a glory to the city; but the friar, divining his thoughts, sternly refused to commit himself.

He was escorted for three miles beyond the city gates by a great company of ecclesiastical dignitaries, the magistrates and a number of fine gentlemen, and when they parted from him there was not a dry eye in all that distinguished gathering.

5

It is unnecessary to deal at such length with the other sons of Don Juan de Valero.

The second son, Manuel, was several years younger than his brother and though far from stupid was neither so intelligent nor so industrious. He was more interested in the sports of the field than in the acquisition of learning. He grew into a handsome, stalwart man, with great strength of body and an uncommonly good opinion of himself. He had dash, courage and ambition. He was a great hunter and could ride horses which others found unmanageable. From his earliest youth he had played at bull-fighting with the other lads of the town and when he was old enough never missed a chance to jump into the ring and play the bull. At the age of sixteen he managed to be allowed to fight a bull on horseback, and to the admiration of the public killed it with one thrust of his lance. He had long decided upon a career of arms, for at that time in Spain, if you did not go into the Church, there was no other way to advance yourself. Though poor, Don Juan de Valero was highly respected, and it chanced that one of the nobles of the city was distantly related to the great Duke of Alva; and so one fine day, with a letter of recommendation in his pocket, young Manuel rode off to seek his fortune. He reached the great man at a favourable moment, for, banished from Court, he was then confined to his Castle of Uzeda. He was taken with the gallant bearing of the youth who sought his favour when he was in disgrace, and when shortly afterwards he was recalled by Philip II to assume command in the war with Portugal he took him in his suite. The Duke defeated Don Antonio, the King, and drove him from his kingdom. He seized a great treasure at Lisbon and gave his soldiers permission to sack the city and its suburbs. Manuel acquitted himself bravely in battle, and later, in the looting, picked up a good many valuable objects which he promptly converted into ready money. But Alva was old and near his death, and since the young man was eager to continue his military career he gave him letters to such of his old captains as had served under him in the Low Countries and who were now under the command of Alexander Farnese.

For twenty years Manuel fought with distinction to regain the Northern Provinces for the King of Spain. He proved himself not only courageous but astute, and he was advanced first by Alexander Farnese and then by the generals who on his death replaced him. He was as unscrupulous as he was intrepid, as ruthless as he was able, and as devout as he was brutal, so that in due course he was given important commands. It had not taken him long to discover that when you serve your country you are unlikely to be rewarded for having deserved well of it unless you ask for what you want. This he had no hesitation in doing, and since by the loot he acquired in captured cities, by the extortion he practised on the merchants of the towns he administered, and by the granting of favours in return for hard cash he amassed considerable sums, he was able eventually to substantiate his claims in a manner that made it hard not to acknowledge them. He received the coveted order of Calatrava and proudly wore its green ribbon. Two years later he was created Count of San Costanzo in the Kingdom of Naples with the right to dispose of the title as he chose. It was the thrifty habit of the Spanish Kings so to reward the deserving, and since they could sell their titles to rich commoners who desired thus to ennoble themselves the Crown was able to provide financially for those that had served it well without expense to the treasury. But the Knight of Calatrava had invested his money judiciously and had no need to do this. He had been wounded several times, the last time so severely that only his strong constitution enabled him to survive. His wound gave him a reasonable excuse to leave the King's service, and he determined to go home and marry into a family of the old aristocracy of his native town, which with his rank and fortune he had little doubt he could do, and then go to Madrid where he could use his energy and gifts for intrigue to achieve his inordinate ambition. Who knew but what, if he played his cards well, cultivating the right people, he might in the end rise to great heights? He was at this time forty years old, a fine figure of a man, with bold black eyes, a handsome moustache, an air of insolent virility and an agile tongue.

6

Of the third son, Martin, even less need be said. Every family has its black sheep, and the family of Don Juan de Valero was no exception. Martin, the youngest of the three and the last child that Doña Violante bore her husband, had neither the fiery zeal that had enabled Blasco de Valero to reach eminence in the Church nor the ambition and dexterity that had brought fame and fortune to Don Manuel. He seemed content to devote himself to the cultivation of the few beggarly acres by the produce of which his father and mother kept body and soul together. At that time, owing to the constant wars and the attraction of America for the young and adventurous, there was a shortage of labour in Spain. The Moriscos, who were clever and industrious, had never been numerous in the region, and by then all but a very few had been forced to leave it. Martin was a sad disappointment to Don Juan, and though his wife urged that there was a certain advantage in having a son who was strong, active and willing to put his hand to any sort of work, he continued to chafe.

But a greater blow was in store for him. At twenty-three Martin married, and married beneath him. True, his bride was an Old Christian, the testimony was convincing that for four generations there had been no intermarriage with persons of Jewish or Moorish blood, but her father was a baker. Consuelo was his only child and would inherit whatever he had, but the fact remained that he was a tradesman. Some years passed, and Consuelo had children, and then still another blow befell Don Juan; the baker died; Don Juan heaved a sigh of relief, for now the bakery could be sold and the stigma of this connection with a menial occupation might be lived down. But no sooner was the baker decently buried than Martin informed his parents that he proposed to move into the city and run the shop himself. They could hardly believe their ears. Don Juan stormed, Doña Violante wept. Their son pointed out to them that if they had lived somewhat less meagerly than before it was owing to the dowry Consuelo had brought him; this was now spent; he had four children and there was no reason why he should not have four more; cash was scarce in Spain and he could not expect to get more for the business than would support them all for a few years, and then they would have nothing to look forward to but starvation. He put forward the ridiculous argument that there was nothing more disgraceful in baking bread than in ploughing a barren field or pressing olives.

Martin installed his family over the shop. He got up long before dawn to bake the bread and then rode out to the farm and worked there till dusk. He prospered, for his bread was good, and in a year or two was able to hire a man to take his place on the farm, but he never let a day pass without going to see his parents. He seldom came without bringing them something, and soon they were able to eat meat every day that the Church allowed it. They were getting on in years, and Don Juan could not deny that the presents his son brought were a comfort to his old age. Though there had been some surprise in the city when the son of Don Juan de Valero thus demeaned himself and the boys in the streets called after him mockingly *Panadero, Panadero,* which means Baker, Baker, his good nature and his unconsciousness that he had done anything odd presently disarmed everyone. He was charitable, and no poor person ever came to his door asking for alms without being sent away with a loaf of new bread. He was pious, went to Mass every Sunday, and confessed regularly four times a year. He was now a hale and hearty man, thirty-four years of age, somewhat corpulent, for he liked good food and good wine, with an open red face and a cheerful, happy look.

'He's a good fellow,' people said of him, 'not very intelligent and not very cultured, but kind and honest.'

He was pleasant of approach, fond of a joke, and in course of time, when he was able to take things more easily, men of respectability often came to his shop for a chat, and indeed it became a sort of meeting-place where one could see one's friends and have a talk.

It was fortunate that he had taken upon himself the charge of his parents, since Friar Blasco had never in the twenty years he had been away sent any money to help them, for everything he had went in charity, while Don Manuel never sent them anything since it never occurred to him that anyone could make better use of his money than he could himself. They were thus in their old age entirely dependent on Martin. They were still ashamed of him and could not but regret that he had made such a miserable business of life. It was a constant irritation that he seemed quite content with it. They treated his plebeian wife with the stately courtesy which they felt their own self-respect demanded of them, and grew fond of their grandchildren. But their fondest thoughts went to the two sons who had brought honour and glory to their ancient name.

7

It is not hard to imagine with what joy Don Juan and Doña Violante looked forward to seeing them after a separation of so many years. The friar had written at rare intervals, and since neither Don Juan nor his son the baker was handy with his pen, or would in any case have trusted himself to write with the elegance due to a learned ecclesiastic, they had got Domingo Perez to answer his letters. This he had done with complete satisfaction both to them and to himself, for he took pride in the elegance of his style. Don Manuel, on the other hand, had never communicated with them except when he was intriguing to get the order of Calatrava and was obliged to offer proof of his unsullied ancestry. Here again the good offices of Domingo were requisitioned and he prepared a genealogy, duly sworn to by the magistrates of the city, in which he traced the origins of the family, without a single admixture of Jewish blood, to Alphonso VIII, King of Castile, who married Eleanora, daughter of King Henry II of England.

The occasion of the coming of Don Juan's two sons was not only the return of Don Manuel, after his long service in the wars, and the elevation of Friar Blasco to the episcopacy, but also the celebrations of their parents' golden wedding. The two brothers arranged to meet at a town some twenty miles from the city and make their solemn entry together. It was pleasing to Don Juan to think that the grandeur of the reception arranged for them would in some measure counterbalance the long disgrace of poor Martin's degradation. It was of course impossible for him to house his two sons and their suite in his tumble-down grange, and it was arranged that the Bishop should be lodged in the Dominican convent, while the steward of the Duke of Castel Rodriguez, his master being absent in Madrid, offered Don Manuel an apartment in the ducal palace.

The great day arrived. The noblemen of the city rode forth on their horses, the magistrates and the clergy on mules; Don Juan and Doña Violante with Martin and his family followed in a carriage lent them by a person of rank; and presently the anxiously-expected visitors were seen making their way along the dusty, winding road. The Bishop in his Dominican habit, on a mule, rode side by side with his brother on a charger. Don Manuel wore a magnificent suit of armour inlaid with gold. After them came the Bishop's two secretaries, members of his own

29

order, and his servants, and then the captain's in sumptuous livery. Having greeted the important personages who had come to meet them and listened to some eloquent speeches, the Bishop asked for his father and mother. They had been hanging back modestly, but now came forward. Doña Violante was about to kneel and kiss the episcopal ring, but the Bishop, to the admiration of the onlookers, prevented her and taking her in his arms kissed her on both cheeks. She began to weep and many of those present were so affected that tears coursed down their cheeks. He kissed his father and then, while the two old people turned to their second son, he asked for Martin.

'*El panadero*,' someone called. 'The baker.'

Martin made his way through the crowd with his wife and children. They were all in their best clothes, and the jolly, red-faced, corpulent man looked well enough. The Bishop greeted him affectionately, Don Manuel with a certain condescension, and Consuelo and the children knelt on the ground and kissed the Bishop's ring. He graciously congratulated his brother on the number and healthy appearance of his offspring. In their letters to him Don Juan and Doña Violante had told him of their youngest son's marriage and of the children as they were born, but had never dared to inform him that he had become a tradesman. They watched the meeting with apprehension. They knew the truth would have to come out soon, but were anxious that nothing should happen to mar the joyful occasion. After much disputing it had been arranged who should ride on the right of the two distinguished sons of the city and who on the left, and though a good deal of ill feeling remained, the procession was formed and the cavalcade made an imposing entry into the city. As they passed through the gate the church bells were set ringing, crackers were exploded, trumpeters blew their trumpets and drummers beat their drums. The streets were crowded and there was a great shouting and a clapping of hands as they passed through on their way to the Collegiate Church where a *Te Deum* was to be sung.

The service was followed by a banquet, and the Bishop's hosts noticed that though it was a Feast Day he neither ate meat nor drank wine. When it was over he intimated his desire to be for a short time alone with his immediate family, so Martin went to fetch his mother, who had gone with his wife and the children to the baker's home. When he returned he found his brother Blasco alone with his father, but he had only just got into the room with Doña Violante when Don Manuel strode in. His brows were knit, his eyes black with anger.

'Brother,' he said, addressing the Bishop, 'do you know that this Martin, son of a gentleman of ancient lineage, is a pastry-cook?'

Don Juan and his wife started, but the Bishop merely smiled.

'Not a pastry-cook, brother. A baker.'

'Do you mean to say that you knew?'

'I have known it for years. Though my sacred duties prevented me from taking the care of my parents that I wished, I have watched over them from afar and have constantly remembered them in my prayers. The prior of our order in this city has kept me informed of their condition.'

'Then how could you let him bring such shame upon our family?'

'Our brother Martin is a virtuous and a pious man. He is a respected citizen and charitable to the poor. He has taken good care of our parents in their old age. I cannot blame him for taking a step which was forced upon him by circumstances.'

'I am a soldier, brother, and I put my honour before my life. This has ruined my plans.'

'I very much doubt it.'

'How do you know?' blustered Don Manuel. 'You do not know what my plans are.'

31

The shadow of a smile lightened for an instant the Bishop's austere features.

'You cannot be very worldly-wise, brother,' he replied, 'if you are unaware that there is little of our personal affairs that remains hidden from our servants. You forget that we spent two days under the same roof on our way hither. It has reached my ears that you did not come here only to fulfil a filial duty, but also to choose a wife from among the nobility of the city. Notwithstanding the avocation which our brother has chosen to follow, with the title which His Majesty has been pleased to grant you and the money you have won in his service I think you will have no difficulty in achieving your object.'

Meanwhile Martin had listened without any sign that he was in the least ashamed. There was something very like a grin on his good-looking face.

'Do not forget, Manuel,' he said now, 'that Domingo Perez has traced our descent from a King of Castile and a King of England. That should assuredly carry weight with the family whom you are proposing to honour by taking their daughter to your wife. Domingo told me that one of the Kings of England made cakes, so perhaps there is no great disgrace in a descendant of kings making bread, especially as it is by common consent the best bread in the city.'

'Who is this Domingo Perez?' the soldier asked sulkily.

That was not a very easy question to answer, but Martin did his best.

'A man of learning and a poet.'

'I remember him,' said the Bishop. 'We were at the seminary together.'

Don Manuel tossed his head impatiently and turned to his father.

'Why did you allow him thus to disgrace us?'

'I did not approve of it. I did everything in my power to prevent it.'

Don Manuel now turned sternly on his younger brother.

'And you dared to go counter to your father's wishes? They should have been a command to you. Give me one reason, only one, why, flinging decency to the winds, you demeaned yourself by becoming a baker.'

'Hunger.'

The world seemed to crash to the floor like a pile of masonry. Don Manuel smothered an exclamation of angry disgust. Once more a faint smile trembled on the Bishop's lips. Even saints retain some small measure of humanity, and during the two days they had spent together the Bishop had come to the conclusion that he had little love for his military brother. He blamed himself for it, but all his Christian charity was insufficient to overcome his feeling that Don Manuel was a coarse, brutal and domineering fellow.

Fortunately this family reunion was interrupted by persons who came in to tell them it was time to go to the bull-fight. The two brothers were placed in seats of honour. The municipality had spent enough money to get good bulls and the fight was worthy of the occasion. When it was over the Bishop with his attending friars retired to the Dominican convent and Don Manuel to the quarters that had been prepared for him. The people of the city wandered back to their homes, or to the taverns, to talk about the exciting day, and Domingo Perez eventually found his way back to his sister's house.

8

After supper, as was his habit, Domingo went upstairs to his room. In a little while Maria followed him. From the floor below she could hear him reading in loud and dramatic tones, and when she knocked at the door he did not answer. She went in. It was a small bare chamber containing nothing but a bed, a chest for his clothes, a table and a chair. There was a shelf filled with books, and books were lying on the table, on the floor, on the chest. The bed was unmade and on it he had flung his cassock. He was in shirt and breeches. The table was littered with papers and there was a great pile of manuscripts in one corner of the room. Maria sighed when she saw the untidiness which she had never been able to cope with. He took no notice of her entrance, but went on declaiming the speeches of a play.

'Domingo, I want to speak to you,' she said.

'Don't interrupt, woman. Listen to the glorious verses of the greatest genius of our day.'

He ranted on. Maria stamped her foot.

'Put down that book, Domingo. I have something very important to say to you.'

'Go away. What can you have to say to me that is more important than the divine inspiration of the phœnix of the age, the incomparable Lope de Vega?'

'I will not go till you listen to me.'

Domingo threw down his book in vexation.

'Then say what you have to say, say it quickly and begone.'

She told him then Catalina's story, how the Blessed Virgin had appeared to her and told her that the Bishop, Don Juan's son, had the power to cure her of her infirmity.

'It was a dream, my poor Maria,' he said when she had finished.

'That is what I told her. She declared that she was wide awake. I cannot persuade her otherwise.'

Domingo was disturbed.

'I will come downstairs with you and she shall tell me the story herself.'

For the second time Catalina narrated the incident. Domingo had but to look at her to be certain that she firmly believed every word she said.

'What makes you so sure you were not asleep, child?'

'How could I have fallen asleep at that hour of the morning? I had only just come out of the church. I cried, and when I came home my handkerchief was wet with my tears; could I have dried my eyes in my sleep? I heard the bells ringing when the Bishop and Don Manuel entered the city. I heard the trumpets and the drums and the shouts of the people.'

'Satan has many wiles to beguile the unwary. Even Mother Teresa de Jesus, the nun who founded all those covents, was for long afraid that the visions she had were the work of the devil.'

'Could a demon assume the mildness and the loving kindness of Our Lady when she spoke to me?'

'The devil is a good actor,' smiled Domingo. 'When Lope de Rueda got impatient with the members of his troupe he would say that if he could only get the devil to play for him he would willingly give him in payment the souls of all his company. But listen, dear heart, we know that certain pious persons have received the grace of seeing with their own eyes the persons of Our Blessed Lord and His Virgin Mother, but they have received this grace as the reward of prayer, fasting, mortification and a life devoted to the service of God. What have you done to deserve a favour that others are accorded only as the result of long years of self-immolation?'

'Nothing,' said Catalina. 'But I am poor and unhappy, I prayed the Blessed Virgin to succour me, and she took pity on me.'

Domingo was silent for a while. Catalina was determined and self-willed, and he was afraid. She had no notion of the risks she was incurring.

'Our Holy Church does not regard with indulgence individuals who claim to have communications with heaven. The country is infested with persons who declare that they have been granted supernatural privileges. Some are poor deluded creatures who honestly believe what they say; many are impostors who make these pretensions either to gain notoriety or to make money. The Holy Office rightly concerns itself with them, for they cause disturbance among the ignorant and often lead them into heresy. Some the Holy Office imprisons, some it scourges, some it sends to the galleys and others to the stake. I beseech you as you love us not to divulge a word of what you have told us.'

'But, uncle, dear uncle, all my happiness is at stake. Everyone knows that there is no more saintly man in the kingdom than the Bishop. It is common knowledge that even pieces of his habit have a miraculous power. How can I remain silent when the Blessed Mother of God herself told me that he can cure me of the infirmity that has robbed me of the love of my Diego?'

'It is not only you that are concerned. If the Holy Office takes it upon itself to make an inquiry, it may well be that the case against me will be re-opened, for the Holy Office has a long memory, and if we are put into the prison of the Inquisition this house will be sold to pay for the cost of our maintenance and your mother will be thrown into the street to beg her bread. Promise me at least that you will say nothing till we have had time to reflect.'

There was so great a dismay, so deep an anxiety, in Domingo's expression that Catalina yielded.

'Yes, I will promise you that.'

'You are a good girl. Now let your mother put you to bed, for we are all weary after the events of the day.'

He kissed her and left the two women to themselves, but from the stairs he called his sister. She went out.

'Give her a purge,' he whispered. 'If she has a good movement of the bowels she will be more reasonable, and we can persuade her tomorrow that the whole thing was no more than a very unfortunate dream.'

9

But the purge had no effect – at least not the desired one. Catalina continued to assert that she had seen the Blessèd Virgin with her own eyes and had spoken with her. She described her attire with such accuracy that Maria Perez was filled with amazement. Now it happened that the next day was a Friday and Maria went to confession. She had had the same confessor, Father Vergara, for many years and had confidence both in his benevolence and his wisdom. So after she had received absolution she told him Catalina's strange story and much of what Domingo had said.

'Your brother has behaved with a discretion and good sense the more admirable because these qualities could hardly be expected in him. This is a matter that must be treated with caution. We must do nothing in haste. There must be no scandal and you must order your daughter not to speak to anyone of this thing. I will reflect upon it and if needful consult my superior.'

Maria's confessor was also her daughter's, and he knew them both as only a confessor can know his penitents. He knew that they were simple, honest, guileless and God-fearing. Even Domingo had not been able to corrupt their innocence or impair their candour. Catalina was a sensible girl, with a good head on her shoulders, and if she had not borne her injury with resignation, she had certainly borne it with courage. She was too ingenuous to invent such a story for any ulterior motive and, he was convinced, of too material a temper to imagine a spiritual event. Father Vergara was a Dominican and it was in his convent that the Bishop and his suite were lodging. He was a simple man of no great learning and Maria's story of her daughter's adventure troubled him so much that he felt bound to report it to his prior. The prior after some thought came to the conclusion that the Bishop should be informed of it, so he sent a novice to ask if it would be convenient for him to see him and Father Vergara on a matter that might be of importance. In a little while the novice came back to say that the Bishop would be pleased to receive them.

He had been given the most commodious cell in the convent. It was separated by a double archway with a supporting column into two parts, one of which served as a sleeping apartment and the other as an oratory. When the prior and Father Vergara entered they found the Bishop dictating letters to one of his secretaries. The prior explained on what errand they had come and then left Father Vergara to repeat exactly what his penitent had told him. The friar started by telling the Bishop how good and pious the two women were, how blameless their lives, then went on to describe the accident that had caused the unfortunate Catalina to lose the use of her leg and the attentions of her lover, and finished by repeating the story of how the Blessed Virgin had appeared to her and told her that the Bishop could cure her of her infirmity. As an afterthought he added that Domingo Perez, her uncle, had exacted a promise from her to keep the episode a secret until the matter had been well considered. By the time he had come to an end the Bishop's face had assumed an expression of such severity that the friar, his voice faltering, sweated at every pore. Silence fell.

'I know this Domingo,' said the Bishop at length. 'He is a man of evil life and one with whom no one who values his salvation should associate. But he is not a fool. When he exacted a promise of secrecy from his niece he acted with prudence. You are the child's confessor, Father?' The friar bowed. 'You would be well advised to refuse to give her absolution until she promises that she will not speak of this affair to anybody.'

The poor friar stared at the Bishop in confusion. Was he not by common consent a saint? Father Vergara thought he would have welcomed the opportunity to exercise his miraculous powers and thereby not only glorify God, but bring many sinners to repentance. The Bishop's eyes were cold. You might have thought that he was controlling his anger only by an effort of will.

'And now if you will permit me I will go on with my work,' he said, and then turning to the secretary: 'Read over the last sentence I dictated.'

The two friars sidled away without another word.

'Why is he vexed?' asked Father Vergara.

'We ought not to have spoken to him about it. I am to blame. We have offended his humility. He does not know how great a saint he is and does not look upon himself as worthy to perform a miracle.'

This seemed a very reasonable explanation and since it only redounded to the Bishop's credit Father Vergara made haste to tell his brother friars all about it. Soon the convent was buzzing with excitement. Some praised the Bishop's modesty, others regretted that he had not taken occasion to do something that would so greatly add to his renown and to the credit of the order.

Meanwhile, however, the story reached another quarter. The church in which Catalina had prayed and from which, if she was to be believed, the Blessed Virgin had come was attached, as has been mentioned, to the Carmelite Convent of the Incarnation. The convent was richly endowed and for a good many years the Lady Prioress had been in the habit of giving Maria Perez work to do, partly from charity and partly because she was very skilful in the difficult and laborious handicraft she exercised. Maria had thus come to be on friendly terms with many of the nuns. Since it was a convent of the mitigated order they enjoyed a good deal of freedom and it was not seldom that one of them came to her house for a meal and a talk. Two or three days after Maria's confession she had occasion to go to the convent and after doing her errand began to chat with the nun who was her most intimate friend. Swearing her to secrecy she told her of her daughter's strange experience. The nuns were great gossips and such a story was bound to be an event in the pious but monotonous routine of their lives, so that within twenty-four hours every inmate of the convent heard it and eventually it reached the ears of the Lady Prioress. Since this lady plays a not unimportant role in this narrative it is necessary here, even at the risk of boring the reader, to tell her history.

10

Beatriz Henriquez y Braganza, in religion Beatriz de San Domingo, was the only daughter of the Duke of Castel Rodriguez, a grandee of Spain and a Knight of the Golden Fleece. He had great wealth and great power. He managed to retain the confidence of the morose and distrustful Philip II and filled with distinction important positions in Spain and Italy. He had vast estates in both countries, and though his duties forced him to sojourn here and there he loved nothing better than to dwell with his wife and children, for he had three sons and a daughter, in his native city with its salubrious air and noble prospects. It was from there his race had sprung, and it was through the successful repulse by one of his ancestors of the Moors who were besieging the city that his family had first become eminent. There none was greater than the Duke of Castel Rodriguez and he lived in a state that was almost royal. Throughout its history the members of his family had made great alliances, so that he was related to all the grandest nobles in Spain. When Beatriz, his daughter, was thirteen he looked round to find a suitable mate for her and after reviewing various possible candidates settled on the only son of the Duke of Antequera who was descended, on the wrong side of the blanket, from Ferdinand of Aragon. The Duke of Castel Rodriguez was prepared to give his daughter a magnificent dowry and so the matter was arranged without difficulty. The young people were betrothed, but since the boy was only fifteen it was decided that the marriage should not take place till he had reached a suitable age. Beatriz was allowed to see her future husband in the presence of the parents on both sides, their uncles and aunts and other more distant relatives. He was a squat little boy, no taller than herself, with a mass of coarse black hair, a snub nose and a sulky mouth. She took an instant dislike to him, but she knew it was useless to protest and so contented herself with making faces at him. He responded by putting out his tongue at her.

After the betrothal the Duke sent her to finish her education at the Carmelite Convent of the Incarnation at Avila where his sister was prioress. She enjoyed herself. There were other girls, daughters of noblemen, in the same situation as herself, and a number of ladies who for one reason or another boarded in the convent, but were not subject to its discipline. The mitigated rule of the Carmelites was not strict and though some of the nuns devoted themselves to prayer and contemplation, many of them, while not neglecting their duties, went out and about to see their friends and sometimes stayed away for weeks at a time. The parlour was always filled with callers, male and female, so that there was a cheerful social life; matches were made, the state of the wars discussed, the gossip of the city exchanged. It was a peaceful, harmless existence, with modest diversions, and to the nuns a not too strenuous way to attain eternal happiness.

At the age of sixteen Beatriz was taken away from the convent and went down with her mother, and a host of attendants, to Castel Rodriguez. The Duchess was in poor health and had been ordered by the doctors to live in a climate less severe than that of Madrid. The Duke, occupied with affairs of state, unwillingly remained behind. The time was approaching when the marriage of Beatriz might take place, and her parents thought it well that she should learn something of the conduct of a great establishment. So for some months the Duchess devoted herself to teaching her daughter the social observations which she could not be expected to have learnt in the convent of the Carmelite nuns. Beatriz had grown to be a tall girl of great beauty, with a clear skin unblemished by smallpox, features of classical regularity and a lithe, slender figure. The Spaniards admired a greater opulence of form than she then possessed and some of the ladies who came to pay court to the Duchess lamented her thinness, but the proud mother promised them that marriage would soon remedy that defect.

Beatriz at that age was gay, passionately fond of dancing and aglow with animal spirits. She was mischievous and wilful. She was even then of an imperious temper, for she had been spoilt and had very much her own way all her life, and from her earliest years had realized that she was born to great station and that the rest of the world must submit to her caprice. Her confessor, not a little disturbed at this desire for domination, spoke to her mother of it, but the Duchess was somewhat cool toward his admonition.

'My daughter was born to rule, Father,' said she. 'You cannot expect from her the servility of a laundress. If there is an excess of pride in her disposition her husband, if he has character, will doubtless modify it, and if he has not, then her sense of what is due to her will be of assistance to him.'

At the convent Beatriz had taken a great fancy to the novels of chivalry which some of the lady boarders were fond of, and though not permitted to read them by the nun who had charge of the pupils she managed now and then to snatch a glance at one or other of those interminable romances. On coming to Castel Rodriguez she found several in the palace and, with her mother often indisposed, her duenna complacent, she devoured them with avidity. Her young imagination was inflamed and she looked forward with distaste to her inevitable marriage with the boy whom she still saw as a scrubby, black-browed and uncouth urchin. She was well aware of her beauty and at High Mass with her mother missed none of the admiring glances that the young blades of the city cast on her. They would gather on the steps of the church to see her come out, and though she walked with eyes modestly cast down, the Duchess by her side, followed by two footmen in livery carrying the velvet pillows on which they had knelt, she was conscious of the excitement she caused and her ears caught the praises that the young men in the Spanish manner uttered as she passed. Though she never looked at them she knew them all by sight and it was not long before she found out their names, what families they belonged to, and in fact all there was to know about them. Once or twice the more venturesome serenaded her, but the Duchess immediately sent out her servants to drive them away. Once she found a letter on her pillow. She guessed that one of her maids had been bribed to place it there. She opened it and read it twice. Then she tore it into little pieces and burnt it in the flame of her candles. It was the first and only love letter she ever had in her life. It was unsigned and she could not tell from whom it came.

Owing to her bad health the Duchess thought it enough to go to Mass on Sundays and on feast days, but Beatriz went every morning with her duenna. It was very early and not many people attended, but there was a young seminarist who never failed. He was tall and thin, with decided features and dark passionate eyes. Sometimes, going on an errand of mercy with the duenna, she passed him in the street.

'Who is that?' asked Beatriz one day when she saw him slowly walking towards them reading a book.

'That? Nobody. The eldest son of Juan Suarez de Valero. *Hidalguía de Gutierra*.'

That may be translated as gutter nobility, and was the scornful term applied to gentlemen by birth who had not the means to live according to their station. The duenna, a widow and vaguely related to the Duke, was proud, devout, censorious and penniless. She had lived at Castel Rodriguez all her life till, when Beatriz left the convent, the Duke had chosen her to attend his daughter. She knew all about everyone in the city, and though so pious was not above a tendency to speak evil of her neighbours.

'What is he doing here at this time of year?' Beatriz inquired.

The duenna shrugged her thin shoulders.

'He fell ill at the seminary from overwork and his life was despaired of, so he was sent home to regain his health, which through the mercy of God he has done. He is said to be very talented. I presume that his parents hope that through the influence of the Duke your father he will obtain a benefice.'

Beatriz said no more.

Then for no reason that the doctors could discover she lost her appetite and her high spirits. She lost her fresh colour and grew pale. She was listless and would often be found bathed in tears. She, whose gaiety, charming wilfulness and irresponsibility had given life to that grim, magnificent palace, now was mopish and dejected. The Duchess was at her wits' end, and fearing that the child was going into a decline wrote to her husband to ask him to visit them so that they might consider what was best to do. He came and was shocked at the change in his daughter. She had grown thinner than ever and there were dark smudges under her eyes. They came to the conclusion that the best thing to do was to get her married at once, but when that was proposed to Beatriz she was seized with shrieking hysterics so that they were more alarmed than ever and for the time dropped the subject.

They dosed her with medicine, fed her with asses' milk and ox-blood, but though she obediently swallowed everything they gave her nothing served. She remained wan and despondent. They did what they could to distract her. They hired musicians to play for her; they took her to a religious play in the Collegiate Church; they took her to bull-fights; she continued to fail. The duenna had become greatly attached to her charge, and since Beatriz no longer cared to read the romances which had been her greatest entertainment, she knew no other way to amuse the sick girl than by telling her the gossip of the city. Beatriz listened politely, but without interest. On one occasion she happened to mention that the eldest son of Juan Suarez de Valero had entered the Dominican order. She went on chatting away about one person and another till suddenly Beatriz fainted. She called for help and Beatriz was put to bed.

A day or two later, when she was better, she asked permission to go to confession. She had for several weeks refused to go, saying she did not feel well enough, and the Duchess's confessor, who was also hers, had agreed that it was better not to insist. Now, however, both her parents tried to dissuade her, but she was so urgent, she cried so bitterly, that at length they yielded; so the great carriage, used only on state occasions, was brought out, and accompanied by the duenna she went to the Dominican church. When she returned she looked more like her old self than she had looked for many weeks. There was a faint flush on her pale cheeks and her fine eyes shone with a new light. She knelt at her father's feet and asked his permission to enter religion. This was a great shock to him, not only because he did not want to lose his only daughter to the Church, but because he was unwilling to forgo the important alliance which he had planned; he was, however, a kind and a devout man, and he answered without harshness that it was a manner not to be undertaken lightly, and in any case out of the question while she was in such poor health. She told him then that she had spoken of it with her confessor and that the scheme had his full approval.

'Father Garcia is no doubt a very worthy and a very pious person,' said the Duke, with something of a frown, 'but his profession has perhaps prevented him from knowing how great are the responsibilities attached to noble birth and high rank. I will talk to him tomorrow.'

So next day the friar was summoned to the ducal palace and ushered into the presence of the Duke and Duchess. They knew of course that he would not reveal anything that Beatriz had said to him in the confessional, and they did not attempt to find out whether she had given him any reason for taking a step which was so unwelcome to them; but they told him that though she had always followed the observances of the Church she had been light-hearted, fond of every kind of amusement and had never shown any inclination to the life of a religious. They told him of the great marriage that had been arranged for her and the inconvenience it would be, the ill feeling it might cause, if it were broken off; and finally, with all due respect to his habit, they suggested that it was unwise of him to approve of her wish when it was so obviously due to her mysterious illness. She was young and her constitution was sound; there was no reason to suppose that when she regained her health she would be of the same mind. They found the Dominican strangely obstinate. he thought that Beatriz's desire was too strong to be opposed, and that her vocation was real; he went so far as to tell these great personages that they had no right to prevent their daughter from taking a step that would bring her peace in this world and happiness in the next. This was the first of many discussions. Beatriz remained firm in her determination and her confessor supported her desire with every persuasive argument at his command. At last the Duke agreed that if at the end of three months she still wished to enter a convent he would give his consent.

From then on she grew better. Three months passed, and she joined the community of the Carmelites of Avila as a novice. Arrayed in all her finery of satin and velvet, wearing her jewels, she was accompanied to the convent by her family and a number of the noblest cavaliers of the city. At the door she bade them all a gay farewell and was admitted by the portress.

But the Duke had made plans of his own to deal with the situation. He decided for his own honour and to the glory of God to found a convent at Castel Rodriguez to which his daughter could come as soon as she had finished her novitiate and where in due course she would be prioress. He owned property in the city and he chose a site just within the wall which was suitable to his purpose. There he built a handsome church, a cloister, and suitable edifices for conventual life, and laid out a garden. He employed the best architect he could find, the best sculptors, the best painters, and when everything was ready Beatriz, now known as Doña Beatriz de Santo Domingo, came to stay at the palace, with several nuns from Avila who had been chosen for their virtue, intelligence and social consequence. The Duke had decided that no nun should be eligible unless she were of noble birth. A prioress was chosen with the understanding that as soon as Beatriz de Santo Domingo was of a suitable age to take her place she should retire. The duenna, on the Duke's somewhat urgent persuasion, had entered a convent at Castel Rodriguez at the same time as Beatriz had gone to Avila, and was now ready to join her old charge. Mass was said by Father Garcia, the Blessed Sacrament was enthroned, and the nuns took up their abode in the new foundation.

At the time with which this narrative is concerned Doña Beatriz de San Domingo had been prioress for many years. She had won the respect of the citizens of Castel

Rodriguez and the admiration, if not the love, of her nuns. She never forgot her great rank, but neither did she forget that her daughters were of noble birth. In the refectory they sat in their proper order of precedence, but when, as sometimes happened, there were disputes on this point Doña Beatriz dealt with them firmly. She was a strict disciplinarian and however well born a nun might be she did not hesitate to have her whipped if her orders were disobeyed. But so long as her authority was unquestioned she was affable and even indulgent. The convent was under the mitigated rule of Pope Eugenius IV, and provided that the nuns performed their religious duties she saw no reason to deprive them of the privileges they had been thus accorded. They were allowed to visit their friends in the city, and indeed, if the reason were good, to go and stay with their relations in other places for quite long periods. Many visitors, both lay and clerical, came to the convent; several ladies, as at Avila, lived there for their pleasure; so that there was a good deal of agreeable intercourse. Silence was only obligatory from Compline until Prime. Lay sisters did the menial work in order to give the nuns more time for their devotions and for occupations of more honour. But with all this liberty and with these temptations to worldliness no breath of scandal had ever tarnished the good name of these virtuous women. The reputation of the community was so great that there were more applicants for admission than the prioress could do with, so that she was able to be very particular in her examination of candidates.

She was a busy woman. Besides her religious duties she had to supervise the economy of the convent and keep an eye on the behaviour of the nuns, and on their health, bodily and spiritual; the foundation had been richly endowed both with houses in the city and with lands, and she had to deal with the factors who collected the rents and with the farmers who farmed the lands. She visited them frequently to see that everything was well and that the crops were in good condition. Since the rule allowed her to own private property the Duke had turned over to her several houses and a handsome estate, and on his death she had inherited much more. She managed it to such advantage that she was able to give away every year a considerable sum in charity. What remained over she spent on beautifying the church, the refectory and the parlour, and on building oratories in the garden to which the nuns could retire for meditation. The church was magnificent. The vessels for the sacred offices were of pure gold and the monstrance was studded with jewels. The paintings over the various altars were heavily framed in gilt wood elaborately carved, and the images of the Saviour and of the Blessed Virgin had great cloaks of velvet, richly embroidered with gold (by Maria Perez), and their crowns blazed with stones, precious and semi-precious.

To celebrate the twentieth year of her profession Doña Beatriz built a chapel to St. Dominic, for whom she had a special cult, and hearing from one of the sisters, a native of Toledo, that there was a Greek there who painted pictures that wonderfully exalted the devotion of the worshipper, she wrote to her brother, the present Duke, to order one for an altarpiece. Being a businesslike woman she gave him the exact dimensions. But her brother wrote back to tell her that the King had ordered from that very Greek a picture of St. Maurice and the Theban legion for his new church at the Escorial, but when it was delivered was so dissatisfied that he would not have it placed. In these circumstances the Duke thought it would be indiscreet of her to give that painter a commission, and so sent her as a gift a picture by Lodovico Caracci, an artist celebrated in Italy, which by a happy chance was of precisely the right size.

The late Duke, her father, when constructing the convent had arranged an apartment for her to occupy when she was lady prioress which was as elegant as was fitting

to the office and her rank. There was a cell on one floor
to which no one was admitted but the lay sister whose
business it was to keep it clean and in order, and from it
a small stair-way led to an oratory on the floor above.
Here she performed her private devotions, attended to
affairs and received visitors. It was severe, but stately.
Above the little altar at which she prayed was a great
crucifix with a figure of Christ, carved in wood, almost
life-size and painted with great realism; while over the
table at which she worked was a picture by a Catalan
painter of the Virgin in glory. Doña Beatriz at this time
was between forty and fifty, a tall, gaunt, pale woman,
with hardly a line on her face, and great sombre eyes. Age
had refined her features and thinned her lips so that she
had the calm and severe beauty of a knight's lady on
a Gothic tomb. She held herself very erect. There was
something imperious in her air which suggested that she
looked upon no one as her superior and few as her equals.
She had a grim, even a sardonic sense of humour, and
though she often smiled it was with a sort of grave indulgence; when she laughed, which was seldom, you had the
feeling that it was with pain.

Such then was the woman to whose ears it came that
the Blessed Virgin had appeared to Catalina Perez on the
steps of the Carmelite church.

II

Doña Beatriz was not only a fine organizer with a good
head for business, but also a highly intelligent and level-
headed woman. She had always discouraged visions, raptures and special graces among her nuns. She did not
allow them to indulge in excessive austerity or in mortifications other than the Rule provided for; nothing escaped
her notice, and when one of them showed signs of a
religiosity that the Lady Prioress thought excessive she

was promptly purged, forbidden to fast, and if that did not serve sent away to pass a few pleasant weeks with friends or relations. The strictness of Doña Beatriz in this respect was caused by her recollection of the trouble and scandal that had been caused at the Convent of the Incarnation at Avila by a nun who asserted that she had seen Jesus Christ, the Blessed Virgin and various saints and had received special graces from them. The Prioress did not reject the possibility of such occurrences since it was certain that some saints had been the recipients of similar favours, but she could not bring herself to believe that the nun of Avila, Teresa de Cepeda, with whom she had herself often spoken when she was a pupil at the convent, was anything but the hysterical and deluded victim of a disordered fancy.

It was highly improbable that there was anything in Catalina's queer story, but since the nuns were so excited about it that they could talk of nothing else, Doña Beatriz thought it advisable to send for the young woman and get it from her own lips. She called one of her nuns and told her to fetch the girl. In a little while the nun came back and informed her that Catalina was dutifully prepared to obey the Reverend Mother's order, but her confessor had forbidden her to repeat her story to anyone. Doña Beatriz, unused to being crossed, frowned; and when she frowned everyone in the convent trembled.

'Her mother is here, Your Reverence,' said the nun, catching her breath.

'What should I want with her?'

'She had the story from the girl's own lips immediately after Our Lady appeared to her. The Father did not think to forbid her to speak of it.'

A grim smile appeared on the Prioress's pallid lips.

'A worthy, but not a far-seeing man. You did well, my daughter. I will see the woman.'

Maria Perez was ushered into the oratory. She had often seen the Prioress, but had never spoken to her, and she was flustered. Doña Beatriz sat in a high chair, with a leather seat and a leather back, the top of which was decorated with acanthus leaves in gilt wood. Maria Perez could not imagine that a queen could look more remote, dignified and proud. She knelt and kissed the thin white hand that was offered her. Then, bidden to tell what she had come to say, she repeated word for word what Catalina had told her. When she had finished the Prioress gave a slight inclination of her distinguished head.

'You may go.'

For some time she pondered. Then she sat down at the table and wrote a letter in which she begged the Bishop of Segovia to do her the honour of coming to see her since she wished to speak to him on a matter that seemed to have some importance. She sent the letter and within an hour received a reply. The Bishop with equal formality said that he would be pleased to obey the command of the Reverend Mother and would visit the convent on the following day.

The nuns were in a turmoil when they learnt that this eminent and saintly person was expected, and they instantly jumped to the right conclusion that his visit had to do with the miraculous appearance of the Blessed Virgin on the steps of their own beautiful church. He came in the afternoon, after the siesta which the nuns took in the heat of summer, accompanied by two friars who were his secretaries, and was received by the sub-prioress in the parlour. The nuns, much to their chagrin, had been told to keep to their cells. After the sub-prioress had kissed his ring she said that she would lead him to the Lady Prioress. The two friars started to go with him.

'The Reverend Mother desires to speak with your lordship in private,' she said humbly.

The Bishop hesitated for a second and then slightly inclined his head in assent. The friars fell back and the Bishop followed the nun through cool white passages and up a flight of stairs till he came to the oratory. She opened the door and fell back to allow him to enter. He went in. Doña Beatriz rose to meet him and falling to her knees kissed the episcopal ring; then she motioned him to a chair and sat down.

'I was hoping your lordship would see fit to visit this convent,' she said, 'but since you did not come I ventured to invite you.'

'My teacher of theology at Salamanca told me to have as little to do with women as possible, to be polite to them, but to keep them at a distance.'

She did not utter that tart reply that was at the tip of her tongue, but instead looked at him intently. He cast his eyes down and waited. She was in no hurry to speak. It was nearly thirty years since she had last seen him, and these were the first words they had ever exchanged. His habit was old and patched. His head was shaven except for a ring of black hair, only just touched with grey, that represented the Crown of Thorns. His temples were hollow, his cheeks sunken, his face, deeply lined, bore the mark of suffering; only the eyes, luminous with a strange light, darkly passionate, remained to remind her of the young seminarist she had known so long ago – known and loved so madly.

It had begun as a frolic. She had noticed him when first he served the Mass, as on occasion he did, at the church she attended with her duenna. He was thin even then, his hair was black and thick, for he wore only the tonsure of minor orders, his features were clean cut and there was a singular grace in his bearing. He looked like one of those saints who have received the call in their boyhood, so that they become an object of veneration to all, and die in youth and beauty. When he was not serving the Mass he knelt in the small chapel among the few who attended it at that early hour. He was attentive to his devotions and his eyes never left the altar. Beatriz in those days was light-hearted and full of fun. She knew the devastating power of her splendid eyes. She thought it would be a merry prank to make the serious young seminarist conscious of her, and she fixed him with her gaze, willing him with all her might to look at her. For days she gazed in vain and then a day came when she had an intuition that he was uneasy; she could not have told what gave her the impression, but she was certain of it; she waited, holding her breath; he looked up suddenly, as though he had heard an unexpected sound, and catching her eye turned quickly away. From then on she ceased to throw him even a glance, but a day or two later, though her head was bent as though she were praying, she was conscious that he was staring at her. She remained quite still, but she felt that he was looking at her, bewildered, with a look that he had never given anyone before. She knew a thrill of triumph and then, raising her head, deliberately met his eyes. He turned away as quickly as before and she saw his face suffused with a blush of shame.

Two or three times in the street with her duenna she saw him coming towards them, and though he passed them with his head averted she knew that he was shaken. Once indeed, catching sight of them, he turned on his heel and walked back the way he had come. Beatriz giggled so that the duenna asked what was amusing her and she had to tell the first lie she could think of. Then one morning it chanced that they entered the church just as the seminarist was dipping his fingers into the holy water to cross himself. Beatriz put out her hand to touch his fingers and thus receive the holy water on her own fingers. It was a common and a natural action and he could not refuse. He went very white and once more their eyes met. It was only for an instant, but in that instant Beatriz knew that he loved her with a human love, the love of a passionate boy for a beautiful girl, and at the same moment she felt a sharp pain in her heart, as though it were pierced with a sword, and she knew that she loved him with the same human love, the love of a passionate girl for a lovely youth. She was filled with joy. She had never known a happiness so great.

He was serving Mass that day. Her eyes never left him. Her heart beat so that she could hardly bear it, but the pain, if pain it was, was greater than any pleasure she had ever known. She had discovered before this that some errand or occupation took him every day past the Duke's palace at a certain hour and she found means to sit at a window from which she could watch the street. She saw him come, she saw his steps linger, as though unwillingly, as he passed, and then she saw him hurry on as though flying temptation. She hoped he would look up, but he never did, and once, to tease him, she let a carnation fall just as he was approaching. Instinctively he glanced up then, but she drew back so that she could see him without him seeing her. He stopped and picked up the flower. He held it in both hands, as though it were a precious jewel, and for a moment stood looking at it like a man entranced. Then with a violent gesture he flung it to the ground, stamped it in the dust and ran, ran as fast as his legs would carry him. Beatriz broke out laughing and then on a sudden burst into tears.

When he did not come to the early Mass for several days running she could bear her anxiety no longer.

'What has happened to that seminarist who used to serve Mass?' she asked her duenna. 'I haven't seen him lately.'

'How should I know? I suppose he's gone back to his seminary.'

She never saw him again. She knew by then that what had started as a comedietta had turned into tragedy, and she bitterly regretted her folly. She loved him with all the passion of her young body. She had never been crossed in anything and it enraged her to think that now she could not have her will. The marriage that had been arranged for her was a marriage of convenience and she had accepted it as the consequence of her station. As was her duty, she had been prepared to bear her husband children, but was decided to be no more troubled by him otherwise than if he were a flunkey; but now the thought of being united to the dwarfish, dull-witted creature filled her with loathing. She knew that her love for young Blasco de Valero could result in nothing. True, he was only in minor orders and could be released from them, but she did not even have to remember that her father would never consent to such a misalliance; her own pride would not have allowed her to bestow her hand in marriage on the gutter nobleman that he was. And Blasco? He loved her, she was certain of that, but he loved God more. When he had stamped with rage on the flower she had dropped at his feet it was to stamp out the unworthy passion that horrified him. She had terrible, frightening dreams, dreams of lying in his arms, her mouth against his, his breast pressing against her, and she awoke with shame, anguish and despair. It was then she began to sicken. They could make nothing of her malady, but she knew what it was, she was dying of a broken heart. It was then she heard that he had entered a monastic order that she had her inspiration; she knew as if he had told her in so many words that in flying the world he was seeking to escape her, and it gave her a strange joy, a sense of triumphant power. She would do the same thing; to enter a convent would release her from a hateful marriage and in the love of God she might find peace. And at the back of her mind, hardly even hinted at in unspoken words, was the feeling that in that life, widely separated as they would be, each devoted to the service of the Highest, they would in some mystical way be united.

All this that has taken so long to tell passed through the mind of the grim, severe Prioress in a flash. She saw it as though it were one of those vast frescoes painted on the long wall of a cloister which yet you embrace in a comprehensive regard. All that passion that in her foolish youth she imagined would endure to the end, was long since dead. Time, the pious monotony of convent life, prayer and fasting, the multifarious duties of her position, had gradually dulled it till it was now no more than a bitter recollection. As she looked at the man now, so worn and haggard, with that look of suffering on his face, she wondered if he remembered that once he had loved against his will, yes, but with all his heart, a beautiful girl whom he had never even spoken to, but who tormented his dreams. The silence weighed upon the Bishop and he moved uneasily in his chair.

'Your Reverence said that she had a matter of importance on which she wished to consult me,' he said.

'Yes, but first permit me to offer your lordship my felicitations on the dignity to which it has pleased His Majesty to advance you.'

'I can only hope that I shall prove worthy to perform the duties of so great an office.'

'There can be no doubt of that in the mind of anyone who knows with what zeal and discretion you acted during the ten years you spent at Valencia. Though this small city in the mountains is remote we managed to keep acquainted with what passes in the great world, and the fame of your lordship's austerity, virtue and unremitting diligence in defence of the purity of our faith has not escaped us.'

The Bishop glanced at her for a moment from under beetling brows.

'Madam, I am obliged to you for your courtesy, but I must beg you to spare me your compliments. It has never been to my liking that people should talk of me to my face. I shall be grateful if you will tell me without further delay for what reason you requested me to visit you.'

The Prioress was not at all abashed by this reproof. A bishop he might be, but as her duenna, now with God, had once said *Hidalgo de Gutierra*, a gutter nobleman; and she was the daughter of the Duke of Castle Rodriguez, a grandee of Spain and a Knight of the Golden Fleece.

A word from her to her brother, confidant of King Philip the Third's favourite, would relegate this prelate to an obscure bishopric in the Canaries.

'I am sorry to offend your lordship's modesty,' she answered coolly, 'but it is your virtue and your austerity, your sanctity, if I may say so, which are the immediate occasion for my requesting the honour of a visit from you. Have you been informed of the strange experience of a girl called Catalina Perez?'

'I have. Her confessor, doubtless a worthy man, but neither learned nor intelligent, reported her story to me. I dismissed him. I have forbidden the friars in the convent to mention it to me or to talk about it among themselves. The girl is either an impostor, looking for notoriety, or a deluded fool.'

'I do not know her, Señor, but from all accounts she is a good, sensible and pious girl. Persons of good judgment, who know her are convinced that she is incapable of inventing such a story. She is truthful and, I am told, far from fanciful.'

'If she had such a vision as she describes it can only be by a machination of Satan. It is well known that demons have the power of disguising themselves in celestial forms in order to tempt the unwary to perdition.'

'The child suffers from an unmerited misfortune. We must not ascribe to the devil more cleverness than he has. How could he be so stupid as to think her soul would be endangered by having a saintly man lay his hand on her in the name of the Father, the Son and the Holy Ghost?'

During this conversation the Bishop had kept his eyes on the floor, but now he glanced at the Prioress, and there was anguish in them.

'Madam, Lucifer, son of the morning, fell through pride, and how could it be but through pride that I, a very wicked and a very sinful man, should take it upon myself to work miracles?'

'It may be fitting that in your humility you should regard yourself as a sinful and wicked man, my lord, but the rest of the world is well aware of your great virtue. Listen, Señor, this story has been bruited abroad and the whole city is talking about it. Everyone is excited and expectant. In some way satisfaction must be given to the people.'

The Bishop sighed.

'I know the people are disturbed, groups stand outside the convent as though they were waiting for something, and when I am forced to go out they kneel as I pass to ask me for my blessing. Something must be done to let them see reason.'

'Would your lordship allow me to give you advice?' the Prioress asked with great respect, but with a glint of ironical amusement in her eyes which somewhat modified it.

'I should be grateful.'

'I have not seen the girl because her confessor ordered her not to repeat her story, but you have the power to overrule his order. Wouldn't it be well if you saw her? With your discernment, your knowledge of character and the skill you acquired in the Holy Office in the examination of suspects, you should be able to tell very quickly if she is an impostor, if she is deceived by the devil or if, finally, it was indeed the Blessed Virgin who condescended to appear to her.'

The Bishop raised his eyes and looked at the image of the Redeemer nailed to the Cross in the shrine at which the Prioress was wont to pray. His face was very sad. He was torn by indecision.

'I need not remind you, Señor, that this convent is under the special protection of Our Lady of Carmel. We poor nuns are doubtless unworthy of the honour, but it may be that she regards with peculiar favour this church which my father the Duke built for her in this city. It would be a great grace and a great glory to our house if

by your lordship's intercession our heavenly patroness
cured this poor child of her infirmity.'

For a long time the Bishop was sunk in thought. At last
he sighed again.

'Where can I see this girl?'

'Can there be a better place than in the chapel of our
church dedicated to the worship of the Blessed Virgin?'

'What must be done had better be done quickly. Let
her come tomorrow, madam, and I will be here.' He rose
from his seat and as he bowed to take his leave of the
Prioress there was the shadow of a smile, but so rueful,
on his lips. 'A sorrowful night awaits me, Your Reverence.' She knelt down once more and kissed his ring.

12

Next day, at the appointed hour, the Bishop, accompanied
by his two secretaries, entered the richly-decorated
church. Catalina, with one of the nuns, was waiting in
the Lady Chapel; with the help of her crutch she was
standing, but when the Bishop appeared the nun touched
her arm and she started to kneel. He prevented her.

'You may leave us,' he said to the nun, and then when
she had gone he turned to the two friars. 'You may withdraw, but remain close at hand. I will speak to this girl
alone.'

They silently slid away. The Bishop watched them go.
He knew they were curious and he did not wish them to
hear what was said. Then he took a long look at the
crippled girl. He had a tender heart and was always moved
by distress, want or infirmity. She was trembling a little
and she was very pale.

'Do not be frightened, child,' he said gently. 'You have
nothing to fear if you tell the truth.'

She looked very simple and very innocent. He saw that
she had a singularly beautiful face, but he noticed it as

indifferently as he might have noticed that a horse was roan or grey. He began asking her about herself. She answered at first very shyly, but as he continued to press her with questions, after a little with greater confidence. Her voice was soft and melodious and she expressed herself with correctness. She told him the simple little story of her life. It was the story of any poor girl, a story of hard work, of harmless amusements, of church-going, of falling in love; but she told it so naturally, with such an ingenuous air that the Bishop was touched. He could not think this was a girl who had invented something to make herself important. Her every word suggested modesty and humility. Then she told him about her accident and how her leg had become paralysed and how Diego, the tailor's son, whom she was going to marry and whom she loved, had abandoned her.

'I don't blame him,' she said. 'Your lordship doesn't know, perhaps, that the life of the poor is hard, and a man doesn't want a wife who isn't able to work for him.'

As tender a smile as the Bishop's haggard features permitted flitted briefly across his face.

'How is it you have learnt to speak so sensibly and so well, my daughter?' he asked.

'My uncle Domingo Perez taught me to read and write. He took great pains with me. He has been like a father to me.'

'I knew him once.'

Catalina was well aware of her uncle's bad reputation and she was afraid that her reference to him would do her little good in the eyes of that saintly man. There was a silence and for a moment she thought he was going to end the interview.

'Now tell me in your own words the story you told your mother,' he said, fixing her with searching eyes.

She hesitated and he remembered that she had been ordered by her confessor not to speak of it. He gravely

61

told her that he had authority to override the confessor's prohibition.

Then she repeated it exactly as she had told it to her mother. She told him she had been sitting on the steps weeping because everyone in the city was happy and she alone wretched, and how a lady had come out of the church and talked to her and how she had said that his lordship had the power to cure her infirmity, how she had vanished before her very eyes, and how then it had been borne in upon her that the lady was the Blessed Virgin herself.

She finished and there was a long silence. The Bishop was shaken, but at the same time distracted with indecision. The girl was no impostor, of that he was convinced, for her innocence, her sincerity were unmistakable; it could not have been a dream, for she had heard the bells ringing, the beating of drums and the blare of trumpets when he and his brother entered the city, and at that moment she was in speech with the lady who she had no reason then to suppose was more than she seemed; and how could Satan have the power to put on a false semblance when the girl had been pouring out her poor little heart to the Mother of God and beseeching her to succour her in her distress? She was a pious creature and there was no presumption in her. Others had had their prayers answered, others had received spiritual grace, others had been cured of their ills. If he refused to do what it looked as if he had been bidden to do, because he was afraid, might he not be committing a grave sin of omission?

'A sign,' he muttered to himself. 'A sign.'

He took a step or two forwards till he came to the altar above which in a great cloak of blue velvet, all stitched in gold, with a golden crown on her head, stood an image of the Mother of God. He knelt and prayed for guidance. He prayed passionately, but his heart was dry and he felt that the darkness of night shrouded his soul. At last, with a sad sigh, he rose to his feet and stood, his arms outstretched in supplication, with his despairing gaze fixed on the mild eyes of the Blessed Virgin. Suddenly Catalina gave a little startled cry. The two friars had withdrawn out of sight but, though they could not hear what was said, not out of earshot, and when they heard this they scuttled forth as quickly as rabbits into their burrow; but what they saw rooted them to the ground. They uttered no sound. They stood, their mouths open, as if like Lot's wife they had been turned to pillars of salt. Don Blasco de Valero, Bishop of Segovia, was slowly rising into the air, as slowly as oil slides down a plate ever so slightly inclined, rising with an even, almost imperceptible motion, as the water rises in a tidal river; the Bishop rose till he was face to face with the image over the altar and for a moment was suspended in the air for all the world like a falcon motionless on its outstretched wings. One of the friars, fearing he would fall, made as if to start forwards, but the other, Father Antonio, restrained him; and the Bishop, slowly, slowly, so that you were barely conscious of movement, descended till his feet once more touched the marble floor in front of the altar. His arms fell to his sides and he turned round. The two friars ran up and falling on their knees kissed the hem of his habit. He seemed not to be aware of their presence. He walked down the three steps that led from the altar, and like a man in a daze groped his way out of the chapel. The two friars, in case he stumbled, kept close to him. Catalina was forgotten. They emerged from the church. The Bishop paused at the top of the steps, the steps on which Catalina had sat when Our Lady appeared to her, and looked at the little plaza dazzling in the light of the August sun. The unclouded sky was so blue, so bright that it was blinding. The white houses, shuttered against the heat, seemed to sparkle with a gem-like brilliance of their own. The Bishop shuddered although the day had the heat of a furnace. He came to himself.

'Have the girl told that she will hear from me.'

He descended the steps and the friars followed him at a respectful distance. He walked through the plaza, his head bent, and they dared not speak to him. When they arrived at the Dominican convent he stopped and turned to them.

'Under pain of excommunication you will not utter a single word of what you have seen today.'

'It was a miracle, Señor,' said Father Antonio. 'Is it fair that such a signal mark of divine favour should be kept secret from our brothers?'

'When you made your profession, my son, you took the vow of obedience.'

Father Antonio had been the Bishop's pupil when he taught theology at Alcalá and it was through the Bishop's influence that he had entered the Dominican order. He was quick and intelligent, and when Father Blasco was made Inquisitor at Valencia he took him with him as his secretary. He was grateful for the young friar's devotion, and though he often tried to reason him out of the inordinate admiration the youth had for him everything he said seemed to increase it. Father Antonio, though as devout and careful to observe his religious duties as the Bishop could desire, blameless in his life and industrious in the service of the Church, suffered from a disease which Juvenal called *cacoëthes scribendi*: not content with acting as amanuensis for the Inquisitor's great correspondence and writing the multitudinous reports, documents, decisions and so forth that were necessary in the conduct of the affairs of the Holy Office, he spent all his spare moments scribbling; and the Inquisitor discovered, as he discovered everything that concerned him or his office, that Father Antonio was keeping a minute record of his actions, of every word he said and of the various events of his career. He was humbly conscious that the secretary held him in exaggerated esteem, and in his self-examination often asked himself whether he should not put a stop to this work, for he could not but know with what purpose the friar was writing. He had got it into his clever, foolish head that he, Friar Blasco de Valero, was the stuff of which saints are made, and that such a document as he was producing would be of value to the Curia when after his death proceedings for his beatification were instituted. Though so well aware of his unworthiness the Inquisitor was human enough to feel a little thrill of pious exultation when he thought there was a possibility, however remote, that one day he might he counted among the saints of the Church. He scourged himself till the blood flowed for his presumption, but could not bring himself to deprive the good and pious creature of an employment that was certainly harmless. And who could tell? It might be that the writer's simple piety would enable him to produce a work which, of however little account was the subject, might prove edifying to the faithful.

And now, looking into the friar's heart, Bishop Blasco was positive that though no word of what had happened in the Carmelite church would cross his lips, a full account of it would be written in the book. The marvel, now known as levitation, of which he had been the instrument was familiar to him from his reading of the lives of various saints, and it was known throughout Spain that in recent years this sign of divine favour had been granted to Peter of Alcantara, Mother Teresa of Jesus and to more than one nun of the Discalced Carmelites. The Bishop could not expect Father Antonio to omit such a remarkable occurrence from his book, he did not even known if he had the right to do it, so without another word he entered the convent and went to his cell.

13

But it had not occurred to him to bind Catalina to secrecy, and no sooner had the three religious left the church than she hurried home as fast as her disabled state allowed. Domingo had gone on an errand to one of the outlying villages and so only her mother was there. Catalina in awestruck tones told her the wonder of what she had been a witness, and when she had finished she told it over again.

Maria Perez had something of the dramatic sense which was apparently denied to the playwright her brother, and so, restraining her impatience with an effort, she waited for the recreation hour at the convent when she knew that most of the nuns would be assembled talking with the lady boarders and visitors from the city and she thus could relate the amazing occurrence to the greatest possible effect. She had quite an audience when she told her story and the astonishment it caused highly gratified her. The sub-prioress was so much impressed with it that she felt not a moment should be lost in telling it to Doña Beatriz. In a little while Maria Perez was summoned to the presence. She repeated her narrative. The Prioress listened with a satisfaction she saw no reason to conceal.

'After this there can be no hesitation,' she said. 'It will be a great glory not only to this convent, but to the Order of Our Lady of Carmel.'

She dismissed the two women and taking up her quill wrote a letter to the Bishop in which she told him that she had learnt of the grace that had been accorded him that morning. No further proof was needed that what the girl Catalina Perez had said was true, to be ascribed to no machination of the Evil One, but to the compassion of

Our Blessed Lady. She conjured him to put aside his doubts and uncertainties, for nothing could be plainer than that it was his Christian duty to accept the charge laid upon him. It was a good letter, succinct but well argued, respectful but firm, and she requested, with great humility, that he would deign to perform the miracle in the church in which he had been granted this divine favour and for which it was evident the Blessed Virgin had conceived a particular affection. She sent the letter by messenger.

Two of the gentlemen who were in the parlour when Maria Perez told her story were so much struck with it that they went at once to the Dominican convent to inquire into its truth. The friars there of course knew nothing of it, but when it was repeated to them were far from surprised. They knew very well that the Bishop was a man of great sanctity, and nothing was more likely than that God should have accorded him the signal honour of levitation. Meanwhile one of the lady boarders went to see friends in the city and told them of the miraculous event. In a couple of hours the whole city knew about it. More gentlemen came to the Dominican convent in order to get information at first hand. The friars were in a tremor of religious enthusiasm. At last Father Antonio was obliged to go to the Bishop and tell him that though neither he nor his fellow friar had opened his mouth the occurrence was now common knowledge. The Prioress's letter was open on the table. The Bishop pointed to it.

'These wretched women, they cannot hold their tongues,' he said. 'It is a great humiliation to me that this thing should have become known.'

'Our brothers of this convent hope that your lordship will now consent to cure the unhappy girl of her infirmity.'

There was a knock at the door. Father Antonio opened it. A friar brought a message to ask if the Prior might see the Bishop.

'Let him come.'

Father Antonio was present at the interview and he wrote an account of it at very tedious length. In the end the Bishop allowed himself to be convinced that it was the will of God that he should do what the Blessed Virgin required of him. He made conditions, however, which the Prior, much against his will, found himself obliged to accept. The Prior wanted a ceremony with all his friars assembled, in the presence of the notabilities of the city, both lay and clerical; but this the Bishop sternly refused to allow. He insisted on secrecy. He was prepared to go to the Carmelite church and say Mass there on the following morning. The doors must be closed so that no one should be admitted. He would himself be accompanied only by his secretaries. The Prior, not a little incensed at what he considered a slight on his dignity, left him. The Bishop then sent Father Antonio to inform Doña Beatriz of his decisions. He gave her permission to bring her nuns, but forbade the lady boarders to come. He instructed her to make Catalina prepare herself to partake of Holy Communion after Mass and requested her and her nuns to pray for him that night.

Within an hour an excited nun came to Maria Perez and asked to see Catalina since she had something very private and important to tell her. When Catalina was called the nun put her fingers to her lips to emphasize the silence that was required.

'It's a great secret,' she said. 'You mustn't tell anyone. His lordship is going to cure you and tomorrow you'll be running about on your two feet like any other Christian.'

Catalina gasped and her heart began to beat like mad.

'Tomorrow?'

'You're to take Holy Communion, so you mustn't eat anything after midnight. You know that.'

'Yes, I know that. But I never do eat anything after midnight.'

'And you must put yourself in a state of grace. After

you've received Communion he'll make you whole just as Our Blessed Lord did the leper.'

'Can Mamma and Uncle Domingo come?'

'Nothing was said about them. Surely they can come. It may well turn your poor uncle from his evil ways.'

Domingo did not get back from the country till late that evening, but he was no sooner in the house than Catalina in a tremor of agitation told him her thrilling news. He stared at her with consternation.

'Aren't you glad, Uncle?' she cried.

He did not speak. He began pacing the room. Catalina could not understand his strange behaviour.

'What's the matter with you, Uncle? Aren't you pleased? I thought you'd be as happy as I am. Don't you want me to be cured?'

He shrugged his shoulders irritably and went on pacing the room. He had never been quite sure that the apparition was not a construction of his niece's distracted mind and he dreaded the consequences to her if the Bishop's intervention were vain. The Holy office might well think then that the matter required investigation. That meant ruin. Suddenly he stopped and faced Catalina. He looked at her with a sternness she had never seen in him before.

'Tell me exactly what it was that the Blessed Virgin said to you.'

She repeated her story.

'And then the lady said: The son of Don Juan de Valeró who has best served God has it in his power to cure you.'

Domingo interrupted her harshly.

'But that is not what you told your mother. You told her that Blasco de Valero had it in his power to cure you.'

'It's the same thing. The Bishop is a saint; all the world knows that. Which of the sons of Don Juan has served God so well?'

'You fool!' he shouted. 'You little fool!'

'It's you who are the fool,' she answered hotly. 'You never believed that the Blessed Virgin had appeared to me and spoken to me and then vanished from my sight. You thought it was a dream. Well, listen to this.'

She told him then how she had seen the Bishop rise from the floor and stay suspended in the air and then sink down once more to the floor.

'That wasn't a dream. The two friars who were with him saw it with their own eyes.'

'Stranger things have happened,' he muttered.

'And yet you refuse to believe that Our Blessed Lady appeared to me.'

He looked at her now with a twinkle in his eyes.

'I don't. I didn't believe it before, but I believe it now, not for what you saw this morning, but for the words the Blessed Virgin spoke to you. There is a meaning in them that convinces me.'

Catalina was perplexed. She could not understand how the insignificant difference between the two versions could make any odds. He gently patted her cheek.

'I am a great sinner, my poor child, and what makes my situation desperate is that I have never yet succeeded in repenting of my sins. I have lived a hazardous and a worthless life, but I have read many books, ancient and modern, and I have learnt many things which perhaps it would be for my soul's good if I did not know. Be of good heart, my dear, perhaps all may yet be well.'

He took up his hat.

'Where are you going, Uncle?'

'I have had a busy day and I am in want of relaxation. I am going to the tavern.'

In this he departed from the truth, for instead of going to the tavern he went to the Dominican convent. Though it was still light, the hour was advanced and the porter would not admit him. Domingo insisted that he must see the Bishop on a matter of grave importance, but the porter, speaking through the judas, would not even open the door. Domingo told him that he was the uncle of Catalina Perez and begged him at least to fetch one of his lordship's secretaries. The porter was unwilling to do this, but Domingo was so urgent that at last he consented. In a few minutes Father Antonio came to the door. Domingo besought him to let him see the Bishop, since he had a communication to impart to him that it was vital for him to hear. The friar had evidently been informed who he was and of what a bad reputation, for he answered coldly. He said it was impossible to disturb his lordship, for he was spending the night in prayer and had given orders that he was on no account to be disturbed.

'If you do not let me see him you will be responsible for a terrible mishap.'

'Drunkard,' said Father Antonio scornfully.

'A drunkard I am, but now I am not drunk. You will bitterly regret it if you will not let me in.'

'What is this message that you wish me to deliver?'

Domingo hesitated. He was at his wits' end.

'Tell him that for the love he bears him Domingo Perez sends him this message: The stone which the builders rejected is become the head of the corner.'

'*Hijo de puta*,' cried Father Antonio, in a rage that this dissolute scamp should quote scripture.

He slammed-to the shutter of the judas. Domingo turned away. He was in a black mood. Habit bent his steps to the tavern and he went in. He was a sociable creature and had, if not many friends, at least a goodly number of drinking companions. He got drunk, and when he was drunk his tongue was loosened. He liked to hear himself talk and it was on this occasion as on many others no difficult for him to find listeners.

14

Next morning, when, as Domingo would have put it in a poem, Aurora rubbed the sleep from her eyes with rosy fingers and Phoebus harnessed to his golden chariot the swift coursers of the sun, or in plain language at break of day, three Dominican friars with their hoods drawn over their shaven heads, partly for concealment, partly to protect themselves from the noxious vapours of the lingering night, slipped out of the convent. But though it was so early the townspeople had gathered that there was something in the wind and there was already a group at the convent gate. In the tall cowled figure between the other two they at once recognized the saintly bishop. The three friars, followed at a respectful distance by the curious, walked swiftly to the Carmelite church. Here more persons were waiting. One of the friars knocked at the door. It was opened just enough to let them pass through one after the other, and closed behind them. When the onlookers tried to enter they found it locked, and though they knocked, they knocked in vain.

Catalina was waiting in the Lady Chapel. Maria Perez and Domingo had accompanied her, but had been refused admittance. Doña Beatriz received the Bishop at the church door with her nuns, twenty in all, for that was the limit the Duke of Castel Rodriguez in his foundation had set to their number. The Bishop, with his two attendants, went into the sacristy and donned the sacred vestments. They walked slowly to the Lady Chapel. The nuns were on their knees. Catalina, supporting herself on her crutch, knelt at the foot of the altar steps. The Bishop said Mass. The nuns joined in the responses in awed undertones. He administered Holy Communion to Catalina. After the benediction and the reading of the last Gospel he knelt at the altar and prayed in silence. Then he rose to his feet and with his great tragic eyes upon Catalina walked down the steps. He placed his thin, brown hand on her head.

'I, the unworthy instrument of the Most High, in the name of the Father, the Son and the Holy Ghost bid you throw aside your crutch and walk.'

He had begun tremulously, in so low a voice that the

nuns could hardly hear, but he spoke the last words loud and clear in a tone of command. Catalina, her face pale with emotion, her eyes shining, raised herself to her feet, cast the crutch aside, took a step forward and with a cry of anguish crashed to the floor. The miracle had failed.

Immediately there arose a hubbub among the nuns. Some of them screamed, two of them fainted. The Prioress stepped forward. She gave Catalina a glance and then her eyes met the Bishop's. For a while they gazed intently at one another. Behind them the nuns were sobbing. Then the Bishop walked out of the chapel, the two friars at his heels, and returned to the sacristy. He did not utter a word. When they had discarded their vestments and wore once more their conventual habits they went back into the church. The portress was waiting to unlock the door. The Bishop, his cowl once more over his head, stepped out into the sunlight of the summer morning.

The news had spread that he was even then performing a miracle and the windows in the plaza were crowded with spectators. They were thick on the church steps and the square was filled with them. For a moment the Bishop was dismayed to see that great throng, but only for a moment; he pulled his habit close to him and drew himself up. He no sooner appeared than a shudder of consternation passed through the crowd, for in some strange way they knew at once, though they could not have said how, that the miracle had failed. Way was made and the Bishop, with the two friars following, walked down the steps. The people in the plaza pressed one another back, and as he passed along the path they thus made for him, his face hidden, his tall figure huddled in the black and white habit of his order, a dreadful silence fell upon them. You would have said that they were terrified as though some horrifying and unavoidable catastrophe impended.

15

The friars of the Dominican convent had been angered because the Bishop had refused to allow them to attend the ceremony, and when, with his two attendants, he returned to it they were loitering about to look at him. The news had already reached them. He passed as though he did not see them.

On hearing that they were to lodge such a distinguished guest they had furnished his cell with such luxury as they thought suitable to his grandeur. But he had immediately had everything removed that offended his austerity. He forced them to change the soft mattress on the bed for one of straw no thicker than a blanket, and he had the two armchairs they had put in the oratory replaced with three-legged stools. They had given him a handsome teak table to write at, but he asked that he should be given instead one of unpainted deal. He would have nothing that appealed to the senses and turned out the pictures they had hung on the walls. They were bare now but for a plain black Cross, without the figure of Our Lord either painted or carved, and this was so that he might more exactly picture himself nailed to it and so in his body feel the pain that the Redeemer for the sake of mankind had suffered.

When the Bishop entered his cell he sank on to the hard wooden stool and stared at the stone floor. Slow, painful tears trickled down his sunken cheeks. Father Antonio's heart was filled with compassion to see his master plunged in what looked very like despair. He whispered to his companion, who forthwith left the cell and in a few minutes returned with a bowl of soup. Father Antonio handed it to the Bishop.

'Señor, here is something for you to eat.'

The Bishop turned his head away.

'I could eat nothing.'

'Oh, my lord, no food has passed your lips since the morning of yesterday. I beseech you to take at least a few mouthfuls.'

He knelt, filled a spoon with the steaming soup and held it to the Bishop's lips.

'You are very good to me, my son,' he said. 'I am not worthy of the care you take of me.'

Not to appear ungracious he swallowed the contents of the spoon, and then the monk fed the broken man as though he were a sick child. The Bishop was well aware of his faithful attendant's deep attachment and had more than once warned him of its danger, for a religious should always be on his guard against conceiving affection for any one person, since it could not but hamper his wholehearted devotion to God who was the only real object of love; and as for human beings, whether clerical or lay, he should regard them with good will, because they were God's creatures, but since they were perishable with an indifference that made it of no moment if they were present or absent. But the affections are difficult to control, and however hard he tried, Father Antonio could not destroy the love, the ecstatic devotion, with which his poor heart was filled.

When the Bishop had eaten, Father Antonio put aside the bowl and, still on his knees, ventured to take his hand.

'Do not take it so hard, Señor. The girl was deceived by demons.'

'No, the fault was mine. I asked for a sign and the sign was given me. In my vainglory I thought myself not unfit to do what is vouchsafed to the saints whom God has chosen for His own. I am a sinner and I am justly punished for my presumption.'

The Bishop was so broken that the friar dared to speak to him as otherwise he would never have done.

'We are all sinners, Señor, but I have been privileged to live close to you for many years and no one knows better than I your unfailing kindness to all men, your ceaseless charity and your loving kindness.'

'It is your own goodness that speaks, my son. It is the affection you have for me which I have so often warned you against and which I so little deserve.'

Father Antonio gazed with pity on the Bishop's agonized face. He still held his cold, emaciated hand.

'Would it not distract your mind if I read to you a little, my lord?' he said after a pause. 'I have lately written something which I should value your opinion of.'

The Bishop knew how bitterly grieved the poor friar was that the miracle, which he had anticipated with complete assurance, had not been performed, and he was touched when the dear, simple man mastered his own terrible disappointment to minister to him and to console him. He had never before consented to listen to a word of the book his secretary was so industriously writing but now he had not the heart to refuse him a pleasure that he so ardently desired.

'Read, my son. I will listen gladly.'

The Father, his cheeks flushed with delight, scrambled to his feet and took, from among the many papers his office required him to deal with, several sheets of manuscript. He sat down on a stool. The other friar, since there was no other place for him, sat on the floor. Father Antonio began to read.

He was an erudite and an elegant writer and none of the artifices of rhetoric was unfamiliar to him. His style was rich in simile and metaphor, metonymy, synecdoche and catachresis. He never let a noun go by without an escort of two stalwart adjectives. Images sprang to his mind as profuse and fat as mushrooms after rain, and being well read in the Scriptures, the works of the Fathers and the Latin moralists, he was never at a loss for a recondite allusion. He was learned in sentence-structure, simple, complex, compound and compound-complex, and could not only compose a period, with clauses and sub-clauses, of the most choice elaboration, but bring it to a conclusion with a triumphant clang that had all the effect of a door slammed in your face. This manner of writing, to which an ingenious critic has given the name of Mandarin, is much admired by those who affect it, but it has the trifling disadvantage of taking a long time to say what can be said in brief; and in any case it would be discordant with the plain, blunt style in which this narrative is written; and so, instead of making a vain attempt to reproduce the good Father's grandiloquence, the author of these pages has thought it better to give the gist of the matter in his own simple way.

Father Antonio, not without tact, had chosen to read his account of the great *auto de fé*, which had been the crown of Friar Blasco's career in the Holy Office, and which, as before mentioned, had given so much pleasure to the Prince, now Philip III, and had in due course been at least the occasion for the saintly inquisitor's elevation to the important See of Segovia.

The impressive ceremony, devised to inspire awe for the authority of the Inquisition and edify the people, took place on a Sunday, so that none should have an excuse not to attend it, since to do so was a pious duty; and to secure as large an attendance as possible an indulgence of forty days was granted to all who came. Three stagings had been erected in the great plaza of the city, one for the penitents with their spiritual attendants, one for the inquisitors, the officials of the Holy Office and the clergy, and a third for the civil authorities and the dignitaries of the city. The proceedings, however, began the night before with the procession of the Green Cross. First, with a standard of crimson damask embroidered with the royal arms, came a crowd of familiars and gentlemen; then the religious orders with the White Cross; the Cross of the parish church borne by the secular clergy; and finally the Green Cross carried by the Prior of the Dominicans, accompanied by his friars with torches. They sang the *Miserere* as they marched. The Green Cross was planted above the altar on the staging reserved for the inquisitors and it was guarded through the night by Dominicans. The White Cross was taken to the place of execution, where it was guarded by the soldiers of the Zarza, a body of men whose duty it was to keep watch over the quemadero or burning-place and provide wood for the bonfire.

One of the duties of the inquisitors was to visit during the night those condemned to death, inform them of their sentence, and assign two friars to each one to prepare him to meet his God. But on this occasion Father Baltasar, the junior inquisitor, was sick in bed of a colic, and so that he might be well enough to take part in the proceedings of the following day begged Friar Blasco to excuse him from accompanying him on this grim errand.

Dawn broke and Mass was celebrated in the audience chamber of the Holy Office and at the altar of the Green Cross. Breakfast was given to the prisoners and to the friars, doubtless glad of it by then, who had attended those about to die. They were then ranged in order according to the gravity of their offence against the Faith and dressed in *sambenitos*. The *sambenito* was a yellow tunic painted on one side with flames for those who were to be burnt, and on the other inscribed with their names, places of residence and crimes. Green crosses were given them to carry and yellow candles put in their hands.

Another procession was formed. The soldiers of the Zarza, who led it, were followed by a religious bearing a cross shrouded in black and an acolyte who from time to time tolled a bell. Then came the penitents one by one, with a familiar on either side; then the effigies and chests of bones of those whose flight or death had robbed the Holy Office of its rightful prey; then those who were to die, accompanied by the friars who had been with them throughout the night. Mounted officials followed, familiars in pairs, the magistrates of the city, and the ecclesiastical dignitaries, according to their official precedence. A noble of high rank bore a box of red velvet fringed with gold which contained the sentences of the condemned. Then came the standard of the Holy Office borne by the Prior of the Dominicans, followed by his friars and finally the inquisitors.

It was a fine, sunny day, the sort of day that elates the heart of young and old so that they feel it good to be alive.

The procession moved slowly through the tortuous streets till it reached the plaza. There was a vast concourse. People had streamed into the city from the fertile haciendas that surround it, from rice fields and olive groves; others had come from as far as Alicante with its vineyards and from Elche with its date trees. The windows of the surrounding houses were filled with nobility and gentry, and the Prince with his suite watched from a balcony in the town hall.

The culprits were seated on the staging created for them in the order in which they had marched, the least guilty on the lower benches and the most guilty on the highest. There were two pulpits on the staging that accommodated the tribunal, and from one of these a sermon was preached. Then a secretary in a voice so loud that he could be heard by all read the oath by which the officials and all present swore obedience to the Holy Office and pledged themselves to persecute heretics and heresy. Everyone said Amen. After this the two inquisitors went to the balcony in which sat the Prince, and on the Cross and Gospels administered to him an oath constraining him to obey the Catholic Faith and the Holy Office, to persecute heretics and apostates and help and assist the Inquisition to seize and punish, whatever their rank and station, the miscreants who rejected true religion.

'This I swear and promise on my faith and royal word,' solemnly replied the Prince.

There was a bench between the two pulpits to which the penitents were brought one by one; their sentences were read to them from alternate pulpits. With the exception of those condemned to the flames this was the first announcement of their fate, and since some fainted when they heard it the Holy Office in its mercy provided a rail to the bench in case they fell and hurt themselves. On this occasion one man, broken by torture, died there and then of the shock. The last sentence was read and the culprits were delivered to the secular arm. The Holy Office rendered no judgment that involved the shedding of blood and indeed went so far as to urge the civil authorities to spare the life of the criminal. They were, however, required by the canon law promptly to punish the heretics consigned to them by the Inquisition, and an indulgence was accorded to the pious who contributed wood to the bonfire that was to burn them.

This ended the work of the inquisitors and they retired. The soldiers of the Zarza marched into the plaza and discharged their muskets. They then surrounded the prisoners and marched with them to the place of execution to protect them from the fury of the populace who in their hatred of heresy would otherwise ill-treat and sometimes even kill them. The friars attended them and strove to the end to bring about their repentance and conversion. Among them were four Morisco women whose beauty excited the admiration of all, an impenitent Dutch merchant who had been caught smuggling into the country a Spanish translation of the New Testament, a Moor convicted of killing a chicken by cutting off its head, a bigamist, a merchant who had harboured a fugitive from the Holy Office, and a Greek found guilty of holding opinions condemned by the Church. An alguazil and a secretary went with the civil authorities to see that the sentences were duly executed. The secretary on this occasion was

Father Antonio, so that he had an opportunity to make his account of the day's proceedings complete.

The *quemadero* was outside the city. Garrottes were attached to the stakes so that those who had professed a desire to die in the Christian faith, even those who did so at the last moment, might be spared death by fire and killed by the more merciful method of strangulation. The crowd had surged after the soldiers and the prisoners, and a great many, in order to get a better view of the proceedings, had hurried beforehand to the open space where the final scene was to take place. There was a vast multitude. This was natural, for it was a sight well worth seeing, a very proper entertainment for a royal guest; and the spectator had besides the satisfaction of knowing that he was performing an act of piety and a service to God. Those who were to be garrotted were garrotted and then the flames were kindled and the quick and the dead were burnt to ashes so that their memory might perish for ever. The people shouted and clapped their hands as the flames soared, so that the shrieks of the victims were almost drowned, and here and there a woman broke into a shrill chant to the Blessed Virgin or to the crucified Christ. Night fell and the crowd streamed back into the city, tired with long standing and the excitement, but feeling that they had had a happy day. They flocked to the taverns. The brothels did a roaring trade and many a man that night put to the proof the efficacy of the fragment of Friar Blasco's habit that he wore round his neck.

Father Antonio was tired too, but it was his first duty to report the proceedings to the two inquisitors, and then, notwithstanding his fatigue which tempted him to go to bed, since he was a conscientious man he sat down and wrote a circumstantial account of all that had happened that day while every detail was fresh in his mind. He wrote rapidly, with an eloquence that seemed inspired by heaven, and when he read over what he had written he found that there was not a word that needed to be altered.

Then at last, happy in the consciousness of having done his duty and besides contributed his small share to a pious work, he went to bed and slept the innocent sleep of a child.

All this then, giving dramatic emphasis to the most significant episodes, he read to the despondent Bishop in a loud, sonorous voice. He read with his eyes glued to the script. He felt strangely exalted. Thus was God served and thus was the purity of the Catholic faith maintained. He finished. He could not but feel that he had done the great ceremony justice. He had himself been struck by the vividness of his description and the artful way in which he had built up the narrative, he himself did not know how, to an impressive climax. He looked up. Like many another author who submits his work to a listener he would have been pleased to be rewarded with a word of praise. But this was merely a passing wish; his main object was to dispel the sombre fancies of his revered and beloved superior by reminding him of the most glorious incident of his career. Saint though he was, he could not but feel a thrill of pride when there appeared before his mind's eye that wonderful day when he had been the means of consigning to eternal torment so great a number of cursed heretics, thereby serving God, discharging his conscience and edifying the people. Father Antonio was surprised, more than surprised, aghast, to see that tears were coursing down the Bishop's withered cheeks and that his hands were clenched to control the sobbing that tore his breast.

He threw aside his manuscript, and jumping up from his stool on which he had been sitting flung himself at his master's feet.

'My lord, what is it?' he cried. 'What have I done? I read only to distract your thoughts.'

The Bishop thrust him aside and rising to his feet stretched out his arms in supplication to the black Cross on the wall.

'The Greek,' he moaned. 'The Greek.'

And then able to contain himself no longer he broke into passionate weeping. The two friars gazed at him in consternation. They had never before seen that austere man exhibit emotion. The Bishop with the palm of his hand impatiently brushed the tears from his eyes.

'I am to blame,' he moaned, 'terribly to blame. I have committed a fearful sin and my only hope of forgiveness is in the infinite mercy of God.'

'My lord, for God's sake explain. I am all confused. I am like a mariner in a storm when his bark is dismasted and he has lost his rudder.' With his reading still ringing in his ears Father Antonio found it impossible not to speak like a book. 'The Greek? Why does your lordship speak of the Greek? He was a heretic and suffered the just punishment of his crime.'

'You do not know of what you speak. You do not know that my crime is greater than his. I asked for a sign and the sign was given me. I thought it was a mark of God's grace; now I know it was a mark of His wrath. It is right that I should be humbled in the eyes of men, for I am a miserable sinner.'

He did not turn to his companions. He did not speak to them, but to the Cross on which he had so often pictured himself with nails in his hands and nails through his feet.

'He was a good old man, in his poverty charitable to the poor, and in the many years I knew him I never heard him say an evil word. He looked upon all men with loving kindness. He had true nobility of soul.'

'Many men, virtuous in their public and their private lives, have been justly condemned by the Holy Office, since moral rectitude weighs nothing in the balance against the mortal sin of heresy.'

The Bishop turned and looked at Father Antonio. His eyes wee tragic.

'And the wages of sin is death,' he whispered.

The Greek of whom they spoke, Demetrios Christopoulos, was a native of Cyprus, a man of some property, which had enabled him to devote himself to learning. When the Turks, under Selim II, invaded the island, they took Nicosia, the capital, and put twenty thousand of its inhabitants to the sword. Famagusta, where Demetrios Christopoulos lived, was besieged and surrendered after a year of bitter resistance. This was in 1571. He fled from the doomed city and hid in the hills till he managed to escape in a fishing-boat and after many an adventure landed in Italy. He was penniless, but in due course found enough work as a teacher of Greek and an expounder of the ancient philosophy to keep body and soul together. Then in an evil hour he attracted the attention of a Spanish nobleman attached to the embassy in Rome who during his sojourn in Italy had succumbed to the fashionable cult of Plato. The nobleman took him into his palace and they read together the immortal dialogues of the philosopher. After some years, however, he was recalled to Spain and he persuaded the Greek to go with him. He was appointed Viceroy for the Kingdom of Valencia and in the city of that name eventually died. The Greek, almost an old man by then, stranded, left the viceregal palace and found a modest dwelling in the house of a widow woman. He had acquired some reputation for his learning and eked out a meagre living by giving lessons in Greek to those who desired to acquire some knowledge of that noble tongue.

Friar Blasco de Valero had heard of him while he was still giving lectures in theology at Alcalá de Henares and soon after he took up his post as inquisitor at Valencia he made inquiries about the Greek, and hearing that he was a man of good repute and virtuous life sent for him. He was pleased with the old man's gentle approach and modest bearing and asked him if he would teach him the language in which the New Testament was written so that he might read the words with greater devotion. For nine years, whenever his manifold duties allowed him leisure, the Inquisitor and the Greek worked together. Friar Blasco was an industrious and an apt pupil, and after some months the Greek, who had a passion for the great and ancient literature of his country, persuaded him to embark on the works of the classical writers. He was himself a fervent platonist and it was not long before they were reading the dialogues. From them they went on to Aristotle. The friar refused to read the Iliad which he thought brutal or the Odyssey which he thought frivolous, but in the dramatists found much to admire. In the end, however, they always returned to the dialogues.

The Inquisitor was a man of sensibility and he was charmed by the grace, piety and profundity of Plato. There was much in his writings that a Christian could approve. They were the occasion for the pair of them to discuss many serious subjects. It was a new world Friar Blasco thus entered, and he felt a singular exultation in his perusal of these great works and a blissful repose after the labours of the day. In their long and fruitful intercourse he had conceived something very like affection for the unworldly Greek, and all he heard of him, of his simple decent life, his kindliness and charity, increased his admiration for his character.

It was a terrible shock to him when a Dutchman, a Lutheran, arrested by the familiars of the Inquisition for bringing into Spain translations of the New Testament, admitted under torture that he had given a copy to the Greek. Under questioning, emphasized by another turn of the rack, he stated that they had often conversed on religion and on many points were in full agreement. This was enough to oblige the Holy Office to make an investigation. This as always was thorough and secret. The Greek was not allowed to know that he was suspect. When Friar Blasco read the final reports he was horrified. It had never occurred to him that the Greek, so good, so humble, had not during his long years in Italy, his long years in Spain, abjured his schismatic opinions and embraced the Catholic faith of Rome. Witnesses were brought forward who swore that they had heard him utter damnable heresies. He denied the procession of the Holy Ghost from the Son, he rejected the supremacy of the Pope, and though he venerated the Virgin he refused to admit her immaculate conception. The woman of the house in which he lived had heard him say that indulgences were worthless and someone else testified that he did not accept the Roman doctrine of purgatory.

Friar Blasco's fellow inquisitor, Don Baltasar Carmona, was a doctor of laws and a rigid moralist. He was a dried-up little man, with a long sharp nose, tight lips and small restless eyes. He suffered from some malady of the intestines which soured his temper. His situation gave him immense power and he took a savage pleasure in exercising it. When these damning facts were laid before him he insisted in the arrest of the Greek. Friar Blasco did what he could to save him. He claimed that as a schismatic he was no heretic, and therefore did not come under the jurisdiction of the Holy Office, but there was not only the evidence of the tortured Lutheran; a French Calvinist whom he had also incriminated stated that he had heard the Greek utter opinions that savoured of protestantism, and upon this Friar Blasco felt obliged to do his bounden duty at whatever cost to his feelings. Familiars went to the old man's lodging and took him to the prison of the Inquisition. He was examined and freely admitted his charges. He was given the opportunity to abjure his false beliefs and be converted to Catholicism, but to Friar Blasco's dismay he refused to do this. The offence was grave, but the evidence of protestantism was not decisive, and in order to give the Greek a chance of purging his offence Friar Blasco urged upon his fellow inquisitor who was all for condemning him out of hand that to induce his conversion and so save his soul he should be put to the torture.

When torture was applied both inquisitors were required by law to be present, with the episcopal representative and a notary to record the proceedings. It was an exhibition that always filled Friar Blasco with such horror that for nights afterwards he was harassed by fearful dreams.

The Greek was brought in, stripped and tied to the trestle. His feeble old body was emaciated. He was solemnly besought to tell the truth for the love of God, since the inquisitors did not wish to see him suffer. He remained silent. His ankles were tied to the sides of the rack, cords were passed round his arms, his thighs and his calves, and their ends were attached to a garrotte, a stick by which they could be twisted tight. The executioner gave a sharp turn of the garrotte and the Greek shrieked; another, and skin and muscle were cut through to the bone. On account of his great age Friar Blasco had insisted that not more than four turns should be given, since, though six or seven were the maximum, it was unusual even with strong men to exceed five. The Greek begged them to kill him at once and put him out of his agony. Though Friar Blasco was forced to be there, he was not forced to look, and he stared at the stone floor; but the shrieks of pain rang in his ears and tore his nerves to pieces. That was the voice with which his friend had recited those grave and noble passages of Sophocles; that was the voice in which with an emotion he could hardly control he had read the dying speech of Socrates. Before each turn of the garrotte, the Greek was ordered to tell the truth, but he clenched his teeth and would not speak. When he was released from the rack he could not stand and had to be carried back to the dungeon of the Holy Office.

Though he admitted nothing he was condemned on the strength of what he had previously confessed. Friar Blasco sought to save his life, but Don Baltasar, the doctor of laws, contended that he was as guilty as the other

87

Lutherans who had been sentenced to the stake. The episcopal representative and the other officials who were consulted agreed with him. Since the *auto de fé* was not to take place for several weeks Friar Blasco had time to write to the Inquisitor General and put the case before him. The Inquisitor General replied that he saw no reason to interfere with the decision of the tribunal. Friar Blasco could do nothing more, but still the shrieks of the old man rang in his ears and he suffered without respite. He sent spiritual advisers to see him and attempt his conversion, for though nothing now could save his life, repentance, allowing him to be garrotted, might still spare him the agony of death by burning. But the Greek was contumacious. Nothwithstanding the torture and his long confinement in prison his mind remained clear and active. To the friars' arguments he answered with arguments so subtle that they were incensed.

At last came the eve of the *auto de fé*. Previous celebrations of the same kind had not affected Friar Blasco, for the relapsed Judaizers, the Moriscos who continued their devilish practices, the Protestants, were criminals before God and man, and for the safety of Church and State there was every good reason that they should suffer. But no one knew better than he how good, how kind, how helpful to the needy was the Greek. Notwithstanding the authority of his fellow inquisitor, a cruel man with a dry, cold mind, he doubted the legality of the frightful punishment. Acrimonious words had passed and Don Baltasar had accused him of favouring the criminal because he was on friendly terms with him. In his heart Friar Blasco knew that there was at least a particle of truth in this; had he never known the Greek he would have accepted the verdict without protest. He could no longer save his life but he could still save his soul. Those friars he had sent to convince him of his error were not clever enough to deal with that man of learning. He decided to do an unprecedented thing. An hour before dawn he went to the prison of the Inquisition and had himself conducted to the Greek's cell. Two friars were passing his last night on earth with him. Friar Blasco dismissed them.

'He has refused to listen to our exhortations,' said one of them.

A smile hovered over the Greek's lips as they left the cell.

'Your friars are doubtless worthy men, Señor,' he said. 'But their intelligence is not remarkable.'

He was calm and though so frail and old maintained an appearance of dignity.

'Your Reverence will forgive me if I remain on my bed. The torture left me very weak and I wish to preserve my strength for this day's ceremonies.'

'Let us not waste time in idle speeches. In a few hours you must face a dreadful fate. God knows I would gladly give ten years of my life to save you from it. The evidence was damning and I should have been false to my oath if I had failed in my duty.'

'I am the last man who would wish you to do that.'

'Your life is forfeit and that I cannot save. But if you will recant and accept conversion I can at least spare you the agony of the flames. I have loved you, Demetrios, I can never repay the debt I owe you except by saving your immortal soul. Those friars are ignorant and narrow men. I have come here to make a last desperate attempt to persuade you of your error.'

'You will only be wasting your time, Señor. We should employ it to better advantage if we talked as we have so often done before of the death of Socrates. They would not allow me to have books in this dungeon, but my memory is good and I have found solace in repeating to myself that speech in which he spoke so nobly of the soul.'

'I do not command you now, Demetrios, I beseech you to listen to me.'

'That last courtesy I am bound to grant you.'

89

The Inquisitor in earnest tones, with learning and discretion, point by point, expounded the arguments which the Church had devised to substantiate her own claims and to refute the opinions of heretics and schismatics. He was well accustomed to discourse of this nature and he expressed himself ably and with impressive conviction.

'I should deserve little respect if for fear of a painful death I pretended to accept beliefs which I think erroneous,' said the Greek when he had finished.

'I do not ask you to do that. I ask you to believe the truth with all your heart.'

' "What is truth?" asked Pontius Pilate. A man can as little constrain his beliefs as he can constrain the sea to calm when stormy winds assail it. I thank Your Reverence for your kindness and believe me I bear you no ill will for the misfortune that has befallen me. You have acted according to your conscience, and no man can do more. I am an old man and whether I die today or in a year or two is no great matter. I have only one request to make of you. Do not because I am gone relinquish your studies of the sublime literature of ancient Greece. It cannot fail to enlarge your spirit and ennoble your mind.'

'Do you not fear the just vengeance of God for your contumacious obstinacy?'

'God has many names and infinite attributes. Men have called Him Jehovah, Zeus and Brahman. What does it signify what name you give Him? But among His infinite attributes the chief, as Socrates, pagan though he was, well saw, is justice. He must know that man does not believe what he would but what he can, and I cannot do Him so great a wrong as to suppose He will condemn His creatures for what is no fault of theirs. Your Reverence must not think I am wanting in respect if I beg you now to leave me to my own reflections.'

'I cannot leave you thus. I might try to the end to save your immortal soul from the raging fires of hell. Say one word to give me hope that you may be saved. One word to show that you are not unrepentant so that I may at least mitigate your earthly punishment.'

The Greek smiled and it may be that there was in his smile a touch of irony.

'You will do your part and I mine,' he said. 'It is yours to kill, mine to die without quailing.'

The Inquisitor was blinded by his tears so that he could scarcely find his way out.

Much of this, in halting tones, the Bishop told the two friars and at this point he covered his face as though to continue were a shame greater than he could bear. They had listened to him with pain, but with rapt attention, and Father Antonio in his mind carefully noted every speech and every reply so that he could write it in his book.

'Then I did a dreadful thing. Don Baltasar was sick in bed and I knew he would stay there till the last moment, for he was mortally afraid of being too ill to attend the *auto de fé*. He is an ambitious man and wished to bring himself to the notice of the Prince. I was free to act on my own initiative. I could not bear the thought of that poor old man being burnt by those cruel flames. His screams when they tortured him still rang in my ears and I thought I should continue to hear them all my life. I told those it concerned that I had myself spoken with him and he had so far recanted as to accept the procession of the Holy Ghost from the Son. I gave orders that he should be garrotted before he was burnt and I sent money by a servant to the executioner to induce him to do his work with dispatch.'

It should be explained that the executioner by tightening and loosening the iron collar round the victim's neck could prolong the death-agony for hours and so had to be bribed to give the sufferer the quick release of death.

'I knew it was a sin. I was distraught with grief. I hardly knew what I was doing. It was a sin for which I can never cease to reproach myself. I told it to my confessor and

91

performed the penance he imposed upon me. I received absolution, but I cannot absolve myself, and the events of this day are my punishment.'

'But, my lord, it was an act of mercy,' said Father Antonio. 'Who that has worked with you as long as I have does not know the tenderness of your heart and who can blame you because for once you allowed it to override your sense of justice?'

'It was no act of mercy. Who knows but that the Greek was shaken by my reasoning and who knows but that when the fire licked his naked flesh the grace of God might have been vouchsafed to him and so moved his stubborn spirit to recant his errors? Many at that last dreadful moment when they are about to meet their Maker have thus saved their souls. I robbed him of the chance and so condemned him to eternal torment.'

A hoarse sob broke from his throat, a sound like the strangled, mysterious cry of a bird of the night in the dark silence of the forest.

'Eternal torment! Who can picture to himself its pain? The damned writhe in a lake of fire from which rise noxious vapours which they breathe in agony. Their bodies are alive with worms. Raging thirst and ravenous hunger torment them. Their shrieks, wrung from them by the scorching flames, are a tumult and a confusion compared with which the crash of thunder, the howling of the storm-swept sea, are a deathly silence. Devils, frightful to look upon, mock and deride them beat them with insatiable rage, but remorse tears them with a pain more cruel than the tortures of those hideous fiends. The worm of conscience gnaws their vitals. Fire crucifies their souls, and it is a fire compared with which the fire of this world is like the fire of a picture, for it is the wrath of God that lights it and maintains it as the terrible instrument of His just vengeance to all eternity.

'And eternity, how terrible is eternity! As many millions of years pass over the damned as drops of water have fallen upon the earth since the beginning of time; as many millions of years as there are drops of water in all the seas and all the rivers in the world; as many millions of years as there are leaves on all the trees that grow and as many millions of years as there are grains of sand on the shores of all the oceans; as many millions of years as all the tears that men have wept since God created our first parents. And after this incalculable number of years has passed, the anguish of those unhappy creatures shall continue as though it were but a beginning, as though it were the first day; and eternity will remain whole as though not one second had passed. And it is to that eternity of suffering that I have condemned that unhappy man. What punishment can make amends for such a frightful misdeed? Oh, I am afraid, afraid.'

He was a man distraught. Great sobs rent his breast. He stared at the two friars with eyes dark with horror and when they looked into them there was a redness in their depths as though they saw in them, as if from a vast distance, the red flames of hell.

'Call the friars together and I will tell them I have sinned and for my soul's sake command them to inflict upon me the circular discipline.'

This was degrading punishment of scourging in which all present used the lash on the offender. Father Antonio, appalled, flung himself down on his knees and with his hands together as if in prayer implored his master not to insist on such a fearful ordeal.

'The brethren have no love for you, my lord, they are angry because you would not allow them to come to the church this morning. They will not spare you. They will use the lash with all their might. Friars have often died under their strokes.'

'I do not wish them to spare me. If I die justice will have been administered. I command you under your vow of obedience to do as I tell you.'

The friar raised himself to his feet.

'My lord, you have no right to expose yourself to such a mortal affront. You are the Bishop of Segovia. You will cast a slur on the whole episcopate of Spain. You will lessen the authority of all who have been appointed by God to your high station. Are you sure that there is not ostentation in the shame to which you would expose yourself?'

He had never dared to speak to his Father in God in such peremptory tones. The Bishop was taken aback. Was there some shadow of vainglory in his desire thus publicly to abase himself? He looked long at the friar.

'I do not know,' he said at last miserably. 'I am like a man stumbling across an unknown country in the darkness of the night. Perhaps you are right. I was thinking only of myself, I did not think how it would affect others.'

Father Antonio gave a sigh of relief.

'You two shall give me the discipline here and in private.'

'No, no, no, I will not. I could not bear to do violence to your sacred body.'

'Must I remind you of your vows then?' asked the Bishop with all his old sternness. 'Have you so little love for me that you can hesitate to inflict a trifling penance on me for my soul's good? There are scourges under the bed.'

Silently, unhappily, the friar got them out. They were stained with blood. The Bishop slipped out of the upper part of his habit so that it fell to his waist. Then he removed his shirt; it was made of tin and pierced like a grater so that it should lacerate the flesh. Father Antonio knew that the Bishop was in the habit of wearing a hair shirt, not always, for then he would have grown used to it, but only so often as to make the torment of it ever fresh; he gasped when he saw that horrible shirt of tin, but at the same time was edified. This was indeed a saint. He would not fail to take notice of it in his book. The Bishop's back was scarred with the scourging he had at least once a week inflicted on himself and there were open and suppurating sores.

He threw his arms round the thin column that upheld the two arches by which his apartment was divided and exposed his back to the two friars. Each of them in silence took a scourge and one after the other brought it down on the bleeding flesh. At each blow the Bishop shuddered, but not even a groan escaped his lips. They had not given him more then a dozen strokes when he fell to the floor in a swoon. They picked him up and carried him on to the hard bed. They threw water over him, but he did not regain consciousness and they were frightened. Father Antonio sent his fellow to tell a lay brother to hurry for a doctor, since the Bishop was ill, and at the same time he bade him let the brethren know that on no consideration was he to be disturbed. He bathed the lacerated back; he anxiously felt the wavering pulse. For a while he thought the Bishop was dying. But at length he opened his eyes. It took him a moment to gather his senses together. Then he forced a smile to his lips.

'Poor creature that I am,' he said. 'I fainted.'

'Do not speak, my lord. Lie still.'

But the Bishop raised himself on an elbow.

'Give me my shirt.'

Father Antonio looked with a shudder at that instrument of torture.

'Oh, my lord, you couldn't bear it now.'

'Give it to me.'

'The doctor is coming. You would not want him to see you wear a garment of mortification.'

The Bishop sank back on the hard pallet.

'Give me my Cross,' he said.

At last the doctor came, ordered the patient to stay in bed and said he would send medicine. It was a soothing potion and after a while the Bishop fell asleep.

16

Next day he insisted on getting up. He said his Mass. Though weak and shaken, he was calm and went about his affairs as though nothing had happened.

Towards evening a lay brother came to tell him that his brother Don Manuel was in the parlour and desired to see him. Supposing that he had heard of his sickness he sent back word that he thanked him for coming, but pressing business prevented him from receiving him. The lay brother returned to say that Don Manuel refused to go till the Bishop saw him, since he had a communication to make to him that was of moment. With a sigh the Bishop told the lay brother to show him in. Since their arrival at Castel Rodriguez he had seen no more of him then courtesy required. Though he chid himself for his lack of charity he could not overcome the dislike he felt for that vain, brutal and callous man.

He came in, very grandly dressed, plethoric, rudely healthy and full of an aggressive vitality. He carried himself with a swagger. His face bore a look of self-satisfaction, and if the Bishop did not deceive himself there was malice and cunning in his bold bright eyes. He smiled grimly when he looked round the bare and cheerless cell. The Bishop motioned him to a stool.

'Have you nothing more comfortable for me to sit on than this, brother?' he said.

'Nothing.'

'I hear you were taken ill.'

'It was a passing indisposition of no consequence. I am restored to my usual health.'

'That is good.'

There was a silence between them. Don Manuel continued to look at him with a smile that was tinged with raillery.

'You said that you had a communication to make to me,' said the Bishop at last.

'I have, brother. It appears that the ceremony of yesterday morning failed to realize your hopes.'

'Be so good as to state your business, Manuel.'

'What made you think that you were the chosen instrument to cure that girl of her disability?'

The Bishop hesitated. It was his inclination to refuse an answer, but, mortifying himself before the gross coarse man, he gave it.

'I received an assurance that what the girl said was true, and though I knew myself unworthy I felt bound to act upon it.'

'You made a mistake, brother. You should have examined her more carefully. The Blessed Virgin told her that the son of Don Juan de Valero who had best served God had the power to cure her. Why did you jump to the conclusion that you were meant? Were you not a trifle wanting in the Christian humility?'

The Bishop paled.

'What do you mean?' he cried. 'She said to me that Our Lady had told her that it was I.'

'She is an ignorant and foolish girl. She supposed that you must be designated because you are a bishop and, how I know not, the people of this city have heard much of your sanctity and mortifications.'

The Bishop prayed a short mental prayer so that he could master the anger and shame with which his brother's words filled him.

'How do you know this? Who told you that those were the words of the Blessed Virgin?'

Don Manuel chortled at what seemed to him an excellent joke.

'It appears that the girl has an uncle called Domingo

Perez. We used to know him when we were little. If I remember right you were at the seminary with him.'

The Bishop inclined his head in token of assent.

'Domingo Perez is a toper. He goes to a tavern frequented by my servants, and he scraped acquaintance with them, doubtless in the hope of drinking wine at their expense. Last night he was in his cups. As was natural they were all talking of the events of the morning, for your fiasco, brother, is become the common talk of the city. Domingo told them he had expected nothing else and had sought to warn you, but was refused admission to the convent. He repeated then the exact words which Our Blessed Lady had spoken as his niece had reported them to him.'

The Bishop was confounded. He did not know what to say. Don Manuel continued and now there was in his eyes a look of frank mockery. The Bishop asked himself miserably what sort of a man this was who could find so cruel a pleasure in thus humiliating his brother.

'Did it not occur to you, brother, that it was I that was meant?'

'You?' The Bishop could hardly believe his ears. If he had been capable of laughing, he would have laughed then.

'Does it surprise you, brother? For four and twenty years I have served my King. I have risked my life a hundred times, I have fought in glorious battles and my body bears the scars of my honourable wounds. I have suffered from hunger and thirst, from the bitter cold of those accursed Low Countries and from the torrid heat of summer. You have burnt a few dozen heretics at the stake, and I, to the glory of God, have killed the damned heretics by the thousand. To the glory of God I have laid waste their fields and burnt their crops. I have besieged thriving towns and when they surrendered put all their inhabitants, men, women and children, to the sword.'

The Bishop shuddered.

'The Holy Office condemns the accused only by process of law. It gives them the opportunity to repent and purge their sin. It is careful to do justice, and if it punishes the guilty it absolves the innocent.'

'I know those Dutchmen too well to think they are capable of repentance. Heresy is in their blood. They are traitors to their faith and their King and they deserve death. No one that knows me can deny that I have served God well.'

The Bishop pondered. The brutality and boastfulness of his brother filled him with disgust. It seemed incredible that God could have chosen such an instrument for His work, yet it might be that He had done so just because he was the man he was, in order to put him, Blasco de Valero, to shame for his unforgiven sin. If so, it was his to kiss the rod.

'Heaven knows, I am conscious of my unworthiness,' he said at last. 'Should you attempt this thing and fail it will cause a scandal in the city and give a cruel opportunity to the wicked to mock. I beseech you to do nothing rashly; it is a matter that demands anxious consideration.'

'That it has already received, brother,' said Don Manuel coolly. 'I have consulted my friends and they are the most important men in the city. I have asked the opinion of the archpriest and the prior of this convent. One and all, they consent.'

Again the Bishop paused. He knew that there were many in the city who were envious of the positions he and his brother had achieved because, though gentlemen by birth, they were of small account. It might well be that they had agreed to his brother's preposterous demand only to throw discredit on them both.

'You must not forget that there is still the possibility that the girl Catalina Perez was deceived.'

'The proof of the pudding is in the eating. If I fail it will be clear that the girl is a witch and should be handed over to the Inquisition for trial and punishment.'

'If you have the consent of the authorities of the city and are determined to make the attempt I can do nothing to prevent you. But I beg you to do everything as secretly as may be so that greater scandal than has been caused already may be avoided.'

'I am obliged to you for your advice, brother. I will give it the consideration it deserves.'

Upon this Don Manuel withdrew. The Bishop sighed deeply. It seemed to him that his cup of bitterness was filled to the brim. He knelt down before the black Cross on the wall and silently prayed. Then he called a lay brother and bade him fetch the man Domingo Perez.

'If you cannot find him in his house, you will find him in the tavern near the palace in which my brother Don Manuel is staying. You will ask him to do me the favour of coming to see me without delay.

17

After a little the lay brother ushered Domingo into the Bishop's oratory. For a while the two men stared silently at one another. They had not met since they were young men, hardly more than boys, at the seminary of Alcalá de Henares. Both were now middle-aged, almost elderly, and both were emaciated and ravaged. But one was ravaged by austerity, long vigils, fasting and continuous labour; while the other was ravaged by drink and dissipation. Yet if there was a certain similarity in their appearance there was none in their expression: the Bishop's was harassed and anxious while the scrivener's was careless and good-humoured. As a clerk in minor orders he wore a cassock, and it was shabby, green with age and stained down the front with wine and food. But both wore an air of asceticism and of intellectual distinction.

'Your lordship desired to see me,' said Domingo.

A slight, yet gentle smile was outlined on the Bishop's pale lips.

'It is a long time since we last met, Domingo.'

'Our paths have gone very different ways. I should have thought your lordship had long forgotten the existence of so poor and worthless a creature as Domingo Perez.'

'We have known one another all our lives. I am ashamed that you should address me with such ceremony. It is many years since I have heard a friend call me Blasco.'

Domingo gave him his charming, disarming smile.

'The great have no friends, dear Blasco. It is the price they must pay for their greatness.'

'Let us for an hour forget this poor greatness of mine and talk with one another like the old and intimate comrades we once were. You were wrong in thinking I had ever forgotten you; we were too close to one another for that. I have kept myself informed of your life.'

'It has not been an edifying one.'

The Bishop sat down on a stool and motioned to Domingo to take the other.

'But more than that I have kept in touch with you through your letters.'

'How can you have done that? I have never written to you.'

'Not as from yourself, but I read too many of the poems you wrote when we were boys together not to know your handwriting. Do you think I did not recognize it in the letters my father and my brother Martin sent me? I knew very well that they could never have expressed themselves with such elegance and propriety. And there were expressions, turns of phrase, reflections, in which I recognized your wayward spirit.'

Domingo laughed lightly.

'The literary gifts of Don Juan and your brother Martin are not remarkable. When they had said they were in good health and hoped you were also, and that the harvest was poor, they had said all they had to say. For my own credit and theirs I felt bound to enliven their bald statements with the gossip of the town and such conceits and flippant jests as occurred to me.'

'How sad it is that you should have let your great gifts run to waste, Domingo. What I had to learn by application and industry you acquired as it were by intuition. Often you used to terrify me by the audacity of your thought, by that flow of unexpected ideas that seemed to flow from your brain with as little effort as water gushes from a spring, but I never doubted your brilliance. You were born to excel, and but for your restless temper you might by now be a shining ornament of our Holy Church.'

'Instead of which,' returned Domingo, 'I am nothing but a poor scholar, a playwright who can find no actors to act his plays, a hack who writes sermons for priests too stupid to write their own, something of a drunkard and a ne'er-do-well. I lacked the vocation, my good Blasco. Life allured me. My place was neither the cloister nor the hearth, but the broad highway with its adventures and perils, its chance encounters and manifold variety. I have lived. I have suffered from hunger and thirst, I have been footsore, I have been beaten, I have suffered every mischance that can beset a man: I have lived. And even now when age is creeping upon me I have no regrets for the years I have wasted, for I too have slept on Parnassus; and when I walk to some distant village to write a paper for an illiterate clown, or when I sit in my little room surrounded by my books and rhyme the speeches in plays that will never be played, I am filled with such exultation that I would not change places with cardinal or pope.'

'Do you not fear the wrath to come? The wages of sin is death.'

'Is it the Bishop of Segovia who asks me that question or my old friend Blasco de Valero?'

'I have never yet betrayed a friend or an enemy. So long as you say nothing to offend the Faith say what you will.'

'Then this must be my answer: We know that the attributes of God are infinite and it has always seemed strange to me that men have never given Him credit for common sense. It is hard to believe that He would have created so beautiful a world if He had not desired men to enjoy it. Would He have given the stars their glory, the birds their sweet song and the flowers their fragrance if He had not wished us to delight in them? I have sinned before men and men have condemned me. God made me a man with the passions of a man, and did He give them to me only that I should suppress them? He gave me my adventurous spirit and my love of life. I have a humble hope that when I am face to face with my Maker He will condone my imperfections and I shall find mercy in His sight.'

The Bishop looked sorely troubled. He could have told the poor poet that we are placed on this earth to scorn its delights, to resist temptation, to conquer ourselves and to bear our cross; so that in the end, miserable sinners though we be, we may be found worthy of communion with the blessed. But would his words avail? He could only pray that before death claimed him the Grace of God might descend upon that wretched man so that he would repent of his misdeeds. Silence fell between them.

'I did not send for you today in order to urge you to mend your ways,' said the Bishop at last. 'It would not be difficult for me to confute your wrongful opinions, but I know of old how ingenious you are to make the worse appear the better reason and I know too the pleasure you take in uttering sophisms to tease. I am ready to believe that much of what you said you said only to amuse yourself at my expense. You have a niece.'

'I have.'

'What do you make of this story that has brought unrest upon the city?'

'She is a virtuous and truthful girl. She is a good Catholic, but no more than properly religious.'

'Since I understand that she owes her education to you I can well credit that.'

'Nor is she prone to idle fancies. She is indeed, as the poor are bound to be, somewhat matter-of-fact. No one could accuse her of possessing the unfortunately faculty of imagination.'

'Do you believe then that the Blessed Virgin did in fact appear to her?'

'I was in two minds until yesterday when she told me the exact words Our Lady had used. Then I was convinced. That is why I sought to see you. I knew at once what was meant and I wanted to spare you a useless intervention. They would not admit me.'

The Bishop sighed.

'It is not the least of the crosses we are called upon to bear that the companions of our labours in their solicitude for our well-being prevent access to us of those whom it would be profitable for us to see.'

'Time has not diminished the affection that bound me to you in my youth, for you see, I, a sinner, can afford to surrender to the blind impulses of my heart. I wished to save you from a humiliation which I knew would be very bitter to you. The moment the girl repeated to me the Blessed Virgin's exact words I knew who was destined to cure her of infirmity.'

'She told me that Our Lady had named me.'

'That was a natural error for a girl to make who had heard of your mortifications, virtue and austerity. The Blessed Virgin told her that the power to cure her lay in the hands of that one of your father's sons who has best served God.'

'I have but just heard that.'

'Do you not know then who has done that? It is as plain as a pike-staff.'

The Bishop paled. He gave Domingo an anxious glance.

'My brother Martin?'

'The baker.'

Beads of sweat stood on the Bishop's brow. He shivered as though someone were walking over his grave.

'It is impossible. He is no doubt a worthy man, but of the earth, earthy.'

'Why is it impossible? Because he has no learning? It is one of the mysteries of our Faith that God Who gave man reason and thereby raised him above the brutes has never so far as we are told laid great store on intelligence. Your brother is a good and simple man. He has been a faithful husband to his wife and a loving father to his children. He has honoured his father and mother. He has fed them when they were hungry and tended them when they were sick. He bore with submission his father's contempt and his mother's distress because, a gentleman by birth, he followed a calling that lowered him in the estimation of fools. He suffered with good humour the scorn of the gentry and the gibes of the vulgar. Like our father Adam he earned his bread by the sweat of his brow and he took a modest pride in the knowledge that the bread was good. He accepted the joys of life with gratitude and its sorrows with resignation. He succoured the needy. He was pleasant in his discourse and cheerful in his mien. He was a friend to all men. The ways of God are inscrutable and it may well be that in His eyes by his industrious, honest life, his loving-kindness, his innocent gaiety, Martin the baker has served Him better than you who have sought salvation by prayer and penance or your brother Manuel who glories in the women and children he has killed and the thriving towns he has left in desolate ruin.'

The Bishop passed his hand wearily across his forehead. His face was anguished.

'You know me too well, Domingo,' he said, his voice trembling, 'to think that I understood to do the thing I did without anxious searching of heart. I knew I was unworthy and my soul was dismayed, but I took the sign that was granted me as a command to do what I believed to be the will of God. I was wrong. And now my brother Manuel is determined to attempt what I failed to do.'

'Even as a boy he was more remarkable for the strength of his body than for the force of his understanding.'

'He is as obstinate as he is wrong-headed. The notabilities of the town are encouraging him so that they may deride him after the event. He has obtained the approval of the archpriest and of the prior of this convent.'

'At all costs you must prevent him.'

'I have no authority to do so.'

'If your brother should persist in his folly he will seek to avenge himself for his discomfiture on that wretched girl. The people will side with him. They will have no mercy. In the name of our old friendship I beseech you to protect her from his enmity and from the blind violence of the mob.'

'By the Cross on which Our Lord was crucified I swear to you that I will give my life if need be to save the child from harm.'

Domingo rose to his feet.

'I thank you with all my heart. Farewell, my dear. Our paths are different and we shall not meet again. Farewell for ever.'

'Farewell. Oh, Domingo, I am an unhappy man. Pray for me, pray for me in all your prayers that God may vouchsafe to release me from the cruel burden of this life.'

He was so shattered, his mien so piteous, that the old toper was seized with compassion. On a sudden impulse he took the Bishop in his arms and kissed him on both cheeks. The sinner pressed the saint to his heart and was quickly gone.

18

That night a very strange thing happened. The full moon, pursuing its appointed course, shone with such a dazzling brilliance that the cloudless sky shone blue like the velvet cloak that covered the white garment of the Blessed Virgin. The people of Castel Rodriguez slept. Suddenly all the bells in the city began to ring with such a clamour as might rouse the dead. It woke the sleepers and some rushed to their windows, while others half-dressed, snatching up clothes as they passed, ran down into the streets. The ringing of the church bells at that unwonted hour meant that fire had broken out in some part of the town and timorous housewives set about getting their valuables together, for when a fire started none could tell how far it would spread, and it was well to save what one could before the flames caught the house. Some in their panic went so far as to throw their bedding out of the windows and some carried out pieces of furniture and deposited them outside their doors.

People poured out of their houses and the streets were thronged with them. By a common impulse they crowded into the great plaza which was the pride of the city. Each one asked his neighbour where the fire was. Men cursed and women wrung their hands. They rushed to and fro to find where houses were aflame; they looked up to heaven to watch for the tell-tale glow that would mark the spot. There was nothing to be seen. People surging into the plaza from the various quarters of the town said there was no fire where they came from. There was no fire anywhere. Then as though a wind had suddenly blown over them the idea seized them one and all that foolish youths were playing a prank and had mischievously set the bells ringing to get the people out of their beds and frighten them out of their wits. Angry men, determined to beat them within an inch of their lives, rushed to the church towers. They were met, with an amazing sight. The ropes were jerking up and down and not a soul was pulling them. They stared for a moment with astonishment at the strange sight and then, with torches and lanterns, ran up the steep steps of the towers. When they reached the platform where the bells hung they were deafened by their clanging. The bells tossed from side to side in a furious oscillation and the clappers thundered against their brazen sides. No men were there. No men could have moved those heavy bells to such a violent din. You might have thought the bells had suddenly gone mad. They were ringing of themselves.

With short gasps, with terror in their hearts, scuttling down the stairways as though the devil were after them, they ran into the streets and with frantic words and wild gestures told what they had seen.

It was a miracle. It was God that had set the bells ringing and none knew whether it betokened good or ill to the city. Many fell to their knees and prayed aloud. Sinners remembered their sins and thought of the wrath to come. The parish priests had the doors of their churches unlocked and the crowd flocked in and followed the priests in their prayers, which besought the Almighty to have mercy on His creatures. It was long before they quieted down and slunk, silent and sober, back to their homes.

19

None knew how it had started, whether the notion had occurred to one fanciful person or whether it had been independently conceived by many; it was like the cholera; you do not know if it has been brought into the city by a stranger from foreign parts or whether some ill wind has spread the disease; a man here falls sick, a woman there dies, and before you are aware of the danger pestilence sweeps through the streets and the grave-diggers can no longer dig graves fast enough to bury the dead. Before the day was well advanced the conviction had spread among all the people of Castel Rodriguez that the mysterious event of the night was bound up in some way with the appearance to Catalina Perez of the Blessed Virgin. They talked of nothing else. Magistrates discussed it in their council chambers, priests in their sacristies and nobles in their palaces. The common people in the streets, housewives in the market place, shopmen in their shops, spoke of it and wondered. Monks in their monasteries, nuns in their convents were distracted from their prayers.

And presently it was agreed that there could be no doubt who was designated by the Blessed Virgin's enigmatic words. There were not a few, especially among the secular clergy, who asked whether God was not displeased with the extravagance of the Bishop's austerity and whether a certain arrogance in his humility did not indeed merit a divine reproof. But on Don Manuel de Valero there was neither spot nor stain. He had given the best years of his life to the service of God and the King. His Majesty, vice-regent on earth of the Almighty, by conferring conspicuous honours upon him had set the seal of his approval on his valour and virtue. It was evident to all, cleric and lay, rich and poor, nobles and commoners, that Don Manuel was the man chosen to work the miracle ordained by the divine will. A deputation consisting of prominent ecclesiastics, members of the aristocracy and persons of authority in the city council, called upon him and announced their unanimous opinion. Don Manuel in his bluff, soldierly way told them that he was prepared to put himself at their disposal. It was decided that the ceremony should take place on the following day in the Collegiate Church. Don Manuel asked the archpriest to receive his confession that afternoon, and since he proposed to take Holy Communion in the morning, which he must take fasting, he called off the supper party he had arranged to give to his friends that evening. He was a conscientious man and was determined to omit nothing that might render his intervention efficacious on such a solemn occasion. Thrice armed is he, shriven and free from guilt, who puts his trust in God.

The Prior of the Dominican convent himself informed the Bishop of what had been decided and at the same time invited him to head the friars who were going in procession to attend the ceremony. Don Blasco discerned the malice in the Prior's offer, but, thanking him for the honour, gravely accepted. He was helpless. He attached no importance to what Domingo had said about his brother Martin; he knew too well Domingo's love of teasing and the pleasure he took in paradoxical conceits; but for all that he had a firm conviction that Don Manuel was not the man to perform a miracle. He would willingly have escaped the obligation of seeing his brother confounded, but knew that if he refused to go it would be ascribed to pique. It did not become his high office to give evil minds opportunity to think ill of him. But putting that aside there was his promise to Domingo to fulfil. He was well acquainted with the folly and brutality of the rabble, rabble if they were nobly born or basely, and it was only too probable that if they were disappointed of the wonder they expected they would wreak their vengeance on the hapless girl. If he were there he might be able to save her from their savagery.

So next day, heavy at heart, with his two faithful secretaries, he walked at the head of the friars from the convent to the church. It was thronged to the doors and still the people, eager to see a miracle performed before their very eyes, pressed in. Way was made and the Bishop, followed by the friars, proceeded slowly up the nave. He took his seat in a great chair beside, and a little in front of, the high altar. The choir was filled with the notabilities of the city. Presently Don Manuel came forward with a company of gentlemen and seated himself in a chair that had been placed for him on the other side of the altar. He was dressed in a parade suit of armour, his breastplate damascened with gold, and he wore the great cloak, with its green cross, of the Order of Calatrava. The nobles in the choir were in their best array. They were chatting and laughing. They exchanged nods and smiles with one another. In the nave the crowd were talking aloud and calling to one another as though they were at a bull-fight. The Bishop surveyed them with indignation. It was a mockery of religion, and he had it in mind to rise and denounce them for their irreverent levity.

At the foot of the steps, supporting herself with a crutch, knelt Catalina.

From the organ loft fell the first notes of a voluntary and the florid sounds swept blithely over the heads of the congregation. The church was in its architecture large and plain, but successive heads of the great house of Henriquez had enriched it with a plateresque ceiling of painted wood, framed the pictures over the altars with frames massive and gilt, and provided the images with gorgeous robes. The choir stalls were elaborately carved. In the chapels were the tombs, the early ones in stone, grim and austere, the later ones of marble richly sculptured, in which lay the mortal remains of the dead dukes and their consorts. A dim light filtered through the windows of stained glass and the air was heavy with incense.

The priests came in, clad in the costly vestments used on great occasions, which had been presented to the church by devout and noble ladies. The subdeacon held the chalice and the paten enveloped in the humeral veil. Mass was sung. A shiver of awe passed over the vast concourse as all fell to their knees at the thin tinkle of the bell that called attention to the elevation of the Host and Chalice. The archpriest, the celebrant, partook of

Communion and administered it in turn to Don Manuel and to Catalina. At last the moment had arrived which the crowd had been impatiently awaiting. A strange sound came from them, not the sound of voices, not the sound exactly of restless movements, but a sound like the sighing of the wind in a wood of pine trees, as though their expectation itself was made audible.

Don Manuel rose to his feel and strode to the kneeling girl. In his armour, the great cloak of his order hanging from his shoulders, he made an imposing and even splendid figure. The scene, the moment had invested him with an unaccustomed dignity. He was confident in his power. He laid his hand on the girl's head and in a loud voice, as though he were giving his regiment the order to charge, so that he was plainly heard to the remotest corners of the great church, he repeated the words he had been given to say.

'In the name of God the Father, God the Son and God the Holy Ghost I command thee, Catalina Perez, to rise to thy feet, cast away thy useless crutch and walk.'

The girl, spell-bound by the awfulness of the occasion, frightened, staggered to her feet and dropped the crutch. She took a step forward and with a cry of terror fell headlong. Once more the miracle had failed.

Then a great uproar arose and it was as though a sudden madness had seized the crowd. Men shouted and women screamed. They yelled with rage.

'A witch. A witch,' they cried. 'The stake. The stake. The stake. Burn her.'

Then with a sudden impulse they surged towards the sacristy and would have torn the girl limb from limb. In their passion they pushed one another aside. Some fell and were brutally trampled on, and their shrieks were added to the din.

The Bishop sprang to his feet and with a swift sweeping movement strode down the sacristy till he came face to face with the frenzied mob. He raised his arms above his head and his great dark eyes blazed.

'Back, back,' he cried in a voice of thunder. 'Who are you to desecrate this holy place? Get back, I tell you. Get back.'

His aspect was so terrifying that a gasp of horror was wrung from a thousand throats. As though a great abyss had suddenly opened before them the crowd on a sudden stopped dead. They shrank back. For a moment the Bishop eyed them, his eyes black with indignation.

'Vile, vile,' he cried and then, clenching his fists, he flung out his arms as though he would fling at them the thunderbolt of his wrath. 'Kneel, kneel and pray that you may be forgiven for the insult that you have offered to the house of God.'

At his words, dominated by his authority, many fell sobbing to their knees. Others, as though too dazed to move, stood and stared vacantly at that fearful figure. Slowly the Bishop looked from side to side till his gaze had taken in the whole of that vast concourse and each one felt that those angry eyes were fixed upon him alone. Silence fell except for the hysterical sobbing of a woman here and there.

'Listen,' said the Bishop at last. 'Listen to what I say.' And now his voice was no longer menacing, but grave, stern and authoritative. 'Listen. You know the words Our Lady vouchsafed to the girl Catalina Perez and you know the wonders that have occurred in this city and have given rise to confusion and unrest in your minds. The Blessed Virgin told this girl that the son of Don Juan de Valero who had best served God had the power by God's grace to cure her of her infirmity. In our sinful pride and vanity I who speak to you and Don Manuel my brother had the temerity to think that one or other of us was thus designated. We have been bitterly punished for our presumption. But Don Juan has still another son.'

The crowd interrupted him with shouts and laughter.

'*El panadero,*' they cried. 'The baker.'

Then they began to sing derisively in a sort of rude rhythm.

'*El panadero. El panadero.*'

'Silence,' cried the Bishop.

People hushed one another.

'Laugh. As the crackling of thorns under a pot, so is the laughter of fools. What does the Lord require of you, but to do justly, to love mercy and to walk humbly with your God? Hypocrites and blasphemers. Fornicators. Vile. Vile. Vile.'

He repeated the word each time with a more biting scorn so that they who heard him recoiled as a man would if a glass of icy water were thrown in his face. His wrath was terrible to see. He swept that multitude with a glance of withering contempt.

'Are the familiars of the Holy Office here?'

A strange sound, like a startled sigh, swept through the crowd as one and all caught their breath, for these instruments of the Inquisition were terrifying to the people. They did not know what the sinister words portended, and each one shook in his shoes. Behind the Bishop several men started up.

'Let them stand forth,' he said.

Since the familiars of the Holy Office enjoyed power, influence and above all protection from its dread proceedings, theirs was a charge sought after by men of the highest rank. There were eight in Castel Rodriguez. There was a moment's pause while they left their seats and took up positions behind the Bishop. He waited till he knew from the quiet of their shuffling feet that they were behind him.

'Listen,' he said again, and the index finger of his outstretched hand seemed to point in accusation at each one of those shivering creatures. 'The Holy Office does nothing in anger nor in haste. It administers justice to the guilty, but is merciful to the repentant sinner.'

He paused and the silence was awful.

'It is not for you, a generation of vipers, to lay hands on this wretched girl. If she is deceived or possessed of a devil it is for the Holy office to take cognizance of it. If she fails in the test the familiars are here to deliver her to the tribunal. But the test is not complete. Where is Martin de Valero?'

'Here, here,' cried several voices.

'Let him come forward.'

'No, no, no.'

It was the voice of Martin the baker.

'If he will not come of his own free will, constrain him,' said the Bishop sternly.

There was a scuffle as Martin struggled with the men who pushed and pulled him, but after a little the crowd parted and he was urged forward to the sanctuary steps. The men fell back and left him standing alone. He had come in from his shop to see the wonder of which everyone was talking, and he was in his working clothes. His face was red from the heat of the ovens and from his vain effort to escape from the rude hands that hustled him. The day was hot and pearls of sweat stood on his forehead. His plump good-humoured countenance was heavy with consternation.

'Come,' said the Bishop.

As though drawn by a force he could not withstand the baker ascended the sanctuary steps.

'Brother, brother, what is it that you are doing to me?' he cried. 'How can I do what you could not? I am but a working man and no better a Christian than my neighbour.'

'Be silent.'

The Bishop had not even a remote notion that the baker could work a miracle, and he had only thought of him on the spur of the moment as the sole means by which he could save Catalina from the fury of the rabble. He wanted a brief respite which would allow him to calm their passion. He knew now that the girl was safe. The familiars were there to protect her, and since there was in the city no prison of the Inquisition they would take her on his order to a convent and when she was there it would be time to consider what further steps should be taken. The Bishop once more addressed himself to the awed people.

'Hath not the potter power over the clay, of the same lump to make one vessel with honour and another with dishonour? There is no respect of persons with God. He that humbleth himself shall be exalted and the haughty shall be abased. Bring forward the girl.'

Catalina was lying where she had fallen, her face hidden in her arms, and sobs shook her thin little body. No one had paid more attention to her than if she were a dead dog by the roadside. Two familiars raised her to her feet and brought her face to face with the Bishop. As best she could, with the crutch under her armpit, she joined her hands together in supplication. Tears streamed down her face.

'Oh, my lord, my lord, have pity on me,' she cried. 'Not again, I beseech you, it can come to nothing. Let me go home to my mother.'

'Kneel,' he ordered. 'Kneel.'

With a despairing sob the child sank to her knees.

'Lay your hands on her head,' he bade his brother.

'I cannot. I will not. I am afraid.'

'Under pain of excommunication I command you to do as I tell you,' said the Bishop harshly.

A shudder shook the unfortunate man, for he knew that his brother would not hesitate to carry into effect his dreadful threat. He timidly laid a trembling hand on the girl's head. It was not even clean.

'Now say the words that you heard your brother Manuel say.'

'I cannot remember them.'

'Then I will say them and you shall say them after me. I, Martin de Valero, son of Juan de Valero.'

Martin repeated the words.

'I, Martin de Valero, son of Juan de Valero.'

The Bishop spoke the last fateful words in a loud strong voice, but Martin said them after him in a tone that was barely audible. Catalina, as she was bidden, scrambled to her feet and with a despairing gesture flung the crutch away from her. For an instant she wavered. She did not fall. She stood. Then, with a cry and a sob, forgetting the place and the occasion, she turned and ran down the sanctuary steps.

'Mother, mother.'

Maria Perez, who was with Domingo, beside herself with joy, forced her way through the crowd and ran to meet her. Catalina threw herself into her arms and burst out crying.

The dense throng for a moment was too stunned to move. They gasped in amazement; then such a hullabaloo arose as never was heard.

'The miracle. The miracle.'

They shouted. They clapped their hands. Women waved their handkerchiefs. The men cried *olè*, *olè*, as they would have done at a bull-fight when one of the toreros had made a dangerous pass; they flung their hats through the air as they flung them at the feet of the matador when with his *cuadrilla* behind him he walked round the ring to receive the plaudits of the public. Above the din rose the piercing tones of a woman here and there singing to a strange, half Moorish tune a hymn to the Blessed Virgin. It seemed as though the tumult would never cease. Strangers embraced one another. Men and women wept for joy. With their own eyes they had seen a miracle.

Suddenly a hush passed over that wild, madly-excited rout, and all eyes were turned upon the Bishop. Martin, in his shyness, hardly able to take in what had happened, had shrunk back, and the Dominican stood alone at the top of the sanctuary steps with his back to the High Altar. In his habit, patched and worn though it was, emaciated, but tall and erect, he made a figure that was awe-inspiring. But the marvellous thing was that he was bathed in light; it was not a halo that surrounded his head, but an aureole that seemed to clothe him from head to foot.

'A saint, a saint,' cried the people and they stared with all their eyes at the strange and thrilling sight. 'Blessed be the woman that bore you,' they cried. 'Now lettest thou thy servant depart in peace. Oh, happy, happy day!'

The did not know what they said. They were beside themselves with joy and love and fear. Only Domingo noticed that a pane of one of the stained-glass windows was broken and by a fortunate chance a ray of sun passed through the aperture to hit the Bishop and suffuse him with glory.

The Bishop raised his hand for silence and immediately that great noise was stilled. He stood for a moment surveying the sea of faces before him, his face sad and stern, and then, raising his head, his tragic eyes rapt as though with the eyes of the spirit he saw the heavenly host, he began in slow and solemn tones to recite the Nicene Creed. The words were familiar to all his listeners, for they heard them every Sunday at Mass and there was a low buzz, like the distant sound of shuffling feet, as they repeated the words after him. He came to an end. He turned and walked towards the High Altar. The light that had shone upon him was seen no more, and Domingo, looking at the window, saw that the sun in its relentless journey across the sky had passed on and no ray sent its light through the broken pane. The Bishop prostrated himself before the altar and gave thanks to God in silent prayer. A great weight was lifted from his tortured heart, for it was borne in upon him without a possibility of doubt that though it was the hand of Martin that had rested on the girl's head he was but an instrument, a tool as it were of which God had been pleased to make use, so that he, Blasco de Valero, might work a miracle to His glory. Moreover it was a sign, a sure and certain sign, that God forgave him for the grievous sin he had committed when in his weakness he had allowed the Greek to be garrotted before he was burnt. God Who knew all things, past, present and future, knew the hardness of the misbeliever's heart and so condemned him to everlasting death. It was well to pity the damned in their torments, but to repine was to impugn the justice of God.

The Bishop rose and slowly walked down the sanctuary. He walked like a man in a dream. The two religious, his friends and secretaries, saw his intention and followed him, whereupon the Prior, making a sign to his friars to come after him, walked behind them. When the Bishop came to the top of the sanctuary steps, he paused.

'The grace of the Lord Jesus Christ and the love of God and the communion of the Holy Ghost be with you all.'

He descended. The crowd pushed back so as to leave a pathway for him and the religious who followed him. The friars broke in the *Te Deum Laudamus* and their strong deep voices rang through the church. The Bishop, as in a trance, passed through the kneeling multitude and gave the people his blessing as he went. He did not see Domingo's ironical glance.

At that moment the bells in the belfry started to peal and in a little while all the bells in the city were ringing. But this was owing to no supernatural intervention. Don Manuel, like the well-trained soldier he was, paid attention to the smallest detail, and he had seen to it that when the bells of the Collegiate Church were set ringing in celebration of the miracle he was confident of working, the bells of all the other churches should be rung too.

The great doors were swung open as the Bishop approached and he passed out into the blazing sunshine of the August day. The crowd surged out after him and followed the procession of friars till it reached the Dominican convent. The Bishop was about to enter when a great outcry arose in the throng. They wanted him to speak to them. Against the wall of the convent was a pulpit used when a preacher came to the city so celebrated for his eloquence that the convent church was too small to hold the vast congregation that desired to hear him. The Prior advanced and telling the Bishop what the people wanted begged him to accede to their wish. The Bishop looked about him as though he did not know where he was. One might have thought he had not till then been aware of all those devout and anxious creatures that had dogged his steps. He paused for an instant to collect himself and then without a word mounted the pulpit.

His voice was magnificent, rich in tone, and with an infinite variety of inflection. He began.

'Ye cannot find out the depth of the heart of man, neither can ye perceive the things that he thinketh; then how can ye search out God, that hath made all these things, and know His mind, or comprehend His purpose?'

His gestures were powerful and significant. His voice reached to the farthest confines of the serried throng, and when he lowered it in compassion such was the beauty of his delivery that his every word was audible. When in passionate denunciation of the sins of men he raised it to its full splendour it was like thunder rolling in the bleak Sierras. He would pause on a sudden and the silence in that torrent of speech was like the crack of doom. The people winced when he reminded them of the shortness of life, the accidents that beset the sons of Adam from the cradle to the grave, the transitoriness of its pleasures, the anguish of its sorrows; they trembled when he painted the horrors of hell and the endless torture of the damned; and they wept when, his voice melting with tenderness, he described in ecstatic strains the communion of saints and the eternal joy of heaven. Many repented of their sins and from then on were changed men. He ended with a great peroration in praise of the Blessed Virgin and to the glory of God. Never had he spoken with a more fiery eloquence nor with a more heartrending pathos.

When they conducted him to his cell he was so broken that he permitted his two faithful attendants to lay him on his hard bed. He was shattered with emotion and fatigue.

20

That night there was great rejoicing in the city. In the taverns the tapsters could not fill cups and drinking-horns fast enough. Chattering crowds wandered round and round the plaza and talked of the wonderful event of the day. No one doubted but that it was the saintly Bishop who had performed the miracle and all were touched by his modesty in using his brother the baker as an instrument of his power. So he had taught then that in truth the humble would be exalted and the haughty abased. Many vowed that they had seen him rise in the air, two feet from the ground, said some, and four feet others, and remain there suspended in glory.

21

When the multitude flocked out of the church in the Bishop's train, Martin, who had shrunk within himself in the hope that no one would pay attention to him, remained so that in the end there was no one there but he. He waited in order to escape unseen, but with some impatience, since he knew that all this excitement would bring a lot of custom and he had left his shop in the charge of his two apprentices and he was afraid they would not be able to cope with the stream of customers. For he not only baked bread, but also meat for people who brought joints or pies which they could not cook at home. A lot of them would think this was an occasion for a treat. When at last he thought it safe to slip out he noticed Catalina's crutch on the marble floor where she had thrown it, and since he was a tidy soul, who didn't like to see things lying about, he picked it up and carried it away with him.

But when the archpriest got back to his house, as he sat down to a meal which he richly deserved and badly wanted, it occurred to him that the crutch had been left in the church and that it was an object that should not be lost sight of. He immediately sent a servant to fetch it and was vexed when the servant told him that he could not find it. It was too valuable an article to lose, so he had no sooner finished his dinner that he sent people to find out what had become of it; but it was not till next day that he was informed that it was standing in a corner of the baker's shop. He dispatched someone to demand its return. The baker handed it over and the archpriest put it carefully away till he could decide how best to make use of it.

Now Doña Beatriz no sooner heard the great news than she sent two nuns to the house of Maria Perez to demand a circumstantial account of all that had occurred, see the girl for themselves, and if they fund her cured as was reported, make her a present of a gold chain, delicately worked, which she put in their hands, and in return ask for the crutch which she had used in her infirmity so that it might be placed as a votive offering in the Lady Chapel of the convent church. She as far from pleased when the nuns came back to tell her than neither Catalina, her mother nor her uncle had any idea what had become of the crutch. The Prioress was determined to get it, but since it was not a matter that she could entrust to her nuns she sent for the steward of her estates and ordered him to find out who had got possession of the precious object and in her name demand its delivery. It was a couple of days before the steward came back with the information that the archpriest had the crutch and would not give it up.

Doñ Beatriz gave way to a lively irritation and told the steward roundly that he was both a fool and a knave. But she was a woman of discretion. She sat down and wrote a polite and complimentary letter to the archpriest in which she asked him with honeyed words to let her have the crutch so that she might hang it in the church on whose steps the Blessed Virgin had appeared to Catalina. She pointed out to him that this was clearly the place where it should be preserved for the edification of future generations. The archpriest wrote back in terms as courteous as her own, but said that though for Christ's sake he was only too willing to grant her any favour within his power, since the miracle had taken place within the Collegiate Church he felt it his duty to keep for its greater glory this visible sign of God's grace. He pointed out further that the fact of its having been left in the sanctuary showed plainly that it was God's intention that there it should remain. Upon this an exchange of letters passed between the two from which by degrees all expressions of politeness and esteem for one another's virtue and piety were banished. The Prioress grew more and more peremptory, the archpriest more and more stubborn. Various persons took sides and what one said was repeated to the other. The Prioress described the archpriest as an insolent donkey, riddled with concupiscence, and the archpriest described the Prioress as an interfering old hag whose administration of her convent was a scandal to Christendom.

Doña Beatriz decided at last that she had kept her temper as long as Christian charity required and was now free to indulge in the righteous indignation which the archpriest's impertinent behaviour justified. She sent for the steward again. She instructed him to call upon the archpriest and taking care to treat him with the respect due to the cloth make it clear to him that if he did not hand over the crutch forthwith he need not expect the protection of her brother the Duke in the law case he was then engaged in nor such advancement in the Church as her favour at Court might enable her to obtain for him, and that she could no longer ignore the scandalous rumours that circulated about his relations with a certain woman and would be constrained to lay the facts before the bishop of the diocese. The Prioress thus traded on his greed, his ambition and his incontinence. The archpriest through the influence of the reigning Duke of Castel Rodriguez had been appointed to a canonry in the Cathedral of Seville; and the chapter were bringing a suit against him to force his resignation owing to his non-residence. He did not wish to lose the handsome emoluments of the office, but since neither law was on his side he could only hope to win his case by the powerful intervention of his patron. He was besides not without a desire to serve the Church to greater advantage on the episcopal bench. For these reasons he could not afford to make an enemy of the Prioress; and, his bishop being of austere morals, he was uneasy at her threats to expose peccadilloes of which the weakness of his flesh had made him guilty. It did not take him long to see that he was beaten, and since he had to yield he was sensible enough to yield gracefully. He handed the crutch to her messenger and with it a letter in which with protestations of his deep regard for her virtue he said that on mature consideration he was obliged to agree with her that the proper place for the precious object was plainly the Church of Our Lady of Carmel.

The Prioress had it encased in silver and hung in the Lady Chapel for the edification of the faithful.

22

In the confusion that ensued when the crowd streamed out of the church in pursuit of the Bishop, Domingo hustled his sister and his niece through a side door and taking unfrequented alleys brought them safely home. Maria Perez was all for putting her daughter to bed, giving her a purge and sending for a barber to bleed her, but Catalina, rejoicing in the free use of her limbs, would have none of it. Just for the fun of it she ran up and down stairs, and but that decency forbade would have turned cartwheels in the parlour. Neighbours came in to congratulate her and to marvel over and over again how the Blessed Virgin had looked when she appeared to her, what she wore and exactly what she had said. They in their turn told her of the wonderful sermon the Bishop had preached and how, such was his eloquence, they were unable to hold their water, so that their rapture was mingled with embarrassment. In the afternoon the great ladies of the city sent for Catalina and made her walk up and down, giving little cries of wonder as she did so, as if they had never seen anyone walk before. They gave her presents, handkerchiefs, silk scarves, stockings and even dresses which were only slightly worn; a gold pin, earrings of semi-precious stones and a bracelet. Catalina had never owned so many rich and beautiful things in her life. Finally, cautioning her not to become conceited because such a favour had been granted her, but to remember that she was a working girl and would do well not to forget her humble station, they sent her away.

Night fell. Maria Perez, Domingo and Catalina supped. They were tired after the adventures of the day, but restless too. Mother and daughter had talked till they had nothing more to say. Domingo urged them to go to bed, but Catalina said she was too excited to sleep, so to calm them both and at the same time by the magic of art to attune their minds to the contemplation of ideal beauty he started to read them a play he had lately finished. Catalina listened somewhat inattentively, with one ear as it were, but this, absorbed in the dramatic situation and enchanted with the mellifluous sound of his verse, its elegantly-varied pattern, Domingo did not notice. Suddenly she sprang to her feet.

'There he is,' she cried.

Domingo stopped and there was a frown of exasperation on his good-natured face. They heard the twanging of a guitar in the street.

'Who is it?' asked her uncle crossly, for no author likes to be interrupted when he is giving a reading of one of his own compositions.

'Diego. Mother, I can go to the *reja*, can't I?'

'I should have thought you had more spirit.'

The *reja* was the frille that secured the window from the intrusion not so much of thieves as of too enterprising swains. As a well-behaved girl, who knew that men were lascivious and a woman's virginity her crowning glory, it would never have occurred to Catalina to admit an admirer into the house, but it was the custom for a girl to sit at her window at night and with the grille between talk with the object of her affections of the mysterious things lovers are accustomed to entertain themselves with.

'He abandoned you when you were crippled,' Maria Perez went on, 'and now that you are a celebrity and the whole city is talking about you he comes running back with his tail between his legs.'

'Oh, mother, you don't know men as well as I do,' said Catalina. 'They're weak and easily led. How could the world go on if we did not make allowances for their foolishness? Naturally he didn't want to marry me when

I was a cripple. His mother and father had found a good match for him. He has told me a hundred times that he loves me better than his soul.'

'You are a very silly girl. He is a shameless fellow and you should have more self-respect.'

'Let her go,' said Domingo. 'She loves him and that is the end of it. I dare say he is no more worthless than any other young man of this degenerate day.'

With a shrug of her shoulders Maria Perez got up and taking the tallow candle by which Domingo had been reading, said:

'Come into the kitchen and read your play to me there.'

'I will do no such thing,' he answered. 'The thread is broken and I am out of the mood. You are a good woman, Maria, but you do not know a pentameter from a cow's tail and I cannot do myself justice unless I have an appreciative audience.'

Catalina was left alone. She went to the window and against the darkness of the night saw a figure which made her heart beat.

'Diego.'

'Catalina.'

Thus at this late stage is introduced into this story a hero.

His father was a tailor in a very good way of business who made clothes for the most notable persons in the city, and from his earliest years Diego had learnt to ply a needle, to cut out breeches and to fit a doublet. He had grown into a tall, strapping lad, with a fine pair of legs, a slim waist and broad shoulders. He had a handsome head of hair, which shone with the oil he plentifully applied to it, an olive skin, bold black eyes, a sensual mouth and a straight nose. He was in short a youth of a comely presence and Catalina thought him more beautiful than the day. He was of gallant spirit and it irked him to sit cross-legged hour after hour stitching under his father's captious eyes cloth, silk, velvet and damask to be worn by the more fortunate than he. He felt himself born for greater things and in his wayward reveries played many a splendid role on the stage of life.

He fell in love. It was a shock to his parents when he told them that unless they gave him permission to marry Catalina Perez he would go as a soldier to the Low Countries or work his way on a ship to seek adventure in the Americas. Catalina's only fortune was the house she would inherit on the death of her mother, and her only prospects the unlikely possibility that her father would one day return laden with gold from the unknown lands in the west. But Diego's parents were wily; he was but just eighteen and they thought his young man's fancy would in due course lightly turn to a more suitable object for his affections; they temporized; they said very sensibly that it was absurd to enter upon the married state before he was out of his apprenticeship, but that if he was then still of the same mind they would be prepared to discuss the matter. They raised no objection to his going night after night to Catalina's window and entertaining her with little tunes on his guitar and amorous conversation. But when a bull trampled on the girl and left her partly paralysed they could not look upon it as a special interposition of Providence. Diego was distraught with horror at the accident, but he was obliged to agree with his fond parents that it was out of the question to marry a cripple, and when presently his mother told him that according to the reliable information she had received the only daughter of a well-to-do haberdasher had taken a fancy to him and would not be averse to receiving his addresses, he was sufficiently flattered to pay her a good deal of attention. The respective fathers of the young people came together and decided in principle that the match would be mutually advantageous. It only remained to settle the terms and since they were both shrewd business men this led to protracted negotiations.

Such then was the state of affairs when Diego presented

himself once more at Catalina's window. Besides learning to measure, cut and sew he had learnt in the course of his short life that a man should never excuse himself, and she, young though she was, knew that it is vain to reproach a man. However heinous his offences, it only irritates him to have them thrown in his teeth. A sensible woman is content to let them weigh on his conscience if he has one, and if he hasn't, recrimination is wasted. So they lost no time in chiding on her side or apology on his, but went straight to the point.

'Heart of my soul,' he said, 'I adore you.'

'My love, my precious love,' she answered.

But it is unnecessary to repeat the sweet, foolish things they said to one another. They said what lovers say. Diego had a pretty gift of language, and phrases came unbidden to his lips that so enchanted Catalina that she felt it had been almost worth while to endure those long weeks of misery in order to enjoy at that moment such an ecstasy of bliss. The darkness of the room behind her hid her almost completely from his sight, but the sound of her voice, low and soft, and the ripple of her light laughter fired his blood.

'Cursed be this grille that separates us. Oh, why cannot I take you into my arms and cover your face with kisses and press my beating heart to yours?'

She knew very well what that would lead to, and the idea did not in the least displease her. She knew that man was a creature of licentious passion, and it gave her a thrill of pride and at the same time a sort of heartache that Diego should so vehemently desire her. She was a little breathless.

'Oh, my dear, what can you want of me that I do not want to give you? But if you love me you cannot ask me to do what would be a mortal sin and which in any case these iron bars make impracticable.'

'Give me your hand then.'

The window at which she sat was at some little height

from the street, so that in order to do this she had to kneel on the floor. She slipped her hand through the grille and he pressed it to his greedy lips. Her hands were very small, with tapering fingers, hands of a lady of high degree; she was proud of them, and in order to keep them soft and white washed them every night in her urine. She gently stroked his face and she blushed and laughed when he put her little thumb in his mouth.

'Shameless one,' she said. 'What will you do next?' She withdrew her hand. 'Behave yourself and let us talk sense.'

'How can I talk sense when you rob me of my senses? Woman, you might as well ask a river to run uphill.'

'Then you had better take yourself off. It is growing late and I am tired. The haberdasher's daughter must be waiting for you and you have no reason to offend her.'

This she said with perfidious sweetness and it brought the answer she wanted.

'La Clara? What is she to me? She has a hump on her back, a squint in her eye and hair like a mangy dog's.'

'Liar,' she answered cheerfully. 'It is true that she is somewhat marked with smallpox and her teeth are a little yellow and one is missing, but except for that she is not a bad-looking girl and she has a nice nature. I cannot blame your father for wishing you to marry her.'

'My father can go and . . .'

What he said his father could go and do was so coarse that a decorous writer cannot but leave it to the reader's imagination. Catalina was not unused to the direct language of her day and she did not turn a hair. Indeed her lover's emphatic utterance gave her a certain satisfaction.

'I was in the church this morning,' he went on, 'and when I saw you stand there in all your beauty it was as if a sword pierced my heart and I knew that all the fathers in the world couldn't separate me from you.'

'I was in a daze. I didn't know where I was nor what had happened to me. I was giddy. And then it was as if a million pins and needles were pricking my leg so that I couldn't have borne the pain another minute, and I knew nothing more till I found myself in mother's arms and she was laughing and crying and I burst into tears.'

'You ran and as you ran we all shouted with joy and wonder. You ran like a doe that flees from the hunter, you ran like a nymph of the woods because she has heard the voices of me, you ran like . . .' Here his invention failed him and he added rather tamely: 'You ran like an angel of heaven. You were more beautiful than the dawn.'

Catalina listened to this with great content and was willing to hear much more to the same effect, but her mother's voice broke in.

'Come to bed, child,' she said. 'You don't want all the neighbours talking and you should have a good night's rest.'

'Good night, my beloved.'

'Light of my eyes, good night.'

Now it happened that Diego's father and the haberdasher had been for some days at odds over a piece of land which the tailor desired as part of the girl's dowry but which the haberdasher could not bring himself to part with. The matter would in all probability have been amicably settled by compromise if the tailor had not on a sudden shown an unreasonable and to the haberdasher's mind churlish obstinacy. Angry words passed and in the end the marriage was abandoned. It was not without motive that the tailor refused to modify his demands: the miracle had given Catalina a distinction which he realized would be useful in his business; she was not only a good and honest girl, but a clever sempstress; and there was some talk that various ladies of the city, charmed with her modesty and good manners, were prepared to join with one another to give her an acceptable dowry. By consenting to the marriage of which he had formerly disapproved he decided that he could make his son happy and do a good stroke of business into the bargain. Thus the last impediment to the happiness of the fond lovers was removed.

23

They little knew that while, with the iron grille between, they continued every night with little variety but to their mutual satisfaction to talk in the silly way above described, a great lady in her oratory, only a stone's throw away, was contriving a scheme that very much concerned them.

Doña Beatriz was a devout woman who scrupulously performed her duties. The convent she ruled was a model to the community and the inspectors who visited it had never had occasion to find fault with her. She maintained perfect discipline. The services of the church were conducted with exemplary decorum. In conduct and piety she was irreproachable. But she carried in her heart a deadly hatred for a certain nun of Avila, Teresa de Cepeda by name, which neither the precepts of religion nor the repeated censures of her confessor could mitigate. This nun, known in religion as Mother Teresa of Jesus, but by the Prioress never referred to but as La Cepeda, had entered the Convent of the Incarnation at Avila where Doña Beatriz had been first a pupil and then a novice. She had aroused a good deal of indignation by claiming to receive special graces, raptures and the vision of Our Lord, His face blazing with glory; to say nothing of having driven away the devil who was sitting in her office book by throwing holy water at him; but the climax came when, dissatisfied with the laxity of the Carmelite rule, she had left the convent and established a new one where stricter rule was followed. The nuns she had left looked upon this as a slur on themselves and an insult to the order and they did everything in their power to have the new foundation suppressed. But Teresa de Cepeda was a woman of energy, determination and courage, and surmounting ceaseless opposition she founded convent after convent of Discalced Carmelites as they were called, since instead of the stout shoes worn by the other members of the order they wore sandals with rope soles; and before her death, some years before the time with which this narrative deals, she had seen the triumph of the Reform.

No one had fought it with greater tenacity than Doña Beatriz. She had never had any patience with the excessive mortifications, the visions and raptures, which the nuns of La Cepeda professed to have. There was a natural antagonism between these two women of strong will. Who was this proud, meddlesome, presumptuous and wicked creature to set herself up above everybody else? At one time she had gone so far as to ask the Bishop to allow her to make a foundation at Castel Rodriguez; she had by then gained many powerful friends, both at Court and among the clergy, and Doña Beatriz, determined not to allow the woman to gain a foothold in the city which she looked upon as her own domain, had been obliged to use all her influence to combat the scheme. A desperate struggle ensued and the issue was still in doubt when Teresa de Jesus died.

Though she prayed for her misguided soul, Doña Beatriz could not but heave a sigh of relief. She was convinced that now La Cepeda's restless and dominating spirit was no longer active the Reform would soon be forgotten and the nuns in due course return to the old rule. She little knew how strong an impress she had left on her daughters and on the priests who had come in contact with her. In a little while stories began to be told of the miracles she had performed in her lifetime and the marvels that attended her death. As she expired so sweet a smell came from her body that the windows of her cell had to be opened to prevent those present from fainting, and when nine months afterwards it was exhumed the body was found to be intact and uncorrupt, and the whole convent was filled with the same sweet odour. Sick persons were cured by touching her remains. Already many influential people were urging her beatification and it was finally borne in upon Doña Beatriz that sooner or later La Cepeda would be canonized.

The thought of this had for some time gravely disquieted her. It would be, to put it profanely, a feather in the cap of the Discalced Order. It was true that there had been saints in the Carmelites of the mitigated rule; indeed both its founders were canonized; but that was a long time ago, and such was the frivolity of people, they were more inclined to pay their devotions to a saint who had recently achieved that sublime rank than to one who had been for centuries in possession of it. But if the Prioress could do nothing to prevent the upstart order from receiving an honour for which she could see no justification she could do something to restore the balance by providing her own order with a candidate for canonization. Providence had shown her a way and it would be a sin if she did not take it. Lazarus was a saint for no other reason that she knew of than he had been the occasion for one of Our Lord's miracles. Catalina was a pious and a virtuous girl and the miracle by which she had recovered her health had been witnessed not by two or three emotional nuns or self-interested priests, but by a vast concourse. Having received so signal a mark of divine favour it seemed only proper that she should devote the rest of her life to the service of God. Doña Beatriz had heard that she fancied herself in love with a young man of the city, but she brushed this aside; she could not believe that a woman in her sense would think twice of marrying a tailor when she might enjoy the benefits, both spiritual and wordly, which she would have by entering the Convent of the Incarnation of which she was herself the Prioress. If the girl was what the nuns who knew her said she was, she could not fail to be a credit to the convent and the grace she had received would add a further distinction to the foundation. She was young enough to react to training and Doña Beatriz was confident that she could make her a worthy religious. There was no reason to suppose that the Blessed Virgin would cease to take an interest in her and it was far from impossible that she would be the recipient of further graces. Her fame would spread, and when in due course she was released from the martyrdom of life she would surely be as suitable a candidate for beatification as the turbulent nun of Avila.

Doña Beatriz brooded over her project for some days and the more she considered it the more it appealed to her; but being a woman of discretion, she thought it prudent not to embark upon it without the approval of her spiritual director. She sent for him. He was a worthy, simple man whose piety she esteemed, but of whose intelligence she had no high opinion. He applauded her wish to give to Our Lord a bride to whom His Mother had condescended to show so great a favour and who thus would be a credit to the community; and this was natural since, though the Prioress had dwelt on the gratitude which the girl must feel for her miraculous cure and the good disposition she surely had to spend the rest of her life in the service of God, she thought it unnecessary to impart to the good man the hidden motives that were the mainspring of her desire. But he raised an objection.

'By the statutes laid down on the foundation of this convent admission to it is reserved to ladies of noble birth. Catalina Perez, though of untainted blood (*de sangre limpia*), is of modest extraction.'

The Prioress was prepared for this.

'I regard the condescension Our Blessed Lady showed her as a patent of nobility. In my eyes it has made her the equal of the proudest in the land.'

Such an answer in the mouth of so great a lady filled the friar with admiration and if possible increased the veneration in which he held her. This settled, it only remained to consider ways and means. Her plan was to have the girl brought to see her and then put before her the utility to her spiritual welfare of making a retreat of some duration at the convent so that she could give due thanks to the Creator for the blessings that had been bestowed upon her; and since she foresaw that Catalina, owing to the unfortunate attachment she had contracted, might raise objection to this, she begged the friar to disclose her plan to the girl's confessor and get him to urge her, or if necessary order her, to accept the proposition. This the Prioress's director very willingly consented to do.

On the following day, therefore, the Prioress had Catalina brought to her. She had seen her but once before and then had hardly noticed her. She was immediately struck by her beauty, and with a smile, in which there was little of her habitual grimness, amiably remarked on it. She did not like ill-favoured nuns. It had always seemed to her unbecoming to offer the celestial bridegroom brides who did not combine spiritual grace with a comely presence. She was charmed with Catalina's modest demeanour, her sweet voice and the distinction of her carriage. There was nothing vulgar in her manner, and her speech, owing to Domingo's teaching, was not only correct, but elegant. The Prioress could not but be surprised that so fair a flower had grown in such humble earth. Any doubt she might have had of the wisdom of her project was dispelled: the girl was evidently destined to honour, and what honour could be greater than to serve God?

Catalina was very much in awe of the great lady with whose reputation both for virtue and severity she was well acquainted, but Doña Beatriz set herself to put the girl at her ease. Her face wore an expression of benignity which the nuns but rarely saw and Catalina began to wonder why they were all so much afraid of her. She was a voluble young person and, graciously encouraged to talk, she was soon telling her kindly listener the whole story of her short life with its hardship of poverty, its tribulations and joys, and she never suspected with what skill the Prioress guided her recital to make her disclose her disposition, honest nature and charm of character. Without a tremor, but with an indulgent benevolence, the Prioress heard her describe the merit and beauty of Diego, his sweetness and goodness; and tell how his parents, so unkind to her before, had relented so that now no obstacle remained to their happiness. The Prioress desired to hear from her own lips how the Blessed Virgin had appeared to her, the very words she had spoken, and how in the twinkling of an eye she had vanished from her sight. It was then that she gravely but mildly suggested that in common gratitude for the grace she had received Catalina should make a retreat in the convent in order to collect herself and for a little while surrender her spirit to the contemplation of heavenly things. Catalina was taken aback. But she was accustomed to say the first thing that came into her head and by now she had so much lost her fear of the Prioress that she did not hesitate to be frank.

'Oh, Reverend Mother,' she cried, 'I couldn't do that. We've been separated so long, it would break my Diego's heart to be parted from me now. He says that he only lives for the hour when we talk to one another at my window. I should pine away if I didn't see him then.'

'I would not press you, child, to do anything that you do not wish. A retreat could only benefit you if you made it for the love of God and with a sincere desire to amend yourself. I confess I should be disappointed in you if you were so little grateful to the Blessed Virgin for her goodness to you that you grudged her a little time to give her thanks; and I cannot think that this young man, if he loves you as you say and is so good, could take it amiss if for a while, no more than two or three weeks perhaps, in return for the blessing that has reunited you, you devoted yourself to pray for his salvation as well as yours. But we will say no more about it; the only thing I would ask you is to consult your confessor on the matter. It may be that he will think my suggestion of no value and in that case your conscience will be at ease.'

She then dismissed her with the present of a rosary of amber beads.

24

It was no surprise to the Prioress when two or three days later she was informed that Catalina was in the parlour and had come to beg permission to make a retreat. She sent for her, made her welcome, kissed her and put her in charge of the mistress of novices. Catalina was given a cell that looked over the nuns' well-tended garden. Though austerely furnished, it was roomy, clean and cool.

There was no need of Doña Beatriz's request – and her requests were orders – that Catalina should be treated with indulgence and kindness, for her beauty, modesty and charm immediately captivated all hearts. Nuns, novices, lay sisters and lady boarders, all joined in making much of her. They liked her gaiety; they spoilt her like a favourite child. Though the bed she slept in was such as the rule of the order directed, it was luxurious compared with that to which she was accustomed, and the food she ate, simple and unspiced as was proper, was such as in the poverty of her home she had never tasted. Fish, chickens, game were provided from the Prioress's estates, and the lady boarders invited her to their rooms to partake of sweetmeats and other delicacies.

Doña Beatriz kept her own counsel; she was content to let the girl see for herself the delight of conventual life, with its peace, its pleasant activity and its security from the turmoil and trouble of the world. Its monotony was relieved by the visits during the recreation hour of distinguished ladies of the city and of worthy gentlemen, for the most part relations of the Prioress and her nuns, whose conversation was not entirely restricted to religious topics. Catalina was not a little flattered by the attentions they paid her. She had entered upon her retreat somewhat rebelliously on the order of her confessor reinforced by the persuasion of her mother, but she found it far from unpleasant. It would have been strange if she had not compared to its advantage the happy, ordered life of the nuns with that she led at at home, with its constant drudgery darkened always by the spectre of want. There had been periods when there was no call of the special work she and her mother did, and then they were saved from starvation only by the uncertain earnings of Domingo. She enjoyed the services which she attended with all the members of the community in the small but beautiful church attached to the convent. The Prioress had an ear for music and she had seen to it that the singing was good and the rites conducted not only with devoutness but with ceremony. Catalina, with her keen sensibilities, found in them not only a delight to her senses, but a spiritual enrichment. Very much to her surprise she found the life of the convent not an imprisonment as she had feared but a liberation. She liked to please, and she pleased; she wished to be loved, and loved she was. Although she missed Diego and thought of him constantly, she was obliged to admit to herself that she would look back later on her retreat as one of the most agreeable] episodes of her life.

Every day, towards evening, Doña Beatriz sent for her and kept her for an hour. She never mentioned her wish that Catalina should enter the religious life; though soon she wished it not only for the motives that have already been related, but because with her insight into character she had quickly realized that besides being virtuous Catalina was intelligent and quick to learn, that she had personality and would be an ornament to the order. The Prioress talked to her, not as a great lady and the Mother Superior of a convent, but as a loving friend. She exerted herself to gain an influence over the girl, but she knew she must tread warily. She told her stories of the saints to edify her and stories of the Court to show her that even a religious could play a part in matters of state. She talked to her of the affairs of the convent and the management of her properties not without a notion that it might favourably affect Catalina to see what a responsible and important position it was to be the Prioress of the Carmelite convent at Castel Rodriquez. The possibility of attaining it might well dazzle the daughter of Maria Perez the sempstress.

But very little can be kept secret in a convent, and though Doña Beatriz had never told anyone of her plan, it was not long before it was generally known among the nuns and the lady boarders to what end tended the privileges Catalina enjoyed and the notice the awe-inspiring Mother Superior took of her. An effusive nun one day told her how much they all loved her and how much they wished that she would remain with them for good. A lady boarder who was staying at the convent because her husband was at the wars told her that she only wished she were free to become a religious.

'If I were in your place, child,' she said, 'I would ask the Reverend Mother tomorrow to accept me as a novice.'

'Oh, but I am going to be married.'

'You will never cease to regret it. Men by their nature are brutal, neglectful and faithless.'

The lady was pasty-faced, lethargic and corpulent. Catalina could not but think that if her husband was as bad as that there were excuses for him.

'How can you hesitate when the heavenly bridegroom holds out his arms to receive you?' the lady went on as she put a sweet into her mouth.

On another occasion during the recreation hour a lady from the city pinched Catalina's cheek and archly said:

'Well, I hear that we are going to have a pretty little saint in the convent very soon. You must promise to remember me in your prayers, for I am a great sinner and I shall count on you to get me into paradise.'

Catalina was frightened. She had no wish to become a nun and much less a saint. She remembered a number of casual remarks to which at the time they were made she had paid no attention. On a sudden it became clear to her that they all expected her to enter the religious life. That evening when as usual she entered the Prioress's oratory it was with a mind ill at ease. Doña Beatriz noticed that something was wrong. She was direct.

'What is the matter, child?' she asked, suddenly interrupting Catalina in what she was saying.

The girl started and flushed.

'Nothing, Reverend Mother.'

'Are you afraid to tell me? Do you not know that I love you as if you were my own daughter? I was hoping you had at least a little affection for me.'

Catalina burst into tears. The Prioress held out her arms in an affectionate gesture.

'Come and sit here, child, and tell me what is troubling you.'

Catalina went and sat at the feet of the Prioress.

'I want to go home,' she sobbed.

Doña Beatriz stiffened, but in an instant recovered herself.

'Are you not happy here, my dear? We have done all we could to make you so. You have gained the love of all.'

'Their love imprisons me. I'm like a trapped hare. The nuns, the ladies, they seem to take it as a matter of course that I shall enter the convent. I don't want to.'

The Prioress was seized with a sudden anger because those foolish women in their zeal had betrayed her, but she did not let a trace of it appear on her grave face. She answered gently.

'No one can wish to force you to do what should only be an act of free will under the inspiration of God. You must not blame the ladies because in the attachment they have formed for you they do not want to lose you. For my own part I will not deny that I have permitted myself to wish that Our Blessed Lady might arouse in your heart the wish to become one of us in gratitude for the great mercy that has been shown you. You would be an honour and a glory to our convent. I know that not only are you humble and pious, but you have a clever head on your shoulders. Too many of our nuns, alas, fail to combine goodness with intelligence. I am an old woman, the burden of my office begins to be more than I can bear; perhaps it was a sin to indulge in idle dreams, but it would have been a great happiness to me if I could have had you by my side, with your tact, your natural kindliness and your good sense, to share my labours with me and to know that when in the fullness of time my Heavenly Father called me to Himself you would occupy my place.'

She paused and waited for a reply. She gently stroked the girl's cheek.

'You are very good to me, Reverend Mother. I cannot thank you enough for your kindness. It would break my heart if you thought me ungrateful. I am unworthy of the great honour you have in mind for me.'

Though in words there was no blunt refusal of the dazzling offer, the Prioress was too clear-sighted not to see that this was what they implied. She had the sensation that along with the fear she felt in the girl there was a stubbornness, and she had a notion that to try further persuasion would only increase her obstinacy. She was not beaten, but discretion suggested for the moment retreat was wise.

'It is a matter for you to decide for yourself according to the dictates of your conscience and I am far from wishing to influence you.'

'Then may I go home, Reverend Mother?'

'You are free to go whenever you like. I ask you as a

favour out of respect to your confessor to stay for the period he appointed. I am sure you cannot be so unkind as to deprive us of the charm and grace of your presence for the few days that remain.'

Catalina could do nothing but say that she would be happy to stay. The Prioress dismissed her with a fond kiss. Once more alone in her oratory she gave herself up to intensive thought. She was not the woman to accept defeat. She had a flash of impatience with Catalina, but since this was an emotion of no profit she immediately suppressed it. Her mind was strong and inventive and several plans suggested themselves to her. She deliberately weighed their advantages and disadvantages. She felt herself justified in using any means, so long as there was no sin in them, to secure the girl's welfare in this world and salvation in the next and at the same time to achieve an object which would bring credit to the order. The first thing evidently was to try whether by persuasion more efficacious than her own Catalina could not be brought to a more proper state of mind. She could think of no one more capable of doing this than Don Blasco de Valero, Bishop of Segovia; he had performed the miracle that had cured her, his high office was impressive, his sanctity awe-inspiring. She sat down and wrote a letter in which she begged him to come and see her on a matter on which she needed advice.

25

He sent back a message to say that he would come next day, and with a punctuality unusual in Spain presented himself at the appointed hour. The Prioress went straight to the point.

'I desired to see your lordship about the girl Catalina Perez.'

The Bishop took the seat Doña Beatriz offered him, but

he sat on the edge of it as though unwilling to surrender to its scant comfort. He waited in silence and with downcast eyes for the Prioress to go on.

'On the advice of her confessor she has been making a retreat in our house. I have had occasion to talk with her. I have examined her character and dispostion. She has a better education than many ladies of noble birth. Her manners are excellent and her behaviour exemplary. She has a very sincere devotion to Our Lady. She is in every way fitted to the religious life, and after the signal mercy which God at your hands was so gracious as to show her it seems only common gratitude on her part to devote her life to His service. She would be an ornament to our order and I should have no hesitation notwithstanding her modest extraction in admitting her to this house.'

The Bishop made no reply. Without looking up he slightly inclined his head, but whether in approval or merely to indicate that he heard was not evident. The Prioress raised her eyebrows.

'The girl is young, she does not know her own mind and perhaps it is only natural that she should be attracted by the vain delights of the world. I am an ignorant and a sinful woman, I have not thought that I could speak to her with profit on the matter; it has occurred to me that it would be a worthy act on your lordship's part if you would see her and point out to her, as no one can do better than you, where her duty and at the same time her happiness lie.'

Then he spoke.

'I do not choose to have commerce with women. I have made it a rule, which I have never broken, to refuse to receive their confessions.'

'I am well aware of your lordship's disinclinations to have any dealings with my sex, but this is an exceptional case. You brought her back to life, you cannot leave her now to endanger her soul for want of a word of admonition. It is as though you had saved a man from drowning and then left him to perish of cold and hunger on the shore.'

'If she has no vocation for a religious life it can be no duty of mine to urge her to enter upon it.'

'Your lordship must know that many women have done so on account of a bereavement, because for one cause or another it has been impossible to marry them suitably, or even because of a disappointment in love. It has not prevented them from becoming excellent nuns.'

'I have no doubt of it, and I am bound to believe that God on occasion dashes the cup from the lips of the worldly in order to call them to His service, but in the case of this girl there is no reason to suppose that any of the grounds you have mentioned exist. I venture to remind Your Reverence that it is no less possible to achieve salvation in the world than in a convent.'

'But more difficult and less safe. Why should Our Blessed Lady have granted you the power to work this miracle to her glory unless with the design of causing this girl's light to shine before all men and lead them to repentance?'

'It is not for us, sinful creatures, to inquire into the motives of God Almighty.'

'But at least we may be sure that they are good.'

'We may.'

Doña Beatriz was none too well pleased with the Bishop's laconic brevity. She was more accustomed to an effusive volubility in those with whom she troubled to converse. There was some sharpness in her tone when she went on.

'It is a very small return I ask for the favour and protection my family has always afforded your order. Will you refuse my request to see this girl, examine her disposition and if you form as high an opinion of it as I have, show her where her true happiness lies?'

The Bishop at last raised his eyes, not to meet those of the Prioress, but to gaze out of the window; it looked on to the garden, but in his preoccupation he saw neither the tall cypresses with which it was planted nor the oleanders in full flower.

He was puzzled by her insistence. He could not believe that this hard, proud woman had no more at heart than the welfare of a little sempstress. What was it that the Prior of the convent in which he was staying had told him about her? She had fought tooth and nail to prevent Mother Teresa of Jesus from founding a convent at Castel Rodriquez. The hatred the Carmelites of the old order bore for those of the new was common knowledge. A suspicion formed itself in his mind that it was for some reason connected with this that Doña Beatriz was trying to induce Catalina to enter the convent; and if she wished to enlist his aid it was because the girl was unwilling. He looked now for the first time at the Prioress and his dark, tragic eyes sought to pierce her innermost thoughts. She bore his gaze with a haughty composure.

'Supposing I saw this young person and came to the conclusion that it was my duty with God's help to persuade her to enter the life of a religious, I should be inclined to think that she would be more at ease in a convent of the Discalced Carmelites than in this house of noble ladies.'

The sudden flash of anger, immediately effaced, that he saw in the eyes of Doña Beatriz told him that he had hit upon something approaching the truth.

'It would be hard on the girl's mother to separate her entirely from her only child,' answered the Prioress blandly. 'The Discalced Carmelites have no house in this city.'

'Only, if I am correctly informed, because Your Reverence persuaded the Bishop to refuse Mother Teresa of Jesus permission to make a foundation here.'

'There are already too many convents in the city. La Cepeda would not accept an endowment, so that her community would have been a charge on the city which can ill afford it.'

'Your Reverence speaks of a very holy woman with small respect.'

'She was a woman of very humble origins.'

'You are mistaken, Señora. She was of noble birth.'

'Nonsense,' said the Prioress sharply. 'Her father received his patent of nobility early this century. You must forgive me if I have no more patience than our late revered King with these people who without any justification assume a rank to which they are not entitled. The country is swarming with this gutter nobility.'

This was the order to which the Bishop belonged, and he smiled faintly.

'Whatever her extraction, it can hardly be denied that Mother Teresa was a pious woman, who received many graces from on high, and whose labours in the cause of religion are worthy of the highest praise.'

Doña Beatriz was too angry to notice that the Bishop was watching every expression of her face, every impatient gesture of her delicate hands.

'Your lordship must permit me to disagree with you. I knew her and had occasion to talk with her. She was an unquiet and restless creature who went about amusing herself with crazy pranks under a pretext of religion. What business had she to leave her convent and to the scandal of her fellow citizens found a new one? There were good and holy nuns at the Incarnation and the Rule was severe.'

This Rule, instituted by St Albert and mitigated by Pope Eugenius IV, ordained fasting from the Feast of Exaltation of the Holy Cross in September till Christmas on four days a week, and in Advent and Lent prohibited the eating of meat. Each nun had to take a scourging on Monday, Wednesday and Friday, and silence had to be observed from Compline until Prime. The habits were black and no shoes were worn. The beds were without linen sheets.

'I must be a very stupid woman,' continued the Prioress, 'but I cannot see how it conduces to greater spirituality to wear rope sandals rather than leather shoes nor why it is to the glory of God to wear habits of sack-cloth rather than of serge. La Cepeda pretended she broke away from our ancient order so that she might have greater opportunity for mental prayer and contemplation, and yet she spent her whole life gadding about from place to place. She enjoined silence on her nuns and was the greatest chatterbox I ever met in my life.'

'If Your Reverence would read the life she wrote of herself you would surely be moved to regard that saintly creature with greater indulgence,' said the Bishop icily.

'I have read it. It was sent me by the Princess of Eboli. It is no business of women to write books; they should leave that to men who have more learning and a better understanding.'

'Mother Teresa of Jesus wrote it in obedience to her confessor.'

The Prioress smiled grimly.

'Is it not remarkable that her confessor never ordered her to do anything but what she had already made up her mind to do?'

'I regret that Your Reverence should think so harshly of a woman who won the affection and esteem not only of her nuns but of everyone who was privileged to come into contact with her.'

'She divided and threatened to destroy our ancient order with her innovations and it is impossible for me not to believe that she was actuated by ambition and spite.'

'Your Reverence is undoubtedly aware that owing to the duly-attested miracles she performed during her life and the miracles that have been performed by her intercession since her death many influential and worthy persons are already urging His Holiness to declare her blessed.'

'I am aware of it.'

'And am I right in supposing that your reason for desiring the girl Catalina Perez to enter your order is that you have conceived the foolish notion that the notoriety which now surrounds her may in some way counterbalance the fame the Discalced Carmelites would acquire if their founder were beatified?'

If the Prioress was startled by the Bishop's discernment no sign of it appeared on her face.

'We have had enough saints in our order to maintain our equanimity if His Holiness should be so misguided by interested persons and superstitious nuns as to confer such an honour on a mischievous rebel.'

'You have not answered my question, madam.'

Doña Beatriz was too proud to lie.

'I should not look upon my life as misspent if in all humility I were enabled to help an aspiring soul to so great a perfection that she became worthy to join the company of saints. I could only look upon it as a good if she were thus enabled to undo the harm caused by Teresa de Cepeda. If you will not help me to do what I am assured is a meritorious service to a poor soul struggling with uncertainty I must help myself.'

The Bishop looked at her long and sternly.

'It is my duty to remind Your Reverence that to compel anyone against his will to enter a religious institution is a crime which incurs a special censure and excommunication *latae sententiae.*'

The Prioress went deathly white, not with fear at the dreadful threat, but with anger that he should venture to make it, and yet it sent a cold shiver down her spine. For the first time in her life she felt the domination of the male. She maintained an offended silence. The Bishop rose to his feet and with the customary expressions of courtesy took his leave. She bowed her head in haughty acknowledgment, but remained seated in her chair.

26

She took part in the offices of the day with decorum, but
it may be surmised with a distracted mind. She had no
intention of abandoning her project and had already considered what to do if the Bishop refused to use his persuasion and authority to help her. Though she thought it
would be to the advantage and glory of her order that
Catalina should enter religion in the convent her father
had founded, she was sincerely convinced that it would
be also to the girl's welfare and to the edification of the
faithful. The Prioress very well knew that the only real
obstacle was the unfortunate attachment the foolish creature had contracted for the young tailor called Diego. It
made her impatient to think that for such a trifling reason
Catalina should be willing to forgo the great advantages,
both here and hereafter, which the religious life offered
her. But a wise person takes things as they are, and knowing the conditions proceeds to deal with them in such a
manner as to achieve the desired result.

First, then, the Prioress sent for her mistress of novices.
This nun, Doña Ana de San José, was discreet, intelligent
and reliable, and she had the interests of the convent at
heart. Her devotion to the Prioress was such, her obedience so perfect, that if she had ordered her to throw
herself into a river she would have done so without a
moment's hesitation. The Prioress began by asking her
what opinion she had formed of Catalina. Doña Ana sang
her praises. She was devout, obedient, kindly and helpful.
She had fallen into the conventual life as though she were
made for it.

'It is a pity that her modest extraction prevents her
from joining our little community.'

'God is no respecter of persons,' said Doña Beatriz gravely. 'In His sight there is no difference between the nobly and basely born. If the girl has the proper disposition that is a difficulty that may be overcome. There is no reason why the rule my father made should not be changed by my brother if the circumstances are exceptional.'

'Your daughters would welcome her as a companion.'

'It would be a source of satisfaction to me to number her among the worthy women over whom by God's will I have the direction.'

The Prioress paused for a while to consider her words. Then she suggested to Doña Ana that it would be a good thing to spread it among the nuns, the lady boarders, *damas de piso* they were called, and among the visitors that she was prepared to accept Catalina as a novice. After the wonderful occurrence that had brought her a fame that would in due course become known throughout Spain it was natural that she should wish to embrace the religious life, and it would be a glory to the city that she should dwell in their midst and by her prayers acquire for it the special favour of the Deity. It would surely require more strength of will than a simple girl could be expected to have, to withstand the pressure of public opinion and to refuse the approbation, the admiration even, with which her decision to abandon the world, with its transitory pleasures, would be received. But Doña Beatriz was a practical woman and she was aware that practical advantages also have their weight. She instructed the obedient nun to see Maria Perez, tell her the good impression she, the Prioress, had formed of her daughter's virtue and aptitude, and what in consequence she was prepared to do for her. She knew that she could trust Doña Ana to make Maria Perez understand how great an honour was thus conferred on her daughter, an honour that would redound to her credit, and how much better a life, materially as well as spiritually, it would offer Catalina than if she married a poor man's son who might well turn out an idler, a drunkard and a gambler. Finally Doña Beatriz told the nun to say that she herself would pay the dowry which was necessary on entering the religious life, and since Maria Perez was growing old and without her daughter's help might find herself in straitened circumstances she would be pleased to give her a pension large enough to keep her in comfort, without the necessity of working, for the rest of her life.

The offers were so handsome that Doña Ana was filled with admiration for her superior's charity and munificence. That wonderful woman forgot nothing. The Prioress dismissed her with the injunction to choose a suitable moment to deliver the message and impress upon Maria Perez the need of absolute secrecy, for she had an inkling that if she talked about it to her brother, the dissolute Domingo, he might be wicked enough to persuade her to refuse her consent.

The mistress of novices executed the commission with dispatch and dexterity and within twenty-four hours was able to tell Doña Beatriz that Maria Perez had received her generous offers with humility and gratitude. Being a Spanish woman, and the age devout, she had no doubt that to serve God in a religious house was the worthiest life anyone could adopt. To have a daughter who was a nun, a son who was a monk, was an honour to a family, and gave it, moreover, as it were a claim on the indulgence of God. But such a distinction as to have a daughter of hers an inmate of a house of noble ladies was something she had never dreamt of. She had a little flutter of pride when her visitor told her that already they looked upon Catalina as a little saint, and half jokingly, for she was a merry, good-natured creature, that if she went on as she had begun, if the Blessed Virgin continued to show her favour, there was no reason why Maria Perez should not one day be the mother of a virgin canonized by the Pope. Then they would paint pictures of Catalina which would be placed over altars and people would come from far and near to be healed of their maladies by touching her relics. It was a prospect dazzling enough to inflame any woman's ambition. Nor was Maria Perez insensible to the pension that was offered to her; the work by which she earned her living was laborious and cruel to the fingers, and it would be wonderful to have nothing to do from morning till night but to go to church and sit at her window watching the passers-by.

'Did she say anything about this young man who, I seem to have heard, has been paying Catalina some attention?' asked the Prioress, when she had listened with satisfaction to the nun's report.

'She doesn't like him. She says he behaved very badly when the poor child had her accident. She thinks he is selfish and has much too good an opinion of himself.'

'It would be difficult to find a man who does not suffer from both those defects,' said the Prioress dryly. 'It is their nature to be selfish and conceited.'

'And she does not like his mother. It appears that when Maria's husband ran away to America the young man's mother told people that it served her right because she led him a dog's life.'

'I dare say she did. That is the sort of life most women lead their husbands. Did you happen to suggest to her that she would be wise to let Catalina know, as though it came from herself, how much she would approve of her deciding to enter religion?'

'I thought there was no harm in it.'

'On the contrary. You have done very well, Doña Ana, and I am pleased with your intelligent conduct of this matter.'

The nun flushed with pleasure. Doña Beatriz was more apt to chide than to praise.

27

The Prioress allowed a few days to elapse so that the news might be spread that if Catalina was moved by the spirit of God to take the veil she would be well received into the convent of the Carmelites. It was received with gratification. There was a general agreement that such a step would redound to the glory of the city and it was eminently fitting that the girl should take it. It was scarcely decent that the recipient of such a prodigious grace should become the wife of a tailor. The mistress of novices accomplished her particular mission with success. She saw Maria Perez again and warned her to deal tactfully with her daughter, not to press her, but when occasion arose to compare the peace and security of the religious life with the dangers, hardships and toils of the married state.

Doña Beatriz had the gift of gaining the devotion and loyalty of her dependants, and of these none was more loyal and devoted than the steward of the convent's properties and her own estates. He was a gentleman, Don Miguel de Becedas by name, and a distant connection of the Prioress's. He knew her bounty, for he administered her charities, and he admired her capacity. She was a good business woman and could drive as hard a bargain as any man. She was prepared to listen to reason, but having once made up her mind never changed it. When this happened there was nothing for it but to obey her, and this Don Miguel was prepared to do blindly. She sent for him and instructed him to make searching inquiries, both in the city and in Madrid, into the antecedents and present circumstances of Don Manuel de Valero, the soldier, and at the same time to find out all that was to be known about the young man Diego Martinez and his father.

By the time Don Miguel brought back the required information the Prioress had sent Catalina home with a handsome present and with the assurance of her unfailing affection. Catalina bade her farewell with tears in her eyes.

'Do not forget, child, that if ever you are in trouble or in any sort of difficulty you have only to come to see me and I will do everything in my power to help you.'

Doña Beatriz listened attentively to everything the steward had to tell her and she was well pleased with the results of his investigations. She then asked him to make an opportunity to see Don Manuel and in the course of a casual conversation tell him that she would be glad to receive a man of whom she had heard so much good.

After the fiasco in the Collegiate Church Don Manuel had shut himself up in his apartments for three days and refused to see anyone. He was vain and thus sensitive to ridicule. He knew too well the mocking spirit of his compatriots and was fully aware that they were making merry at his expense. He did not think anyone would venture to make an allusion to his misadventure to his face, for he was a good swordsman and it would be a brave man who would risk being run through the body for the sake of a quip, but he could not prevent them from talking behind his back. When at last he ventured to show himself in company there was a truculence in his manner that served as ample warning to those present. He was angry, moreover, not only because he had made a fool of himself, but because he had jeopardized his prospects. His intention in coming to Castel Rodriguez, as perhaps the reader will remember, was to find in one of the noble but impoverished families of the place a girl to marry, and he had good reason to think that his handsome fortune would make him an acceptable suitor. But the public humiliation to which he had been exposed greatly reduced his chances. The nobility of the city were proud, pride in those hard times was all they had left them, and they would refuse the hand of one of their daughters to a man who was a common laughing-stock. It looked to Don Manuel as though the only thing left him was to go to Madrid, hoping the lamentable story had not reached it, and see whether he could not find there a suitable bride.

He was not a little surprised when Don Miguel brought him the Prioress's courteous message, and flattered, for it had never occurred to him that she would deign to receive him. She belonged to a world so much above his that she might have been an inhabitant of another planet. Don Manuel said he would look upon it as an honour to be allowed to pay his respects to the Prioress at whatever time was convenient to her. The steward replied that she saw few persons who were not members of her family, and mentioned an hour when her numerous duties left her free.

'I will come and fetch you tomorrow, Señor, if it suits you, and take you to the convent myself,' he said.

It suited Don Manuel very well.

He was ushered into the oratory and left alone with the great lady. She was at her table writing and did not rise to receive him. He looked about for a chair to sit on, but as she did not invite him to take one remained somewhat awkwardly standing. Though a bold, impudent man, he was awed by her dignity. She addressed him with graciousness.

'I have heard much, sir, of the courage, devotion and capacity with which for so many years you have served His Majesty the King, and I was curious to see a fellow citizen who has by his own efforts raised himself to such distinction. I was hoping that you would find time to visit me so that I might congratulate you personally on your great exploits.'

'I never dreamed that I might without offence intrude upon your privacy, madam,' he stammered.

But he began to feel more at his ease. If the daughter of the Great Duke of Castel Rodriquez paid him compliments his state could not be so desperate after all. But her next remark, though made with a smile, somewhat disconcerted him.

'You have gone a long way, Don Manuel, since you were a little barefoot boy running about the streets of your village and tending your father's swine.'

He flushed, but not knowing what to answer, held his tongue. Doña Beatriz looked him up and down for all the world as though he were a lackey she was about to engage. If she noticed his embarrassment she was not concerned with it. She saw a well-set-up man, not unpleasing in appearance, with an erect carriage and an air of virility. She knew his age; it was forty-five but he carried his years well. He was a little taller than his brother the Bishop, who was not a small man, and though his bones were well covered he was far from fat. His eyes were handsome, and though there was some brutality in his face, that was natural enough in a man who had been so long at the wars, and it did not particularly offend the Prioress who had no patience with a milksop. He was doubtless arrogant, boastful and licentious, but these were defects common to her own relations, and though as a religious she deplored them, as a woman she accepted them as masculine traits with the same resignation as she accepted the biting cold of the Castilian winter. Altogether the first impression Don Manuel made on her was not unfavourable.

She appeared for the first time to notice that he was still on his feet.

'Why do you stand, Señor?' she asked. 'Will you not do me the favour of taking a seat?'

'You are very good, madam.'

He sat down.

'I live a very retired life and my religious duties combined with the business of my office keep me fully occupied, but nevertheless from time to time a scrap of news reaches me from the world outside these walls. I have heard, for instance, that apart from performing a filial duty your object of visiting your native place was to choose a wife from among the noble families of this city.'

'After serving my King and country for so many years it is true that I have the desire to make a home for myself and enjoy the delights of domesticity of which I have been hitherto deprived.'

'Your desire is praiseworthy, Señor, and increases the esteem in which owing to your reputation I already hold you.'

'I am strong and active, and my fortune is considerable. I cannot but think that such talents as I am possessed of will be as useful at Court as they have proved to be in battle.'

'And if I understand you, you are aware that a wife with intelligence and important connections can be of service to you there.'

'I will not deny it, madam.'

'I have a widowed niece, the Marquesa de Caranera, whose husband has unfortunately left her ill provided for. She is at present living in this house. I had hoped that she would be moved to adopt the life of a religious so that when at last I lay down my arduous functions she might succeed me, as indeed, being the granddaughter of our founder, she would be entitled to. But she lacks the vocation, so I have come to the conclusion that a suitable marriage should be arranged for her.'

Don Manuel was suddenly alert. But he was a shrewd man; the possibility of being allied with so great a family as that of the Duke of Castel Rodriguez was so far beyond his hopes that he could not but suspect some chicanery. He answered with prudence.

'The Marquesa is twenty-four, which is a very suitable

age for a man of your years,' the Prioress replied somewhat sharply. 'She is not lacking in beauty, and since she had a son by her husband, who died of the same distemper as carried off his father, she is certainly not barren. The fact that I intended her to be Prioress of this convent after my death proves that I have a high opinion of her ability. I need not point out to you that a Don Manuel de Valero could never have aspired to marry the niece of the Duke of Castel Rodriguez. I should in fact have to use all my powers of persuasion to induce my brother to consent to it.'

Don Manuel had been thinking quickly. With the influence of that powerful family behind him there was no knowing to what heights he might rise. To make such a marriage would be a triumph over the fools who had held him up to ridicule.

'The Marquis of Caranera died without heirs to his title. I do not think it impossible that the King might be persuaded to grant it to you. It would be more suitable than this wretched Italian title which you now have.'

That clinched it. Though the Marquesa was old, ten years older than the bride he had desired, and might be homely, the advantages of marrying her were too great for him to hesitate.

'I don't know how to show Your Reverence my gratitude for the honour you propose to confer on me.'

'I will tell you,' she said coolly, 'and indeed it is only if you show your gratitude efficiently that I propose to enter into the matter further.'

Don Manuel smothered a sigh of relief. He was far too astute not to know that this unexpected suggestion was made to him for a better reason than his wealth and his military reputation. Being a coarse man, the idea flashed across his mind that the Marquesa was pregnant and he had been chosen to father an illegitimate child. He would hardly know then whether to accept or decline the

159

invitation, and he waited with some anxiety for Doña Beatriz to continue.

'I desire to enlist your influence on behalf of a young man of this city with the Archduke Albert. I should have no need to do this but for the unfortunate fact that my brother has had a violent quarrel with him and so cannot help me. I have been given to understand that you stand high in the Archduke's favour.'

'He has been good enough to think well of my capacity.'

The Archduke Albert, it should be explained, was at that time commander-in-chief of the Spanish forces in the Low Countries.

'It would be to this young man's advantage to enter the Archduke's service. He is strong and brave and would certainly make a good soldier.'

Don Manuel was much relieved. The Archduke was in various ways indebted to him. He would surely be glad to oblige him by taking into his service anyone in whom he was interested.

'I think there would be no difficulty in effecting Your Reverence's desire. The young man is presumably of a good family.'

'He is an Old Christian of pure blood.'

This of course only meant that there was no taint in him of Jew or Moor. Don Manuel noticed that the answer did not meet his question.

'And what, madam, is the young man's name?'

'Diego Martinez.'

'The tailor's son? Then, madam, what you ask is impossible. The soldiers serving in the Archduke's army are gentlemen, and I could not put such an affront on His Highness as to make the request you wish.'

'I have foreseen that difficulty. I have a small estate some miles from this city which I am prepared to settle on the young man, and through my brother I can get letters of nobility given to him. You would recommend to the Archduke not the tailor's son but the hidalgo Don Diego de Quintamilla.'

'I cannot do it, Your Reverence.'

'In that case there is nothing more to be said, and further discussion is useless on the matter or on that I previously mentioned.'

Don Manuel was a worried man. The marriage that the Prioress had proposed would give him the position that he hankered after to further his ambition and he had an inkling that if he refused to accede to her request he would make a dangerous enemy. On the other hand the consequences might be unfortunate for him if it were discovered that he had lent himself to a plan which the Archduke might very well regard as a personal insult. Doña Beatriz discerned his trouble.

'You are a fool, Don Manuel. Don Diego will be a man of property and, believe me, his estate will compare not unfavourably with the barren acres belonging to your father Don Juan.'

Don Manuel was something of a bully. He cringed under the lash of the Prioress's tongue. She could ruin him and would not hesitate to do it.

'May I ask why Your Reverence takes an interest in this young man?' he asked hesitantly.

'My family have always looked upon it as a privilege as well as a duty to advance the fortunes of deserving persons in this city.'

The guarded answer so far restored his confidence that he smiled, but his glance was shrewd.

'He is the lover of the girl Catalina Perez?'

Doña Beatriz was affronted by the question, his smile and the shrewdness of his glance. She had some difficulty in outwardly controlling her indignation.

'He has been pestering the unhappy girl with his attentions.'

'And is that why you wish him sent to the Low Countries?'

161

The Prioress considered for a moment. It was probable that he knew the circumstances and it was evident that he was a tactless fellow. There were many things that could be understood, but which it was better not to put into words. She answered him, however, with an impressive dignity.

'The girl is young and does not know her own mind. She has admirable dispositions for the life of a religious and there are many reasons which make it highly desirable that she should adopt it. I have no doubt that were it not for the presence of this young man she would soon see the advisability of taking a step which would give so much satisfaction to myself, to the most important personages in the city, and to her mother.'

'But, madam, would it not be more expeditious and less costly to dispose of the young man on the spot? It would be very easy to have his throat cut one dark night.'

'It would be a mortal sin, sir, and I am shocked that you should venture to propose it. It would make a scandal in the city, give rise to unpleasant gossip, and there is no certainty that it would achieve the desired result.'

'Then what would you have me do, madam?'

She looked at him reflectively. For the present at least she felt it necessary to her plan that neither she nor anyone connected with her should be known to be concerned in it; she had to entrust its execution to someone else, and she was not sure that this man had the necessary intelligence or subtlety. She had to risk that, and she answered without further hesitation.

'Order a suit of clothes.'

Don Manuel was so surprised that, thinking she must be jesting, he looked for a smile to hover on her decided lips. Her face was grim. She explained.

'Send for the tailor to take your measurements and to bring samples of materials. He will be flattered and impressed. You must make an opportunity to talk to him about his son and tell him that a person of consequence in the city has heard good reports of him and wishes to advance him. Then, binding him to secrecy, disclose to him the plan suggested for the boy's welfare. Let him send the young man to you on some pretext and put it before him. I am assured he looks upon himself as born for better things than to sit on a tailor's bench, and he will without doubt accept with alacrity.'

'He will be a great fool if he doesn't.'

'Let me see you again when you have something to tell me. I trust you to be discreet and tactful.'

'Never fear, madam. In two days at the utmost I shall be able to inform you that the business is satisfactorily concluded.'

'You may rest assured that in that case I shall perform my part to your satisfaction.'

28

Don Manuel sent for the tailor. He could be very affable when he chose, and when his measurements had been taken and various materials examined he set himself to be so. As natives of the same city they had certain common interests and Don Manuel talked to him good-humouredly of the changes that had taken place in it during his long absence. The tailor was a little dried-up man with a sharp nose and a querulous expression. But he was garrulous. Finding in Don Manuel a sympathetic listener he enlarged upon the hard times. The wars and the heavy taxation had impoverished everyone, and even gentlemen of the highest rank were content to wear their clothes till they were threadbare. It was not so easy to make a good living then as it had been thirty years before when the caravels were arriving regularly with their cargo of gold from America. A few well-directed questions brought out the fact that he was worried about his son. It was only right that he should follow in his father's footsteps, but the boy had silly ideas and it had required the exercise of parental authority to force him to go into the business.

'And now if you please, though he's only eighteen, he wants to marry.'

'That may settle him.'

'That is the only reason I have consented.'

'And I have no doubt the money of the girl's dowry will be useful,' said Don Manuel archly.

'She has no money. There is some talk that certain ladies are prepared to give her a dowry, but how do I know that it will come to anything?'

The tailor then proceeded to tell Don Manuel who the girl was and how it had come about that he had at last yielded to his son's insistence, all of which of course Don Manuel knew already.

'I had another match in view for him, but the young person's father would not accept my very reasonable conditions, so I agreed to let the boy marry Catalina. After all that has happened and the notice that has been taken of her, I think it will bring me a nice lot of custom. My wife blames me. She asks what is the use of making clothes for gentlemen who can't afford to pay for them.'

'A very sensible remark. But if business is so bad why don't you let your son go for a soldier?'

'The life is hard and ill paid. In the shop he can still earn enough to keep body and soul together.'

'Listen friend,' replied Manuel with a frankness that charmed the poor tailor, 'you know that when I left this city I was as poor as a church mouse. Now I am a Knight of Calatrava and a rich man.'

'Ah, but Your Excellency was a gentleman and had friends to help you.'

'A gentleman, yes, but the only friends I had to count on were my youth, my strength, my courage and my intelligence.'

The tailor shrugged his shoulders despondently. Don

Manuel from his greater height looked down upon him with benignity.

'I have heard nothing but good of your son, and if what they tell me is true I cannot but suppose he is fitted for better things than you think. I too have been poor; we are citizens of the same town; I should be glad to give the boy a helping hand if I were sure it met with your approval.'

'I don't think I understand you, Señor.'

'The Archduke Albert is my friend and will do anything for me. If I recommended a young man to him he would put him in his own regiment and would mark him out for advancement.'

The tailor looked at him with gaping mouth.

'Of course we should have to provide him with certain advantages. There is a small estate not far from here of which I would give him the deeds, and with my influence in Madrid I can see that he gets letters of nobility. Your son will enter the service of the Archduke as Don Diego de Quintamilla.'

Since the Prioress had told him that she did not wish her name to be mentioned Don Manuel saw no reason why he should not himself get what credit he could from a generous action. The tailor was so overwhelmed that his face twitched and be began to cry. Don Manuel kindly patted his shoulder.

'There, there, it's nothing to make a fuss about. Go home now, say nothing of this to anyone, and send your son to me. You can tell him that you forgot to bring me a pattern of some stuff you think I may like.'

In a little while the boy came. Don Manuel noticed with relief that he was a youth of pleasing exterior. Suitably dressed he would certainly pass as a gentleman. He was neither pert nor shy. There was a confidence in his bearing which promised that he would be able to hold his own in any company. Already predisposed in his favour, after a few preliminary remarks Don Manuel broached the subject on account of which he had had Diego sent. They talked for an hour, after which they parted and Don Manuel went to see the Prioress.

'I have wasted no time in obeying your commands, madam,' he said. 'I have seen both the boy and his father.'

'You have indeed been prompt, Señor.'

'I am a soldier, madam. The father is in full accord with our plan. He is indeed overwhelmed by the opportunity that the kindness of a benefactor proposes to give his son.'

'He would be a fool to be anything else.'

Don Manuel moved uneasily from one foot to the other.

'I had better tell Your Reverence word for word what passed between me and the boy.'

The Prioress gave him a quick look of inquiry and slightly frowned.

'Go on.'

'He is a very presentable lad and my first impression was good.'

'Your impressions do not interest me.'

'I very soon discovered that he dislikes and despises the trade to which his father has put him. He has only adopted it because there was no help for it.'

'That I already knew.'

'I told him that I could not understand how a young man of spirit and intelligence, endowed with all the qualities necessary for success in the world, could think of wasting his life in a humble occupation. He answered that he had often thought of running away to seek adventure, but was held back by the fact that he hadn't a penny in his pocket. I then told him that the King wanted soldiers and that it was a career that might easily lead a man of courage and resource to position and wealth. After that I disclosed to him little by little exactly what was proposed to enable him to achieve his natural and laudable ambition.'

'Very good.'

'He took the prospect more calmly than I expected, but it was evident that it tempted him.'

'Naturally. He accepted then?'

Don Manuel hesitated briefly, for he knew that what he had to say would not satisfy Doña Beatriz.

'Conditionally,' he answered.

'What d'you mean by that?'

'He said he wanted to marry his sweetheart, but in a year, when she'd had a baby, he wouldn't be unwilling to go to the Low Countries.'

The Prioress was enraged. What use could she make of a married woman with a squalling brat? Catalina's virginity, her perpetual virginity, was essential to her purpose.

'You've bungled the whole thing, you fool,' she cried.

Don Manuel flushed angrily.

'Is it my fault if the young idiot is head over ears in love with this girl?'

'Hadn't you the sense to tell him that it was madness to refuse such an opportunity?'

'Yes, madam, I had. I told him that in this life when you get a chance to better yourself you must take it and take it quickly, because if you let it slip it may never come again. I told him that it was absurd at his age to hamper himself with a wife and that as an officer and a gentleman he could in due course do much better for himself than a penniless daughter of a sewing-woman. And if he wanted a girl to amuse himself with he would find plenty in the Low Countries who would be delighted to oblige a good-looking young man and not a few who would be prepared to show their gratitude in a substantial manner.'

'And what did he say to that?'

'He said he loved his sweetheart.'

'No wonder the world is in a mess and the country is going to the dogs when it's governed by men, and men haven't the elements of common sense.'

Don Manuel did not know what to say to this and so said nothing. The Prioress gave him a look of cold disdain.

'You have failed, Don Manuel, and I can see no profit in our further communication.'

He was acute enough to see that with these words she intimated to him that he need no longer entertain the hope of marrying the widowed marchioness. He was not prepared to give up the chance of so advantageous an alliance without a struggle.

'Your Reverence is easily discouraged. The boy's father is on our side. He does not like the idea of Diego marrying the girl Catalina and I have no doubt that I can get him to withdraw his consent. You can be sure that he will use every effort to persuade the boy to accept our proposition.'

Doña Beatriz made an impatient gesture.

'You know little about human nature. Señor. Parental opposition has never made lovers love one another less. That is not the frame of mind in which I should be prepared to accept the girl into this house. If the boy had fallen in with my proposal she would have seen how worthless is a man's love compared with the love of God. She would have been unhappy, but I should not have regretted it if it taught her where the only real happiness may be found.'

'There are more ways than one of being rid of a troublesome fellow. I have men I can trust. The boy can be seized one night, taken to a sea port and put on a ship. Youth is fickle. Once in the Low Countries, with new sights to see, adventures to be encountered, with the standing of a gentleman and by the Archduke's favour brilliant prospects, he will forget his love and in a short while thank his stars that he has been saved from an unfortunate entanglement.'

The Prioress did not answer for a while. She was a woman of robust conscience and the plan Don Manuel suggested did not outrage her. Unruly sons were often packed off to America just as daughters, unwilling to accede to their parents' matrimonial designs, were placed in a convent until they were prepared to listen to reason. She was fully convinced that to part Diego from Catalina was to the advantage of both of them.

'Your Reverence may be certain that the boy will tell Catalina of the offer that has been made him.'

'Why?'

'To make himself more precious in her sight by showing her what advantages he is prepared to forgo for her sake.'

'You are shrewder than I took you for, Señor.'

'When he is missing one morning she will naturally suppose that he found himself unable to resist the temptation.'

'That is probable enough. There is still his father to consider. It would not do if he made trouble with the authorities.'

'So that he should not do that I propose to take him into my confidence. He is ambitious for his son. He will agree to the plan without hesitation. He will hold his tongue and by the time the boy's absence is noticed he will be safely aboard ship.'

The Prioress sighed.

'I do not like the plan, but it is evident that the young are foolish and it is often better that their fate should be decided by older and wiser heads. I should require to be assured that no unnecessary violence would be used on the boy.'

'I can promise Your Reverence that no harm shall come to him. I will have him accompanied by a man I can rely on to see that he is well treated.'

'It will be to your interest,' she said grimly.

'Of that I am fully aware, madam. You can safely leave everything in my hands.'

'When do you propose to act?'

'As soon as I can make the necessary arrangements.'

For a moment Doña Beatriz was silent. It was evident

that Diego's disappearance would give rise to gossip and it was not unlikely that it would reach the Bishop's ears. She had experienced his perspicacity. He might very well put two and two together and come to the conclusion that she was concerned in the matter. She bitterly regretted that during their interview she had been led by anger to speak without discretion. She did not quite know what he could do, but he was a determined man, and a powerful; she was not frightened of him, but was wise enough to see that it was better to avoid an open breach which would not only cause scandal but might also frustrate her design.

'When does your brother leave the city, Don Manuel?' she asked.

The question surprised him.

'I do not know, Your Reverence, but if it interests you I can inquire.'

'I do not wish anything to be done till after his departure.'

'Why?'

'Because it is my pleasure. Let it be enough for you to know that such is my desire.'

'It shall be as you will, madam. The boy shall be taken on the night of the day on which my brother leaves the city.'

'That will do very well, Don Manuel,' she said graciously.

She gave him her hand to kiss as he took his leave.

29

But though her reason assured her that she was acting for the best and was fully justified, Doña Beatriz could not dispel the peculiar uneasiness that possessed her. It was so compelling that once or twice she was in mind to tell Don Manuel to abandon his scheme. But she chid herself for her weakness. Much was at stake. Yet she fretted and her nuns found her unaccountably irritable. Then one morning the sub-prioress informed her that the Bishop had gone. To avoid attention he had slipped away at crack of dawn with his secretaries and servants. An hour later Don Manuel conveyed a message to her that arrangements were complete and the plan would be carried into effect that night. That settled it. She examined her conscience and knew that her intentions were blameless.

Towards evening she was told that Catalina was asking to be allowed to see her. She was shown into the oratory. The Prioress noticed with dismay that she was violently agitated. She guessed that something had gone wrong.

'What is it, my child?' she asked.

'Your Reverence told me that if ever I was in trouble I could come to you.'

She burst into tears. Doña Beatriz told her to calm herself and tell her what had happened. Sobbing, the girl told her that a principal gentleman of the city had offered to send Diego to the wars, with the promise of giving him an estate and getting the title of Don for him. He had refused for love of her and in consequence had had a violent quarrel with his father. His father had said at last that if he did not accept these magnificent offers as any sensible man would, if he did not go peacefully he should go by force, and added that he withdrew his consent to his marriage to Catalina. The Prioress frowned when she heard of the threat. The man was a fool to have made it. Now if Diego disappeared the girl would know that it was not of his own free will. The Prioress had counted on the effect it would have on her if she thought that he had succumbed to temptation and abandoned her.

'He could never have hoped for such good fortune,' she said, 'It is a chance no young man would hesitate to seize. Men are vain and cowardly and though they act badly they take pains to be thought well of. How do you know that he is not deceiving you and talking of force being applied in order to make you think he has abandoned you through no fault of his own?'

'How do I know? I know because he loves me. Ah, madam, you are a saintly woman, you don't know what love is. If I don't have my Diego I shall die.'

'No one ever died of love yet,' said the Prioress with a savage bitterness.

Catalina fell to her knees and put her hands together in passionate supplication.

'Oh, Mother, Reverend Mother, have pity on us. Save him. Don't let them take him away. I cannot live without him. Oh, madam, if you knew the anguish I suffered when I thought I'd lost him for ever and how night after night I cried until I thought I should go blind! Why did the Blessed Virgin cause me to be freed from my infirmity if not that I should be fit once more to be my lover's wife? She had pity on me, and will you do nothing to help me?'

The Prioress clenched her hands on the arms of her chair, but said nothing.

'All that time I longed for him. My heart was breaking. I am only a poor and ignorant girl. I have nothing in the world but my love. I love him with all my heart.'

'He's nobody. He's only a boy like another,' said Doña Beatriz hoarsely, so that her voice sounded like the croak of a raven.

'Ah, madam, you say that because you have never known the pain and bliss of love. I want to feel his arms round me, I want to feel the warmth of his mouth on mine, the caress of his hands on my naked body. I want him to take me as a lover takes the woman he loves. I want his seed to flow into my womb and to create the child within it. I want to suckle his child at my breast.'

She put a hand to each breast and sensuality poured from her in a flame so fierce that the Prioress shrank back. It was like the heat of a furnace and she put up her hands as though to shield herself from it. She looked at the girl's face and shuddered. It was strangely changed, pale, and one might have thought the features were swollen; it was a mask of desire. She was breathless for lust for the male. She was like one possessed. There was something not quite human about her, something even slightly horrible, but so powerful that it was terrifying. It was sex, nothing but sex, violent and irresistible, sex in its awful nakedness. Suddenly the Prioress's face was contorted in a grimace, a grimace of unendurable agony, and tears poured down her cheeks. Catalina gave a cry of dismay.

'Oh, Mother, what have I said? Forgive me. Forgive me.'

She clasped the knees of the Prioress. She was startled by this exhibition of emotion in one whom she had never seen but calm, grave and dignified. She was bewildered, She didn't know what to do. She took the thin hands in hers and kissed them.

'Madam, why do you cry? What have I done?'

Doña Beatriz withdrew her hands and clenched them in the effort to regain her self-control.

'I am a wicked and unhappy woman,' she moaned.

She leant back in her chair and covered her face with her hands. Memories of long ago crowded upon her and she gritted her teeth to choke back the sobs that tore her throat. The little fool, the silly little fool had said she had never known love. How cruel it was that after all these years that old wound should be so green! She gave the ghost of a bitter chuckle as the humour of it struck her that she had eaten her heart out for a boy who was now a wasted, haggard priest. She brushed away the tears that dimmed her eyes and taking Catalina's face in her hands gazed at her as though she had never seen her before. There was no trace now of the carnality that for an instant had so hideously changed the comely features. She was all tenderness, solicitude and purity. The Prioress was entranced by her loveliness. So young, so beautiful and so passionately in love. How could she break that poor little heart as hers had been broken? She, who thought she had conquered every human weakness, felt weak, pitifully weak, and yet there was in the feeling something strange and uplifting, something that warmed her heart and at the same time, oh, so comfortingly, crippled her will; it was as though a knot had been loosened deep within her breast, and she rejoiced to be relieved of the aching pain. She bent down and kissed the girl's red mouth.

'Have no fear, my sweet,' she said. 'You shall marry your lover.'

Catalina gave a cry of joy and broke into voluble expressions of gratitude, but the Prioress harshly told her to be quiet. The situation was delicate and she had to think. In a few hours they were to spirit Diego away; it was true that she could send for Don Manuel and tell him that she had changed her mind; she could cut his expostulations short; but that would not solve the difficulties she had got herself into. The seed she had sown had been sown well. There was a feeling widespread in the city that it behoved Catalina to become a religious. Doña Beatriz knew well the passionate devotion the people had for the Faith; they would not only be disappointed if she did not do what was expected of her, they would look upon it as an indecency, almost as an insult to religion if after receiving such a grace she married a tailor. The worldly would laugh and make bawdy jokes; the pious would be incensed. Catalina was regarded now with admiration, even with awe, but that could easily change into indignation and contempt. The Prioress knew the violent nature of her countrymen; they were capable of burning down the house in which she lived, they were capable of stoning her as an abandoned wanton and driving a dagger into Diego's back. There was but one thing to do and that must be done quickly.

'You must leave the city, you and this boy, and you must go tonight. Fetch Domingo, your uncle, and come back here with him.'

The girl, inflamed with curiosity, wanted to know what

the Prioress had in mind, but the Prioress very peremptorily told her not to ask questions, but do as she was told.

When Catalina in a few minutes came back with her uncle, the Prioress sent her down to wait in her own cell so that she could speak to him alone. She told him such of the facts of the situation as she thought it needful for him to know, gave him certain instructions and with them a short note which she had already written for her steward. She then told him to get hold of Diego, let him know what had been decided, and see that he followed the directions given him. Having dismissed him she called Catalina.

'You will spend the evening with me, my child. At midnight I will let you out by a door in the city wall and you will find Domingo with a horse which I have ordered my steward to let him have. He will ride with you to a spot which has been arranged, and there Diego will be waiting. He will change places with Domingo and you are to ride South till you come to Seville. I will give you a letter to friends I have there and they will find suitable work for you and him.'

'Oh, madam,' cried Catalina, wild with excitement, 'how can I show my gratitude for what you are doing?'

'I will tell you,' answered the Prioress with some severity. 'Ride fast and on no account linger on the way. You have desperate men to deal with and it may be they will pursue you. Chastity is a woman's crown, and you must preserve it till the Church has blessed your union. Intercourse between unmarried persons is a mortal sin. You will seek out a priest at the first village you come to after day-break and ask him to join you to Diego in holy matrimony. Do you see what I have here?'

Catalina looked and saw a plain gold ring.

'It is the ring I had destined for your consecration on your profession. It will be your wedding ring.'

She put it on the palm of Catalina's hand. It made

her heart beat nineteen to the dozen. The Prioress then proceeded to instruct her on the duties and responsibilities of married life. She listened with becoming gravity, but with some distraction, for she was in a flutter and her mind was more occupied with its delights. They prayed together. The hours passed slowly. At last the convent clock struck midnight.

'It is time,' said Doña Beatriz. She took a small bag from a drawer in her writing-table. 'Here are some gold pieces. Put the bag in a place where you are sure you will not lose it and do not let Diego get hold of it. Men do not know the value of money and when they have any spend it on foolishness.'

Catalina modestly turning her back pulled up her skirt and put the bag inside her stocking, and tied the strings round her leg.

The Prioress lit a lantern and told the girl to follow her. They walked softly through silent passages till they came out into the garden. Then, in case some wakeful nun happened to see the light and wondered what it meant, she extinguished the lantern and taking Catalina's hand led her along the pathways. They came to the small door that the Prioress had caused to be cut in the city wall so that if need be she could leave the city unobserved or receive persons whose visit for some reason had to be secret. She alone had the key. She unlocked the door. Domingo on horseback was waiting in the shadow of the wall, for the moon was shining and the night was bright.

'Now go,' said the Prioress. 'God bless you, my child, and remember me in your prayers, for I am a sinful woman and I need them.'

Catalina slipped out of the door and the Prioress closed and locked it behind her. She listened till she heard the horse's hoofs. They sounded very loud in the silence of the night. Doña Beatriz with lagging steps walked back to the convent building. She could hardly see her way, for she was almost blinded by her tears. She returned to her oratory and spent the rest of the night in prayer.

30

Domingo gave Catalina his hand and helped her up on to the horse so that she could sit on the pillion behind him. It was still and warm, but high up in the heavens there was wind, and little clouds sped across the sky, black but edged with silver of the shining moon. The countryside was deserted and they might have been riding in a world of which they were the only inhabitants.

'Uncle Domingo.'

'Yes?'

'I'm going to be married.'

'Make quite sure of it, child. It is a sacrament necessary to salvation, but one which men in general hesitate to avail themselves of.'

They passed a sleeping hamlet and beyond it was a clump of trees. As they came to it a figure detached itself from their shadow. Catalina slipped off the horse and flung herself into Diego's arms. Domingo dismounted.

'Come, come,' he said. 'You'll have plenty of time for that sort of thing later. Get on the horse both of you and be off. There's food and a bottle of wine in the saddlebags.'

He kissed Catalina and Diego, saw them start, and then, since the city gates were shut and he could not get in till dawn, settled himself down as comfortably as he could under a tree. He had taken the precaution to bring wine and he put the bottle to his mouth. It was the very place to compose poetry and he prepared to await daybreak in commerce with the Muse. But before he had made up his mind whether to indite a sonnet to the moon or an ode to love triumphant he fell sound asleep and did not wake till sunrise.

The lovers rode for an hour and Catalina talked her

head off. It seemed that she had a thousand things to say, much to tell Diego, plans to divulge, and since she had a pretty way of putting things she made it all sound very delightful and amusing. Diego was so happy he was prepared to laugh at everything she said. And she was enraptured. She could not imagine anything more like heaven than to ride through the night in the open country with her arms clasped round her lover. They had to be, of course, for that was the only way to hold on, but it was very pleasant.

'I could ride like this to the end of the world,' she said.

'I'm hungry,' he answered. 'Let us stop here and see what is in those saddlebags.'

They were passing a wood and he reined in the horse. Catalina was well aware that his appetite just then was not for food and drink, and a tremor of desire tingled down her body; but it needed the admonitions neither of the Prioress nor of Domingo to tell her that it was very imprudent to let a man have his will of you until the Church had sanctified the union. She knew that men have an instinctive disinclination to marry and she had known cases of girls who had yielded to their lovers only to have them refuse afterwards to fulfil their promises. Then nothing was left them but the brothel.

'Let us ride on, dear,' she said. 'The Prioress said we might be pursued.'

'I'm not frightened,' he said.

He passed his leg over the horse's head and slipping to the ground lifted Catalina off the horse's back. She was in his arms and he kissed her on the eyes and on the mouth. He took hold of the bridle and with his arm still about Catalina's waist made for the wood. But at that moment a sharp shower of rain fell upon them. They were both startled, for the night seemed fair and they had not noticed the black cloud over their heads. Now Diego was as brave as a lion and would have faced armed men with intrepidity, but he was terrified of rain. Moreover he had put on his best clothes before starting and could not bear to get them wet.

'It's not raining over there,' he said, pointing a little way down to the other side of the road. 'Let's run.'

But they had no sooner reached the spot he indicated than the rain suddenly began to fall there too and more heavily. Diego gave an exclamation of annoyance.

'It's only a local shower,' he said. 'If we ride quickly we shall get out of it.'

He mounted, helped Catalina up, and clapping his spurs to the horse's flanks galloped down the road. But no sooner had they got away from the wood than the rain stopped as abruptly as it had begun. He looked up at the sky. There were dark clouds behind them, but ahead the sky was blue and serene. They rode in silence. After a little while, perhaps half an hour, they came to a little copse.

'This'll do,' said Diego, reining in the horse.

The words were hardly out of his mouth when a heavy drop of rain fell on his nose.

'It's nothing,' he said, and once more swung his leg over the horse's head; but he had no sooner done this, he had not even got to the ground, when the drops began to fall more and more frequently. 'The devil's in it.'

He put his foot back in the stirrup and rode on. The rain stopped. Catalina pondered.

'It's not the devil,' she said.

'What is it then?'

'It's the Blessed Virgin.'

'You're talking nonsense, woman, and in a little while I'll prove it.'

He kept a sharp look-out. For some time they did not pass a tree to which he could tie up the horse.

'I ought to have brought a rope to hobble him,' said Diego.

'One can't think of everything,' she answered.

'The horse ought to have a rest. It wouldn't hurt us to have a bit of a sleep by the roadside.'

'I couldn't sleep a wink.'

'I dare say you wouldn't want to,' he grinned.

'Look,' she said, 'it's going to rain again.' And in fact several drops began to fall. 'We shall only get wet through.'

'A few drops of rain won't do us any harm.'

As he spoke, the rain on a sudden fell heavily. He uttered a curse and spurred his horse.

'This is the strangest thing I've ever seen in my life,' he said.

'Almost a miracle,' she murmured.

Diego gave it up as a bad job. Though the rain stopped they were both pretty wet by then and Diego's amorous ardour was sensibly mitigated by his concern for his clothes. In extenuation it should be stated that it was not only his best but his only suit that he wore, for Domingo had told him it would be unwise to leave his home with anything but what he stood up in. They went on through the night, passing no one, but occasionally in the moonlight catching a glimpse of a farmhouse or a few cottages. At last the sun rose. They were on the top of a little hill and looking down saw in the grey dimness of dawn a small village. There could not but be an inn there where they could get something to eat and drink, for by this time they were both quite honestly hungry and thirsty. They rode on and now encountered peasants going to work in their fields. They entered the village and suddenly the horse stopped dead.

'What's the matter with you, you brute? Get on with you,' cried Diego, digging in his spurs.

The horse did not move. Diego hit him over the head with the ends of the reins and again sharply kicked him. It made no impression on the horse. He stood stock still. He might have been turned to stone.

'You shall go, you brute.'

Diego was angry now and he slapped the horse's neck as hard as he could. The horse reared up on his hind legs and Catalina gave a shriek. Diego hit him on the head with his closed fist and the horse got back on to his four legs, but still nothing Diego could do got him to move a step forwards. He stood as if rooted to the ground. Diego, red in the face, was sweating profusely.

'I can't make it out. Is the devil in the horse too?' Catalina began to laugh and he turned on her furiously. 'What is there to laugh at?'

'Don't be cross with me, my love. Don't you see where we are? The church.'

Diego, frowning, looked and noticed for the first time that the horse had stopped in front of the church, which was on the very edge of the village.

'What of it?'

'The Prioress made me promise that we'd get married in the first church we came to. That's it.'

'There's plenty of time for that later,' he said.

Once more he dug his spurs savagely into the poor brute's flanks and as he did so the horse humped its back, kicked up his hind legs, and before they knew what had happened the two riders were flying through the air. Fortunately they fell on a pile of hay and so were not hurt. They lay for a moment somewhat shaken and very much startled. The horse, after this strange show of spirit stood as still as before. Just as this happened the priest, who had been saying his Mass, came out of the church and seeing the accident hurried up to see if he could be of help. They got up, shook themselves, and finding that no harm had come to them brushed off their clothes the hay that stuck to them.

'You're lucky it was there,' said the priest, a short, red-faced man on the plump side. 'If you had come a little later it would have been in my barn.'

'It's providential that this should have occurred at the

church door,' said Catalina, 'for we were looking for a priest to marry us.'

Diego gave her a glance of surprise, but did not say anything.

'To marry you?' cried the priest. 'You are no parishioners of mine. I have never seen you before. I certainly will not marry you. I have had nothing to eat since my supper yesterday evening and I am going to my house now to get some food.'

'Please wait, Father,' said Catalina.

She turned her back on them, raised her skirt and quickly got a gold piece out of the bag the Prioress had given her. With her bewitching smile she showed it on the palm of her hand. The priest looked at it and grew redder in the face than ever.

'But who are you?' he asked doubtfully. 'Why do you want to be married in a strange place and in such a hurry?' He did not take his eyes off the glistening coin.

'Have pity on two young lovers, Father. We have run away from Castel Rodriguez because my father wanted to force me to marry a rich old man for his money; and this youth, to whom I was betrothed, was being forced by his avaricious parents to marry a woman without a tooth in her head and only one eye.'

To make her story more convincing Catalina put the gold piece in the priest's hand and firmly closed it upon the coin.

'You have a very persuasive manner with you, young woman,' said the priest, 'and your story is touching enough to bring tears to my eyes.'

'You will not only be doing a meritorious deed, Father,' Catalina continued, 'but you will be saving two virtuous young people from committing a mortal sin.'

'Follow me,' said the priest and re-entered the church. 'Pepe,' he called in a loud voice as he proceeded towards the high altar.

'What is it?' came back.

'Come here, you idle scoundrel.'

A man, broom in hand, came out from the chapel beside the sanctuary.

'Why can't you let me get my sweeping done?' he asked gruffly. 'Never was a sacristan paid such a miserable wage and then you never give me a moment's peace. How am I to get out to my field if you interfere with me in the middle of my work?'

'Hold your impudent tongue, you son of a bitch. I am going to marry these young people. Ah, but there must be two witnesses.' He turned to Catalina with a smirk on his fat face. 'You will have to wait while this drunken ruffian goes down to the village to find someone and that will give me chance to get something to eat.'

'I will be the second witness.'

It was a woman who spoke. They all turned round and saw her walking towards them. She wore a blue cloak and her head was covered with a great white scarf the ends of which were thrown over her shoulders. The priest looked at her with surprise, for he had not noticed that there was anyone in the church when he said his Mass, but he gave his shoulders an impatient shrug.

'Very well. Let us get it over as quickly as possible. I want my breakfast.

Catalina gave a start when the stranger joined them and tremulously took Diego's hand. The stranger, a faint smile in her eyes, put her finger to her lips enjoining Catalina to silence. The ceremony was speedily performed and Catalina Perez was joined in the bonds of matrimony to Diego Martinez. They went into the vestry to sign the book. The priest wrote down the names of the newly-married couple, and the names of their parents. Then the sacristan laboriously wrote his.

'That's the only thing he can write,' said the priest, 'and it took me six months to drive that into his thick head. Now, madam, it's your turn.'

He dipped the quill into the ink and handed it to the strange lady.

'I cannot write at all,' she said.

'Then make a cross and I will write your name.'

She took the quill and did as he directed. Catalina, her heart beating, watched her.

'Well, I cannot write your name unless you tell it me,' said the priest sharply.

'Maria, daughter of the shepherd Joachim,' she answered.

He wrote it.

'That's all,' he said. 'And now I am going to eat.'

They followed him out of the church, all but the sacristan, who took up his broom and with mutters of irritation resumed his sweeping. But the Spanish have always been a courteous people and the priest, with the gold piece safely tucked away, was no exception.

'If, gentleman and ladies, you will do me the honour of coming to my humble dwelling next door I shall be happy to offer you such refreshment as my poverty can provide.'

Catalina who was well brought up, knew that such an offer should be declined with grace, but Diego was ravenous and did not give her time to speak.

'Señor,' he said, 'neither I nor my wife have had anything to eat since yesterday, and however poor your fare, it will seem a feast to us.'

The priest was a little taken aback at this, but was too polite to say anything but that they would confer a favour on him. They walked the few steps to his house and he showed them into a small bare room which served as refectory, parlour and study. He set before them bread and wine, goat cheese and a dish of black olives. He cut four hunks of bread and filled four horn tumblers with wine. He set about the food greedily and Diego and Catalina followed his example. He looked up to help himself to an olive and noticed that the strange lady had touched nothing.

'Pray eat, madam,' he said. 'It is simple fare, but good, and it is the best I can offer you.'

She gave the bread and wine a smile in which there was singular sadness and shook her head.

'I will eat an olive,' she said.

She took one and delicately nibbled it with white teeth. Catalina gave her a glance, their eyes met, and in the lady's was a look of infinite kindness. At that moment the sacristan burst into the room.

'Señor, Señor,' he shouted, beside himself with excitement, 'they've stolen the Virgin.'

'I'm not deaf, you old fool,' cried the priest. 'What in heaven's name do you mean?'

'I tell you they've stolen our Virgin. I went in there to sweep and the pedestal on which she stood was empty.'

'You're mad or drunk, Pepe,' the priest shouted back at him, jumping to his feet. 'Who would do a thing like that?'

He flung out of the house and followed by the sacristan, Diego and Catalina, ran to the church.

'I didn't do it, I didn't do it,' cried the sacristan, waving his hands distractedly. 'They'll all say I did it and put me in prison.'

They scrambled up the church steps, and ran to the Lady Chapel. The sacristan gave a great cry. The image of the Blessed Virgin stood in its accustomed place.

'What do you mean?' yelled the priest furiously.

'It wasn't there a minute ago. I swear by all the saints the pedestal was empty.'

'You drunken swine. You old wineskin.'

The priest seized him by the neck and kicked the wretched man's backside till he was exhausted and then for good measure slapped his face on both sides with all the strength he had left.

'If I only had a stick I'd break every bone of your body.'

When the three of them got back to the priest's house

to finish their frugal repast they were surprised to find that the strange lady was nowhere to be seen.

'Where can she have gone?' the priest exclaimed. Then he slapped his forehead. 'Fool that I am! Now I see it all. Of course she's one of these Moriscos and when Pepe came in and said the Virgin had been stolen she thought she'd better make her escape. They're all thieves and she thought some of her cursed infidels had taken the image. Did you notice she wouldn't drink the wine? They've been baptised but they keep to their pagan customs. I had my suspicions when she gave me her name; that isn't the name of a good Christian.'

'We got rid of the Moriscos at Castel Rodriguez long ago,' said Diego.

'And quite right too. I pray every night that our good King may be brought to see his duty to the Faith and expel every one of these odious heretics from the kingdom.'

'It will be a great day for Spain when he does.'

It is perhaps worthy of note to add that the worthy priest's prayers were answered, for in 1609 all the Moriscos were driven out of the country.

It was now time for Diego and his bride to resume their journey to Seville, and thanking the priest for his hospitality, they took leave of him. The horse meanwhile had been making a good meal of the hay on to which he had pitched his riders. Diego watered him and as soon as they were on his back the horse without urging set out at a comfortable amble. It was a beautiful day and there was not a cloud in the sky. The priest had told them that some fifteen miles along the road was an inn, patronized by carters and muleteers, where they could get lodging, and there they decided to stay the night. They rode in silence for three or four miles.

'Are you happy, dear?' asked Catalina at last.

'Of course.'

'I will be a good wife to you. For love of you I will work my fingers to the bone.'

'There will be no need for you to do that. There's plenty of money to be made in Seville by a clever man and no one has ever taken me for a fool.'

'I should think not indeed.'

They were silent again for a while and it was Catalina who spoke again.

'Listen, my lover, that was no Moorish woman who came to our wedding.'

'What are you talking about? One only had to look at her to tell that she was no Old Christian.'

'But I'd seen her before.'

'You? Where?'

'On the steps of the church of the Carmelite nuns. It was she who told me how I could be cured of my infirmity.'

He stopped the horse and looked around.

'My poor child, you're crazy. The sun has addled your brains.'

'I'm as sane as you are, my sweet. I tell you it was the Blessed Virgin, and when she refused to eat of the bread and wine I knew why. I knew she remembered her bitter, bitter sorrow.'

Diego stared at her with a puzzled frown.

'The Reverend Mother told me a hundred times it was quite certain I was under the special protection of our most Holy Lady. That is why she pressed me so constantly to enter the convent. Those sudden showers last night and the horse stopping at the church door and refusing to move and then throwing us both. You must see that all that was no accident.'

He looked at her for the moment and Catalina to her distress throught there was some displeasure in his eyes. Without another word he turned round again and with a click of his tongue started the horse off. Somewhat timidly Catalina hazarded a casual remark now and then, but he either answered not at all or with a monosyllable.

'What is the matter with you, darling?' she said at last, trying not to cry.

'Nothing.'

'Look at me, sweetheart. I'm hungry for a glance of your eyes.'

'How can I look at you when the road is full of ruts and holes? If the horse stumbled we might break our necks.'

'You're not angry with me because the Blessed Virgin saw fit to protect my virtue and was so gracious as to be a witness to our marriage?'

'It is an honour to which I would never have ventured to aspire,' he said dryly.

'Then why are you vexed with me?'

He took some time to reply.

'It does not augur well for our future happiness if whenever we have a difference of opinion a miracle will occur to let you have your own way. A man should be master in his own home. It is a wife's duty to yield to her husband's wishes, and it should be her pleasure.'

Catalina had her arms round him and he felt them shaking.

'You won't make it any better by crying,' he said.

'I'm not crying.'

'What are you doing then?'

'Laughing.'

'Laughing? It is no laughing matter, woman. It's very serious and I have the right to be disturbed.'

'You are very sweet, my darling, and I love you with all my heart, but sometimes you are not very sensible.'

'Explain,' he said coldly.

'The Prioress told me that I owed the favours I have received at the hands of Our Blessed Lady to my virginity. It appears that in heaven they set great store on that. It may be that when I have lost it I shall receive no more.'

Upon this Diego turned as far round in the saddle as he could and there was a sly smile on his handsome face.

'Blessed be the mother that bore you,' he cried. 'We will put the matter to the test without delay.'

'The sun is growing warm. It would be pleasant to rest for a while under the shade of trees till the heat of the day is past.'

'That is the very thought that was passing through my head.'

'And unless my eyes deceive me there is a wood not more than a mile away that will do very nicely.'

'If your eyes deceive you my eyes are deceiving me too.'

He gave the horse a touch of his spurs and galloped hell for leather till they came to the wood. He jumped off and lifted Catalina down. While he tied the horse to a tree she got out what the forethought either of the Prioress or Domingo had provided. Bread and cheese, sausage, a cold chicken and a bulging skin of wine. Who could want a better wedding breakfast? It was cool and dark under the trees and a trickle of water flowed down the bed of a tiny, limpid stream. The spot was propitious.

31

When they emerged from the wood, Diego leading the horse, the sunrays flamed less fiercely.

'It was just as well to make assurance doubly sure,' he said.

'Trebly,' she murmured, not without a certain smug self-satisfaction.

'That is nothing, child,' he returned with a very pardonable complacency. 'You do not know yet of what I am capable.'

'You are as shameless as you are adorable,' she said.

'I am as God made me,' he answered modestly.

They rode on slowly, up hill and down dale, not talking very much, but chewing the cud as it were of their happiness; they rode for six or seven miles and then saw in the mellow light of the late afternoon a ramshackle building by the roadside. That was evidently the inn of which the priest had spoken.

'We shall be there very soon. Are you tired, sweetheart?'

'Tired?' she answered. 'Why should I be tired? I'm as fresh as a lark.'

They had ridden a good forty miles and since the day before she had not slept more than an hour. She was sixteen.

They were in the plain now and the country stretched widely on both sides of the road. The harvest had been gathered and the fields were brown and dry. Here and there grew a few gnarled oak trees; here and there a grove of age-old olives. They were less than a mile from the inn when they saw galloping towards them in a great cloud of dust a horseman of such a strange appearance that they were filled with amazement, for he was in full armour. He pulled up sharply as he came to them and posted himself in the middle of the road. Couching his lance he seated himself firmly in his saddle and in a haughty tone thus addressed Diego:

'Stand and whoever you be tell me who you are, whence you come, whither you go, and who is the fair princess you carry pillion behind you. For I have every reason to believe that you are bearing her to your castle against her will and it is requisite that I should be informed of the matter to punish you for the wrong you have done her and return her to her sorrowing parents.'

For a moment Diego was so astonished that he had no answer to make. The horseman had a long cadaverous face, a short ragged beard and an immense moustache. His armour was rusty and old-fashioned and his helmet looked more like a barber's basin than a knight's helmet. His horse was a wretched jade fit for nothing but the knacker's yard and so thin that you could count his ribs. His head drooped so that it seemed as though at any moment he would tumble down from sheer weakness.

'Sir,' said Diego, putting on a bold front to impress Catalina with his valour, 'we are on our way to the inn we see from here and I see no reason to answer your impertinent questions.'

With this he clapped his spurs to his horse and moved forward, but the knight seized the bridle and stopped him.

'Mind your manners, proud, discourteous knight, and give me instantly an account of yourself or I defy you to mortal combat.'

Just then a very fat little man, with an immense paunch, came scampering up on a dappled ass and significantly tapping his forehead sought to indicate to the travellers that the horseman so strangely accoutred was out of his senses. But on hearing those threatening words Diego had drawn his sword and seemed ready to defend himself. The little fat man pressed forward.

'Contain your anger, Señor,' he said to the knight. 'These are inoffensive travellers and that young man has every appearance of being able to give a good account of himself should it come to blows.'

'Peace, varlet,' cried the horseman. 'If the adventure is perilous it will give me greater occasion to exercise my strength and prove my courage.'

At this Catalina slipped off the horse and advanced to the stranger.

'Señor, I will answer your questions,' she said. 'This youth is no knight, but an honest citizen of Castle Rodriguez and a tailor by trade. He is not carrying me by force to his castle, for he hasn't got one, but of my own free will to Seville where we hope to find decent occupation. We have run away from our native city because enemies sought to prevent our marriage, and we were married this morning at a village some miles from here. We are making all the haste we can in case we are pursued, overtaken and obliged to return to our city.'

The knight looked from Catalina to Diego, then handed

his lance to the little man on the ass, who grumbled but took it.

'Put up your sword, young man,' said the fantastic creature, with a grandiose gesture. 'You have nothing to fear, though I am well aware from your appearance that fear is an unworthy emotion to which your noble heart is a stranger. It may suit you to assume the humble guise of a tailor, but your bearing and demeanour betray your illustrious lineage. It is fortunate for you that you have crossed my path. I am a Knight-errant and my employment is to visit all parts of the world in quest of adventure, to right the wrong, relieve injured innocence and punish oppression. I take you under my protection, and should your enemies come ten thousand strong and attempt to take you captive I, single-handed, will put them to flight. I will myself escort you to the inn where it so happens that I too am lodging. This my squire will ride with you. He is an ignorant, garrulous fellow, but well-meaning, and he will obey your commands as if they were my own. I will ride a little behind you so that if I see an army approaching I can attack it and you will be able to escape with this beauteous maiden to a place of safety.'

Catalina jumped up behind her husband and with the squire accompanying them they set out once more. He told them that his master was as mad as a hatter, to which conclusion his remarks had already led them, but added that for all that he was a good and worthy man.

'And when the fit is not on him, poor gentleman, he can talk better sense in an hour than any sane man can talk in a month of Sundays.'

They reached the inn. A group of people were sitting on benches at the door; they gave the two travellers a glance of curiosity, but otherwise took no notice of them. They appeared sunk in a lethargy of gloom. The fat little man tumbled off his ass and called the landlord, but when he came and Diego asked for a room he told him in a surly tone that there wasn't an unoccupied bed in the place. A troupe of actors had arrived the day before to give a performance at a neighbouring castle where its lord, a grandee of Spain, was celebrating the marriage of his son and heir. The people on the benches, evidently the actors of whom he spoke, stared at the young couple with a somewhat hostile indifference.

'But you must find us something, mine host,' said Diego. 'We have ridden far and can ride no further.'

'I tell you, I have no room, Señor. They are sleeping in the kitchen, they are sleeping in the stables.'

The knight now rode up.

'What is this I hear?' he cried. 'You refuse to harbour these gentlefolk? Churlish fellow. Under pain of incurring my displeasure I command you to provide them with a decent lodging.'

'The inn is full,' the landlord shouted.

'Then let them have my room.'

'That they can have if it is your wish, Sir Knight, but where will you sleep?'

'I shall not sleep,' he answered grandly. 'I shall keep guard. This is their wedding-day and the most solemn occasion of a maiden's life. The apostle has taught that it is better to marry than burn. The end of marriage is not to satisfy the lusts of the flesh, but to effect the procreation of children, and for that purpose the blushing bride is called upon to abandon her natural modesty and in the arms of her lawful husband sacrifice the priceless pearl of her virginity. It is a duty of my calling not only to guard the privacy of the nuptial couch from the intrusion of the enemies who pursue these noble creatures with their malignity but also to prevent the horse-play with which the vulgar are apt on these occasions to exercise their humour.'

This speech covered Catalina with confusion, but whether from shame or modesty is uncertain.

In the Spain of that day innkeepers provided only lodging and the traveller had to bring his food with him. But on this occasion the great lord had sent the actors by his steward a kid and a hunk of pork; and the knight's squire by methods of his own had acquired two brace of partridges; so that the company could look forward to a more sumptuous repast than usual, for their evening meal ordinarily consisted of no more than bread and garlic with sometimes a piece of cheese. The innkeeper announced that it would be ready in half an hour and the knight with elaborate courtesy asked the newly-married couple to do him the honour of being his guests. He told his squire to remove his belongings and conduct the bride and bridegroom to the chamber where in due course they would solemnize the sacred rites. The bedrooms were up a flight of stairs and the doors opened on to a gallery round the courtyard. When they had repaired as best they could the disorder of their toilet Diego and Catalina went down again to get a breath of the cool evening air. The actors were sitting as they had left them. They seemed a sullen lot, on edge, and when they spoke to one another it was with bitterness. Presently the knight joined them. He had removed his armour and now wore a pair of breeches and a doublet of chamois leather, stained with the rust of his breastplate, leggings and shoes. His trusty sword hung by his side from a belt of wolf's skin.

The landlord called them in and they sat down to supper. The knight, putting Catalina on one side of him and Diego on the other, took the head of the table.

'And where, pray, is Master Alonso?' he asked, looking round. 'Has he not been told that supper is ready?'

'He will not come,' said a middle-aged woman who played duennas, wicked stepmothers and widowed queens and was also the wardrobe-mistress. 'He says he has no heart to eat.'

'An empty stomach only makes misfortune doubly hard to bear. Go and fetch him. Tell him that I shall look upon it as a grave discourtesy to my honoured guests if he deprives me of the pleasure of his company. We shall not eat till he comes.'

'Go and fetch him, Mateo,' said the wardrobe-mistress.

A skinny little man with a long nose and a big loose mouth got up and went out. The wardrobe-mistress sighed.

'It is a sad business,' she said, 'but as you wisely remark, Sir Knight, going without one's supper will not help it.'

'If you will not think me impertinent,' said Catalina, 'I should like to ask you what the trouble is.'

They were only too glad to tell her, for it was very much on their minds. The company belonged to Alonso Fuentes, who also wrote many of the plays they acted, and his wife Luisa was his leading woman. Early that morning she had run away with the leading man and taken with her all the cash she could lay hands on. It was a catastrophe. For Luisa Fuentes had been a great attraction and they were well aware that it was she that had brought the money into the box-office. Alonso was in despair. He had not only lost a wife, but an actress and a source of income. It was enough to upset any man. Now their tongues were loosened. The men reviled the perfidy of women and wondered how such a fine creature could throw herself away on the indifferent actor their leading man had been. The women on the other hand asked how any woman could be expected to stay with a bald fat man like Alonso when she had the chance of a handsome young fellow like Juanito Azuria. The conversation was interrupted by the appearance of the abandoned husband. He was small and plump, no longer young, with the rubber face of the actor of many parts. He sat down morosely and a great dish of olla podrida was set on the table.

'I have come as a compliment to you, Sir Knight,' he said. 'This is my last meal on earth, for after supper I have every intention of hanging myself.'

'I must insist on your waiting till tomorrow,' answered

the knight gravely. 'This gentleman and his lady whom you see on either side of me were married this morning and I cannot allow their first night to be disturbed by such an unseemly incident as you suggest.'

'I do not care a fig for this gentleman and his lady. I am going to hang myself.'

The knight sprang to his feet and drew his sword.

'If you do not swear to me by all the saints that you will not hang yourself tonight I will cut you into a thousand pieces with my sword.'

Fortunately the sturdy little squire was standing behind his master to wait on him.

'Have no fear, Señor,' he said. 'Alonso will not hang himself tonight because he has to give a performance tomorrow, and once an actor always an actor. He won't disappoint his public. If he will reflect for a moment he will remember that it's a long lane that has no turning, what can't be cured must be endured and every cloud has a silver lining.'

'Stop prattling your pointless proverbs,' said the knight angrily, but he sheathed his sword and sat down. 'It is not becoming to make so much of a misadventure that has happened to many a better man than this Alonso. With a little thought I could give both from Holy Writ and from profane history the names of many great men whose wives have made cuckolds of their husbands; but at the moment the only ones that occur to me are King Arthur whose wife Guinevere betrayed him for Sir Lancelot and King Mark whose wife Iseult deceived him with Sir Tristram of Lyonesse.'

'It is not the injury to my honour that has driven me to desperation, Sir Knight,' said the actor and playwright, 'but the loss both of the money and the two most important members of my company. We have to play tomorrow, and the sum that has been promised me would to some extent compensate me financially, but how can I give a performance without actors?'

'I could very well play the part of Don Ferdinand,' said the skinny fellow who had gone to fetch Alonso.

'You?' cried the actor-manager scornfully. 'How could you with your horse face and your shrill voice play the part of a gallant, audacious, headstrong and passionate prince? No, that is a part *I* could play, but who is going to take the part of the lovely Dorotea?'

'I know the lines,' said the wardrobe-mistress. 'It is true that I am not so young as I was . . .'

'Very true,' Alonso interrupted, 'and I beg to remind you that Dorotea is an innocent virgin of unsurpassed beauty and your mature figure suggests that you may at any moment give birth to a litter of pigs.'

'Is is possible that you are referring to *Truth with Zeal even Heaven can Move*?' asked Catalina, who had been following the conversation with attention.

'It is,' said Alonso, not without surprise. 'But how did you know?'

'It is one of my uncle's favourite plays. We used to read it together. He often said that Dorotea's speech when she indignantly rejects the dishonourable advances of Don Ferdinand is equal to anything that the great Lope de Vega has written.'

'Do you know it?'

'By heart.'

She began to recite, but then, noticing that the company were watching her with curiosity, was seized with shyness and, faltering, stopped.

'Go on, go on,' cried the actor.

She blushed, smiled, and plucking up her courage started again and spoke the long tirade to its end with so much grace, pathos and sincerity that they were all amazed. Several indeed were moved to tears.

'Saved,' cried Alonso. 'You shall play Dorotea with me tomorrow and I will play Don Ferdinand.'

'How could I?' she said in a fright. 'I should die. I have never acted. It is impossible. I should be struck dumb.'

'Your youth and beauty will make up for any deficiences. I will help you. Listen, fair one, you alone can save us. If you refuse we cannot play and there is no money to pay for our lodging in this inn and for our food. We shall be reduced to begging our bread in the streets.'

Then the knight put in his word.

'I can understand, gracious lady, that your modesty makes you hesitate to expose yourself on the stage to the gaze of a company of strangers and it would be unbecoming of you to do so without the permission of the lord your husband.' For the knight had made up his mind that the young couple were of high degree and nothing they said could persuade him to the contrary. 'But remember that it is the part of a noble nature to succour the distressed and relieve the necessities of the needy.'

The rest of the company joined their entreaties to those of Alonso Fuentes and in the end Catalina agreed, with Diego's willing consent, to rehearse the play and if the rest thought she acquitted herself with credit to risk a performance; so after supper the table was pushed to one side and the rehearsal begun. She had a good memory and she had recited the scenes in which Dorotea appeared often enough with Domingo to be tolerably sure of her words. At first she was nervous, but the encouragement of the players helped her, and presently, losing herself in the part, she lost her self-consciousness. She profited then by the lessons she had received from her uncle and spoke her lines with point and sincerity. She did remarkably well and Alonso was confident that with another rehearsal next morning she would be competent to appear before an audience. She was flushed and happy and looked so beautiful that he felt certain her inexperience would pass unnoticed.

'Go to bed, children,' he said to his company, 'and sleep in comfort. Our troubles are at an end.'

But now that they were relieved of their anxieties they were much too excited to do this and so, calling for wine, settled down to make a night of it. The knight, comfortably seated in a chair, had watched the rehearsal with a critical eye. Now, rising somewhat stiffly to his feet, he called the duenna aside.

'Lead the fair Catalina to the nuptial chamber,' he said, 'and since she has no mother to tell her what on this grave occasion it behoves her to know, it is your part to explain to her in terms that will not offend her modesty the ordeal to which as an obedient wife it will be her duty to submit. You must in short prepare her for the mysteries of love which as an innocent virgin she must be unacquainted with.'

The duenna blinked, but promised to do her best.

'Meanwhile,' the knight went on, 'I will explain to the young lord, her husband, that he must restrain his natural impetuosity, for the aversion a virtuous female must feel for the intimacies of sexual congress can only be overcome by patience. The depravity of the times is such that I cannot suppose he has maintained his innocence to this day.'

'Saving your presence, Sir Knight,' said the duenna, 'it is better that the man should not be entirely without experience in the act of love, for in this no less than in the arts and handicrafts practice makes perfect.'

'That is a matter on which I will not venture an opinion, madam. Suffice it to say that after a decent interval I will myself conduct the bridegroom to the threshold of the nuptial chamber and then, after donning my armour, mount guard on the balcony so that the marriage may be consummated in a style fitting the distinction of the parties concerned.'

He dismissed the duenna and called Diego.

'You are now entering upon a state,' he began, 'in which few conduct themselves in such a way as to attain happiness themselves or bring happiness to their partners in life; and the circumstances of your marriage are of a nature that makes it incumbent upon me to give you the advice which otherwise would have been given you by your noble father.' The knight then proceeded to speak to the young man on the lines that he had indicated to the duenna and finished as follows: 'I do not condemn the necessary pleasures of the body, which refresh it in its exhaustion and hinder it from being importunate; but food and drink, and still more, sexual congress are no more than assuagements provided for the body lest the work of the soul be impeded. Yet the love that is sanctioned by marriage has its touch of upward striving, and in so far as it has this leads the souls of the young towards the Good. In the chaste love that has drawn you to this maiden there cannot but be in you a desire for such immortality as lies within mortal reach and, when you clasp her to your heart, through your own kinship with the beautiful, you will sow in beauty and thus sow towards eternity. For the eternal and the beautiful are one.'

Diego listened to this harangue with the politeness natural to him, but with a wandering attention, for he was impatient to be with Catalina. The knight took him by the hand and led him to what he was pleased to call the nuptial chamber; then, summoning his squire, he resumed his martial equipment and spent the night, tramping up and down, occupied with thoughts of the unapproachable object of his own devotion.

32

Early next morning they rehearsed the play again and then carriages arrived to take them to the Duke's castle. The knight and Diego mounted their horses and the squire his ass and set forth. But at the last moment Catalina's heart failed her, and crying that she could never face the ordeal of appearing before an audience, she begged Alonso to let her stay behind; he flew into a passion and telling her it was now too late to withdraw bundled her into a carriage and seated himself beside her. She was in a flood of tears, but with the duenna to help him, he managed presently to calm her and by the time they arrived she was sufficiently composed. The players were honourably received and by the Duke's instructions suitably entertained, but word had reached him of the knight's extravagances, and thinking his conversation would divert his guests, he begged him to favour the Duchess and himself with his company at dinner. A stage had been erected in the courtyard and when the gentry had eaten their fill the actors were summoned to give their performance. The distinguished audience were not a little amused by Alonso in the part of a gay seducer, for it was not one that his appearance made plausible; but they were charmed by Catalina's grace, the music of her voice and the elegance of her delivery, and when the play was over paid her many fine compliments. The knight had given them his own romantic version of the young couple's elopement and this naturally increased their interest. The Duchess sent for them and all were astounded by their beauty, the modesty of their demeanour and their gallant bearing. The Duchess gave Catalina a gold chain and the Duke, not to be outdone, took a ring off his finger and gave it to Diego. Alonso was richly rewarded and the company, tired but happy, returned to the inn. Shortly afterwards the knight and his squire rode up. He dismounted somewhat stiffly and taking Catalina by the hand added his compliments to those she had already received.

'You have come in the nick of time, Sir Knight,' said Alonso, 'to hear me make a proposition to these young people.' He turned to Catalina. 'I invite you to join my troupe.'

'Me?' said Catalina astounded.

'Though you still have everything to learn, you have gifts that it would be a sin to waste. You do not know how to act. You say your lines as you would say them in real life. That is futile. The stage does not deal with truth, but with verisimilitude, and it is only by artifice that the actor can be natural. Your gestures want amplitude and you have yet to acquire authority. The good actor even by his silence dominates his audience. If you will place yourself in my hands I will make you the greatest actress in Spain.'

'Your suggestion is such a surprise to me that I can hardly believe you mean it. I am a married woman and my husband and I are on our way to Seville where we have the assurance of honest occupation.'

Alonso Fuentes had caught the look she gave Diego and now with a smile turned to him.

'You have good looks, young fellow, and a fine presence. There is no reason why with experience you should not be able to make yourself useful in suitable parts.'

The applause that had rewarded her performance and the compliments she had received had excited Catalina and she was not a little flattered by this unexpected offer; but she saw that her husband was displeased by he casual way in which Alonso proposed to include him in the arrangement and so hastened to say:

'He can sing like an angel.'

'All the better. There are few plays in which there is not a song or two to enliven the proceedings. Well, what do you say? The opportunity I offer you is surely more alluring than the occupation, honest perhaps, but certainly modest, that awaits you in Seville.'

During this time the knight had sat silent, listening, but now he spoke.

'The proposition that Master Alonso has put before you is one that should not be hastily rejected, for consider: you are pursued by the rage of your outraged parents and they will stop at nothing to snatch you from one another's arms. But time assuages wrath and the day will come when your respective parents will lament your loss and regret that from ambition or greed they wished you to contract distasteful alliances. You will be restored not only to their love but to the rank and station to which your high birth entitles you. But till this happens you will be wise to remain in concealment, and how better can you be better concealed than in a troupe of actors? Now must you think that you demean yourself by treading the boards. They who write plays and they who act them deserve our love and esteem, for they serve the good of the commonwealth. They set before our eyes a lively representation of human life and show us what we are and what we ought to be. They ridicule the vices and foibles of the times and give praise where praise is due, to honour, virtue and beauty. The playwrights improve our minds by their wit and wisdom and the actors refine our manners by the grace of their demeanour and the dignity of their carriage.'

He went on for some time in this strain and all were amazed that a man so crazy you couldn't account for his actions should yet express himself with such good sense.

'And let us not forget,' he ended, 'that just such a comedy as we see played on the stage of a theatre is played on the stage of the world. We are all actors in a play. To some it is allotted to play kings or prelates, to others merchants, soldiers or husbandmen, and each should see that he acts the part given to him; but to select it belongs to a greater power.'

'What do you think, beloved?' asked Catalina, with her most charming smile. 'As the knight so truly says, it is not an offer to be lightly rejected.'

She had in point of fact by now made up her mind to accept it, but she well knew that men like to think they decide matters for themselves.

'You will not only be helping me in my difficult situation,' said Alonso, 'but you will be benefiting yourselves, for you will visit with me the most famous cities of Spain.'

Diego's eyes sparkled. He could not but see that this would be vastly more amusing than to sit for twelve hours a day on a tailor's bench.

'I've always wanted to see the world,' he smiled.

'And so you shall, my sweet,' said Catalina. 'Master Alonso, we will gladly join your troupe.'

'And you shall be a great actress.'

'*Olé, olé!*' cried the other members of the company.

Alonso called for wine and they drank to the health of their new comrades.

33

Next day, having courteously taken leave of the knight, the strolling players started off for the neighbouring town of Manzanares, where a fair was being held and where consequently they were confident of finding a good audience. Alonso had hired mules for the actors to ride and to carry the chests that contained their clothes and costumes. Catalina and Diego went on the horse Doña Beatriz had given them. Including Master Alonso himself and Diego there were now seven men in the company, and besides the duenna and Catalina there was a boy to play second women's parts. He was also what is now called a barker, and when they reached a town where they wanted to play, while Alonso went to see the mayor to obtain permission, he walked the streets, beating a drum, and announced to all and sundry that the celebrated troupe of Alonso Fuentes would give a performance of the magnificent, witty and immortal play So and So.

Since at that time there were no theatres in Spain plays were given in courtyards where the windows and balconies of the surrounding houses could serve as boxes for the nobility and gentry. The ceiling was the blue heaven except in the height of summer, when awnings against the sun were drawn from roof to roof. In front of the stage were a few benches and round the courtyard others, arranged stepwise, for the respectable middle class. The common people stood on the bare ground, the men in front and the women, squeezed together in a boarded-off space, behind. Partly for fear of fire and partly for morality's sake the performance took place in the afternoon. The scenery consisted of a single backcloth, and change of scene was indicated by the players' words.

The elopement of Alonso's wife with the leading man had caused him to change his route, and when they had played at Manzanares he set forth with his company for Seville, where he knew he would be able to engage an actor for the parts which his own age and appearance prevented him from playing himself. They went first to Ciudad Real, a rich city, and from there to Valdepeñas; they made the ascent of the Sierra Morena and entered Andalusia by the rocky defile called the Puerto de Despeñaperros. They crossed the Guadalquivir and at last reached Cordova, where they played for a week; then, after following for a while the noble river, they came to Carmona, where they gave one performance, and finally reached Seville. Master Alonso engaged the actor he wanted and they settled down for a month. After that they took to the road again. It was a hard life. The inns they slept in were miserable and the beds so bad and filthy that, tired though they were and exhausted by the heat of summer or chilled to the bone by the cold of winter, they often preferred to sleep on the floor. They were bitten by fleas, stung by mosquitoes, tormented by bugs and vexed by lice. When they were playing they rose at dawn to study their parts. They rehearsed from nine till twelve, dined and went to the theatre; they left it at seven; and then, however weary, if they were wanted by persons of consequence, the mayor, a judge, a nobleman who was giving a party, off they had to go and give another performance.

Alonso Fuentes was a slave-driver and as soon as he

discovered that Catalina was skilful with her needle and Diego no mean tailor he set them, whenever they were not otherwise occupied, to making or altering the costumes needed for the repertory, which consisted of eighteen plays. It did not take him long to find out that Diego, notwithstanding his good looks and his self-assurance, would never be much of an actor, so he contented himself with letting him sing the songs with which the plays were interspersed, for his voice was pleasing, and giving him small parts. But on the other hand he took pains to make an actress of Catalina. He knew his business and had a lively sense for theatrical effect; she was an apt pupil and a quick study, so that under his tuition, which was intensive and sometimes brutal, she ceased in time to be a clever amateur and became a competent professional. Alonso was rewarded for his trouble, for she found favour with the public and brought prosperity for the company. He enlarged his troupe and extended his repertory. Among others he engaged a young actress called Rosalia Vazquez, partly to console himself for the loss of his wife and partly to play seconds, for the boy who had been used to play them had by then lost his treble voice and was starting to shave. Moreover Catalina had first one baby and then another, so that it was necessary to have a good enough actress to replace her when childbirth for a period kept her out of the bill.

Thus three happy, strenuous years passed. By then Catalina had learnt all that Alonso Fuentes could teach her, and with two young children to take care of she began to find it irksome to be constantly on the move. Her beauty and her talent had attracted the attention of influential persons and more than one had suggested that she and Diego should form their own company and establish themselves in Madrid. Some in their admiration for her gifts went so far as to offer financial assistance. Now Alonso Fuentes was not only manager, director and actor, but also author, and every year, mostly during Lent when play-acting was prohibited, he turned out two or three plays. It had not escaped Catalina's notice that in the plays he wrote presumably to show *her* off to best advantage the parts he wrote Rosalia Vazquez tended to become more and more substantial. In his last the parts had been of almost equal length and only Catalina's greater talent had enabled her to make it appear the more important. When she expressed her displeasure, which she did not hesitate to do, Alonso shrugged his shoulders and laughed.

'My dear,' he said, 'when you sleep with a woman you have to keep her in a good humour.'

This, though obviously true, was unsatisfactory. Catalina was no prude, but it seemed to her only just that a respectably married woman should have better parts than one who was no more than a baggage.

'Things can't go on like this,' she told Diego.

And he agreed they couldn't. The notion of having a company of her own was tempting, but she was well aware of the difficulties she and Diego would have to cope with. Catalina was greatly loved in the company and she was pretty sure that several of the members would be glad to go to Madrid with her. With sufficient funds she could engage other actors there, buy the necessary costumes and acquire a number of plays. But Madrid audiences were well known to be hard to please: she would need the influence of her friends as well as their money. Diego was all for making the venture, but she knew that, dissatisfied with the small parts alotted to him by Alonso, he would, as manager, look upon it as his right to cast himself for whatever roles took his fancy. Though she loved him as passionately as ever she was not convinced that he was competent to play the leading parts he hankered after, and she guessed that she would have to exercise a great deal of tact to persuade him to engage a well-known actor to play them. She hesitated. They talked and talked, and could not arrive at a decision; then, one day, Catalina conceived the bright idea of sending for Domingo Perez and asking for his advice. He had been an actor himself, he was a playwright, and if they finally decided to go into management for themselves they might put on one or two of his plays and he would certainly be able to put them in touch with authors. Diego approved, so she wrote to him. She had already written three or four times, first to tell him that she was married, well and happy, and then to announce the birth of her children; but knowing how bitterly it would grieve her mother, she had thought it better not to say that she and Diego were becoming strolling players. She asked him now, but without giving any particular reason, to visit them at Segovia. They were spending Lent there, partly because it happened to be Alonso's native city, but chiefly because his company had been engaged to play a religious drama in the Cathedral at Easter and it was not in rehearsal. It was Alonso's latest play and he had chosen the life of Mary Magdalen as his subject.

34

Domingo, always glad of a jaunt, no sooner received Catalina's letter than he hired him a horse, packed food and a couple of shirts in the saddlebags and set out. He was pleased on his arrival at Segovia to find Catalina with her husband and children installed in a decent lodging, and delighted to see that she was even more beautiful than before. She was then nineteen. Success, happiness and maternity had combined to give her self-confidence and a certain dignity, but also a tender voluptuousness that was vastly alluring. Her face had lost its appealing childishness, but had gained perfection of line. Her figure was as slender as ever and she moved with an enchanting grace. She was a woman now, a very young woman certainly, but a woman of character, sure of herself and conscious of her beauty.

'You look prosperous enough, my dear,' he said. 'What do you do for a living?'

'Oh, we'll come to that later,' said Catalina. 'First tell me how my mother is and how is everyone at Castel Rodriguez and what happened after we ran away and how is Doña Beatriz.'

'One thing at a time, child,' he smiled. 'And remember I have come a long way and I am thirsty.'

'Run to Rodrigo's and get a bottle of wine, dear,' said Catalina, and Domingo smiled when he saw her dive into some recess of her petticoats and taking out a purse give Diego a few coins.

'I shan't be a minute,' said Diego as he went out.

'I see that you are prudent, sweetheart,' grinned Domingo.

'It didn't take me long to discover that men can't be trusted with money, and if a man has no money he can't get into mischief,' she laughed. 'But now answer my questions.'

'Your mother is in good health, she sends you her love, her piety is exemplary and it is doubtless for that reason that the Prioress gives her a pension so that she is no longer obliged to work.'

This he said with a twinkle in his eye and Catalina laughed again. Her laughter was so frank and at the same time so musical that Domingo in his poetic way likened it to the purling of water in a mountain stream.

'There was quite a commotion in Castel Rodriguez after you disappeared,' he went on. 'My poor child, no one had a good word to say for you any more and your wretched mother was in despair. It was not till the nun Doña Ana came and told her that the Prioress proposed to come to her assistance pecuniarily that she was able to console herself for your abandoned behaviour. For ten days people talked of nothing else. The nuns were horrified that after

209

all the kindness Doña Beatriz had shown you, after the great favour she was prepared to confer on you, you should have put such an affront on her. The principal persons of the city went to the convent to offer her proper expressions of sympathy, but she was evidently so upset that she refused to receive them. She did, however, consent to see Don Manuel, but what passed between them is unknown; the lay sister who waits upon her heard their voices raised in anger, but though she did her best she could not hear a word they said, and shortly afterwards Don Manuel left the city. I would have written to tell you all this long ago if you had given me an address.'

'It was impossible to do that. You see, we were moving from place to place and I never knew where we should be going next till we were starting to go.'

'Why were you doing that?'

'Can't you guess? How often have you told me of the days when you wandered over Spain under the burning sun of summer, in the bitter cold of winter, barefoot, not to save your boots but because you had worn out your only pair, and with but one shirt to your back.'

'God in heaven, you're not strolling players?'

'My poor uncle, I am leading woman in the celebrated company of Alonso Fuentes and Diego sings and dances and is a much better actor than Alonso will allow.'

'Why didn't you tell me sooner?' cried Domingo. 'I would have brought half a dozen plays with me.'

At this moment Diego returned with the wine and while Domingo drank Catalina told him how it had come about that she and Diego had become actors.

'And everyone agrees,' she finished, 'that I am now the greatest actress in Spain. Is it true, Diego of my soul, or is it not?'

'I would cut the throat of any man who ventured to deny it.'

'There can be no doubt that I am wasting my talent in the provinces.'

'I have been telling the girl that our place is Madrid,' said Diego. 'Alonso is jealous of me and will not give me the parts in which I can distinguish myself.'

It will be seen that neither suffered from that false modesty which may well prove a bane to the artist. They proceeded then to tell Domingo what was on their minds. He was a prudent man and when they had finished said that he was not prepared to advise them one way or the other till he had seen them act.

'Come to rehearsal tomorrow,' said Catalina. 'I am playing Mary Magdalen in Alonso's new play.'

'Are you pleased with your part?'

She shrugged her shoulders.

'Not altogether. It's well enough at the beginning, but it falls off in the last act. I don't appear in the last three scenes at all. I've told Alonso that as the play is about me I should be on at the end, but he says he must follow Holy Writ. The fact is, the poor man has no imagination.'

Diego took Domingo to the tavern to which Alonso Fuentes and other members of his troupe were in the habit of going and introduced him not only as Catalina's uncle, but also as at one time an actor and now a playwright. Alonso received him with civility and the elderly scrivener quickly gained the good graces of the company by his wit, his good humour and his stories of the hardships in the old days of a strolling player's life. Alonso consented to his attending a rehearsal and he went next day.

He was amazed by the naturalness of Catalina's delivery, the eloquence of her gestures and the grace of her movements. Alonso had taught her well. She had an ear for verse and a lovely voice. She had gaiety and pathos. She had sincerity. She had power. It was astonishing that in three years she had learnt so completely the technique of her art. She seemed incapable of uttering a false note. And her native gifts, her acquired skill, the self-control she had learnt by experience, were all wonderfully enhanced by her great beauty.

When the rehearsal was over Domingo kissed her on both cheeks.

'Dearest one, you are very nearly as good an actress as you think you are.'

She flung her arms round his neck.

'Oh, uncle, uncle, who would have thought when I was a child and we used to recite those scenes of Lope de Vega's that the day would come when people would fight to gain admission to see me play? And you have only seen me rehearse. Wait till you have seen me with an audience.'

Diego was playing John, the Beloved Disciple, and the part was small. He was good to look at, but colourless. When there was an opportunity Domingo asked Alonso what he thought of him.

'He has a good appearance, but he'll never be an actor. I only let him play to please Lina. If only actors and actresses wouldn't marry one another! It is that that makes the life of a manager a burden.'

This did not prevent Domingo from advising Catalina and Diego to have no fear, but to leave Alonso and set up for themselves in Madrid. During the twenty-four hours he had been with them he had discovered that Catalina had good sense, and he was confident that she would not jeopardize her own success by letting Diego play parts that he could not do justice to. He felt sure that somehow or other she would arrange matters to their mutual satisfaction.

But it was not only his desire to see his niece and her husband that had led Domingo to undertake the somewhat arduous journey from Castel Rodriguez to Segovia; he hoped too to see his old friend Blasco de Valero. He was curious to know how he fared in his exalted station. So, for the next few days while Catalina and Diego were busy with their rehearsals, he wandered about the city and in one way and another, with his pleasant gift for social intercourse, managed to scrape acquaintance with a good many people. From them he learnt that the mass of the population looked upon their bishop with veneration. They were impressed by his piety and the austerity of his life. News of the miraculous events at Castel Rodriguez had reached them and filled them with wonder and awe. But Domingo learnt also that he had aroused the hostility of his chapter and of the city clergy. He had been shocked by the looseness of their lives and the negligence with which many of them performed their religious duties. With zeal but with little discretion he started upon a passionate campaign of reform. He had no mercy on those who would not mend their ways and as at Valencia was no respecter of persons. The clergy, with very few exceptions, bitterly resented his harsh intolerance and employed every method their subtlety could devise to hamper his activities. Those who dared were openly defiant, the rest contented themselves with passive resistance. The people approved his strictness, justified by his own virtue, and did what was in their power to support him. There had been in consequence unfortunate occurrences and the authorities had been obliged to intervene. He had brought not peace to the city, but a sword.

Domingo had arrived at Segovia at the beginning of Holy Week and he knew that during that period the duties of his office would prevent the Bishop from receiving him, so it was not till the following Tuesday that he presented himself at the episcopal palace. It was an imposing, but severe building with a granite façade. Domingo gave his name to a porter and after waiting some time was led up a flight of stone stairs, through cold, lofty rooms, sparsely furnished, and hung with pictures, dark and gloomy, of religious subjects; but the room into which he was at length shown was no larger than a cell. Its only furniture was a writing-table and two high-backed chairs. On the wall hung the black cross of the

Dominicans. The Bishop rose and took Domingo in his arms and warmly embraced him.

'I thought we should never meet again, brother,' he said with an affectionate cordiality that surprised Domingo. 'What has brought you to this city?'

'I am a restless fellow. I love to wander.'

The Bishop, dressed as ever in the habit of his order, had aged. He was emaciated, his lined face was haggard, and his eyes had lost their fire. But notwithstanding these signs of decrepitude there was in his aspect something luminous, a change in his expression that Domingo was conscious of, but failed to interpret; and he could not tell why, it recalled to his mind the afterglow when the sun has set at last after the long hours of a summer day. The Bishop asked him to sit.

'How long have you been here, Domingo?'

'A week.'

'And you have waited all this time to see me? That was not kind.'

'I did not wish to intrude on you before, but I have seen you more than once. In the processions of Holy Week and in the Cathedral on Good Friday and again at Easter, and at the play.'

'I have a horror of these performances they give in the House of God. In other cities of Spain they give them on the feasts of the Church in the plaza, and I do not disapprove them since they edify the people, but Aragon is tenacious of its old customs and notwithstanding my protests the chapter has insisted that they should be held in the Cathedral as has been done from time immemorial. I attended only because it was a duty of my office.'

'The play was reverent, dear Blasco; there was nothing in it to offend you.'

A frown darkened the Bishop's brow.

'When I came here I found a terrible laxity in those whose charge it is to fulfil their function and give a good example to the people. Some of the canons of the

Cathedral had not been near the city for years, too many of the secular clergy were living in open immorality, in the convents the rule was not obeyed with proper rigour and the Inquisition had renounced its vigilance. I was determined to put a stop to these abuses, but I was met with hatred, malice and obstruction. I have succeeded in restoring a certain decency, but I wanted them to behave well for the love of God: if they behave less scandalously than they did it is only for fear of me.'

'I have heard something of this in the city,' said Domingo. 'I have heard even that efforts have been made to remove you.'

'If they only knew how happy I should have been had they succeeded!'

'But you have this consolation, dear friend, the people love you and reverence you.'

'Poor creatures, they little know how unworthy I am of their reverence.'

'They honour you for the asceticism of your life and your charity to the poor. They have heard of the miracle of Castel Rodriguez. They took upon you as a saint, brother, and who am I to blame them?'

'Do not mock me, Domingo.'

'Ah, dear friend, I have too much affection for you ever to do that.'

'It would not be the first time,' the Bishop said with a smile in which there was something of pathos. 'During these three years I have thought often of our last meeting and of what you said to me. At the time I paid little attention to it. It seemed to me no more than the paradoxical, cynical talk in which you have always indulged. But since I came here, in the loneliness of this palace, your words have haunted me. I have been tortured by doubt. I have asked myself if it is possible that my brother the baker, modestly doing his duty in his lowly station has served God better than I who with prayer and mortification have given my life to His service. If so, whatever others think, whatever I myself thought for one rapt moment, it was not I that performed the miracle, but Martin.'

The Bishop was silent. He looked at Domingo with searching eyes.

'Speak,' he said. 'Speak and by the love you once bore me tell me the truth.'

'What is it you want me to tell you?'

'You were certain then that it was my brother who was chosen to effect the cure of that poor girl. Are you certain of it now?'

'As certain as I was then.'

'Then why, why was I granted the sign that dispelled my trembling hesitations? Why did the Blessed Virgin use words that might so easily give rise to a mistaken interpretation?'

His distress was so great that Domingo, as once before, was moved to pity. He wanted to console him, but scrupled to say what was in his mind. He knew Don Blasco's inflexible integrity, and it was far from improbable that his sense of duty would oblige him to report to the Holy Office things said, even by a friend, that seemed to require examination. The old seminarist had no wish to be a martyr to his opinions.

'You are a difficult man to speak freely to, my dear,' he said. 'I do not want to say anything that may be an offence to you.'

'Say on, say on,' cried the Bishop with something like impatience.

'Do you remember that on the occasion to which you just referred I told you how surprising it seemed to me that among the infinite attributes that men ascribe to God they have never thought of including common sense? But there is another that has even more completely escaped their attention, and yet, if a creature may venture to judge of these things, it is of even greater value.

Omniscience would be incomplete without it and compassion repellent. A sense of humour.'

The Bishop gave a slight start, seemed about to speak, but stopped himself.

'Do I shock you, brother?' Domingo asked seriously, but with a faint twinkle in his eyes. 'Laughter is not the least precious of the gifts that God has granted us. It lightens our burdens in this hard world and enables us to bear many of our troubles with fortitude. Why should we deny a sense of humour to God? Is it irreverent to suppose that He laughs lightly within Himself when He speaks in riddles so that men, deceived in their interpretation, may learn a salutary lesson?'

'You put things strangely, Domingo, and yet I do not know that there is anything in what you say that a good Christian need reject.'

'You are changed, brother. Is it possible that in your old age you have learned tolerance?'

The Bishop gave Domingo a quick, inquiring glance, as though, surprised by his remark, he wondered what he meant; and then looked down at the bare stone floor. He seemed to be plunged in thought. After a while he raised his eyes and gazed at Domingo as though he wanted to speak, yet could not quite manage it.

'A very strange thing has happened to me,' he said at last, 'and I have dared to tell no one of it. Perhaps providence sent you here today so that I might tell you, for you, my poor Domingo, are the only man in the world that I can call my friend.'

Once more he hesitated. Domingo, watching him intently, waited.

'As bishop of the diocese I was obliged to attend the play they gave in my Cathedral; someone told me it dealt with the life of St Mary Magdalen; but I was not obliged to listen or to look. I abstracted my mind. I prayed. But my soul was weary and disquieted. So it has been ever since I came to this city. I have suffered from distraction

217

and dissipation of spirit. I have felt myself despoiled of everything, so that I could neither love nor hope. My understanding has been in darkness, my will dry, and I have found no comfort in the things of God. I prayed, as I had never prayed before, that He might see fit to succour me in my deep affliction. I was oblivious of my surroundings. I was alone with my sorrow. Suddenly I was startled by a cry and I remembered where I was. It was a cry, a cry so moving, so pregnant with significance that against my will I was compelled to listen. Then I remembered that they were acting a play. I do not know what had passed before, but, listening then, I understood that it had reached the point where Mary Magdalen and Mary the mother of James, bringing spices, came to the sepulchre where Joseph of Arimathæa had laid the body of Jesus and found the stone rolled away. And they entered in and found not the body of Jesus. And as they stood there perplexed a traveller, a follower of Jesus, came to them and Mary Magdalen told him what she and the other Mary had seen. And then, because he knew nothing of the terrible events that had taken place, she told him of the capture, the trial and the shameful death of the Son of God. The description was so vivid, the words so well chosen, the verse so mellifluous that even if I had not wanted I should have been forced to listen.'

Domingo, holding his breath, leant forward eagerly.

'Ah, how right was our great emperor Charles when he said that Spanish was the only language in which to address God. The speech rolled on line after line. There was a fiery indignation in the voice of that woman who played the Magdalen when she told of the betrayal of Jesus, and a fierce anger seized the multitude in the Cathedral and they shouted curses on the traitor; her voice was broken with anguish when she told how they had scourged Our Lord, and the people gasped with horror; but when she told of the agony on the cross they beat their breasts and sobbed aloud. The pain in that golden voice, the heartrending pathos in it, were such that the tears ran down my cheeks. There was a tumult in my soul. My spirit quivered as the leaves of a tree quiver with a sudden flurry of wind. I felt something strange was about to happen to me and I was afraid. I raised my downcast eyes and gazed at the speaker of those lovely, cruel words. She was of a beauty I have never seen on earth. It was no woman who stood there, wringing her hands, with streaming eyes, it was no actress, but an angel from heaven. And as I looked, spell-bound, on a sudden a ray of light transfixed the dark night in which I had so long languished; it entered my heart and I was rapt in ecstasy. It was a pain so great that I thought I should die, but at the same time it was a delight so sweet; and I felt myself released from the body and a stranger to the flesh. At that happy moment I tasted of the wonderful peace that passeth all understanding, I drank of the wisdom of God and I knew His secrets. I felt myself filled with all good and emptied of all evil. I cannot describe that bliss. I have no words to tell what I saw and felt and knew. I possessed God and in possessing Him possessed everything.'

The Bishop sank back in his chair and his face shone with the recollection of his great experience.

'The desires of hope no longer afflict my soul. It is satisfied in its union with God, so far as in this life it is possible, and it has now nothing of this world to hope for and nothing spiritual to desire. I have written a letter in which I have begged His Majesty to allow me to resign my ecclesiastical offices and dignities so that I may retire to a convent of my order and spend the remainder of my life in prayer and contemplation.'

Domingo could contain himself no longer.

'Blasco, Blasco, the girl who took the part of Mary Magdalen is my niece, Catalina Perez. When she ran away from Castel Rodriguez she joined the troupe of Alonso Fuentes.'

The Bishop stared at him with amazement. He was dumbfounded. Then with a sweetness Domingo had never seen on his face before he smiled.

'Truly the ways of God are inscrutable; how strange are those He has chosen to lead me to my goal! Through her He wounded me and through her He healed me. Blessed be the mother that bore her, and all glory to God, for when she spoke those heavenly words she was inspired by Him. I shall remember her in my grateful prayers to my dying day.'

At that moment Friar Antonio, still Don Blasco's secretary, came into the room. He gave Domingo a glance, but gave no indication that he recognized him; he went up to the Bishop and whispered in his ear. The Bishop sighed.

'Very well, I'll see him.' Then to Domingo: 'I'm afraid I must ask you to leave me, dear friend, but I shall see you again.'

'I'm afraid not. I leave for Castel Rodriguez tomorrow.'

'I am sorry.'

Domingo knelt down to kiss the Bishop's ring, but he raised him to his feet and kissed him on the cheek.

35

Domingo walked back to his lodging, a skinny, elderly man, with great pouches under his eyes, a reddish nose and not a dozen teeth in his head, an old reprobate in a patched cassock green with age and spotted with wine-stains and the droppings of food; but he walked on air. He would then, as he had once told the Bishop, have changed places neither with emperor nor pope. He talked to himself aloud and waved his arms, so that passersby thought he was drunk: and drunk he was, though not with wine.

'The magic of art,' he chuckled gaily. 'Art also can work its miracles. *Et ego in Arcadia natus.*'

For it was he, the despised playwright, the dissolute scapegoat, who had written those lines that had so profoundly affected the Bishop. It had come about after this wise:

Catalina had not been dissatisfied with the first two acts of the play Alonso had written for her. He had made her the mistress of Pontius Pilate and in the first act she appeared gorgeously arrayed, proud in her sinful life, extravagant, wilful, luxurious and mercenary. Her conversion took place in the second act, and there was a good scene when, knowing that Jesus sat at meat at a Pharisee's house, she brought an alabaster box of ointment, washed His feet and anointed them with the ointment. The last act took place on the third day after the Crucifixion. There was a scene in which Pilate's wife reproached him for having allowed a blameless man to be put to death, another in which the disciples mourned the death of their master, and still another in which Judas Iscariot went to the Elders of the Temple and flung down the thirty pieces of silver they had given him to betray Jesus; but Mary of Magdala did not appear till she and Mary the mother of James went to the sepulchre and found it empty. The play ended with the two disciples walking to Emmaus, when they were joined by a stranger whom they later discovered to be the risen Christ.

Catalina had not been a leading lady for three years for nothing, and when she discovered that she had so little to do in the last act she was incensed. She reproached Alonso with acrimony.

'But what can I do?' he cried. 'You are on the stage almost all the time during the first two acts. In the third there is no occasion for you to appear except in that one scene.'

'But this is out of the question. Is the play about me or

221

is it not about me? The audience will want to see me and if they don't it will simply ruin your play.'

'But, my dear child, this isn't a play in which I can give free rein to my imagination. I must stick to the facts.'

'I don't deny it, but you are an author. If you know your business you ought to be able to think of something that will bring me in. Now, for instance, there is no reason why I shouldn't come on in the scene between Pontius Pilate and his wife. You have only to exercise a little ingenuity.'

Alonso began to get angry.

'But, my poor Lina, you were Pilate's mistress. Is it likely that you would be in his palace and present when he is having an intimate conversation with his wife?'

'I don't see why not. I could have had a scene with Pilate's wife first and it is on account of what I have said to her that she reproaches Pilate.'

'I never heard of anything so ridiculous. If you had attempted to approach Pilate's wife he would have had you whipped.'

'Not when I threw myself on my knees, and begged her pardon for my past wickedness. I would be so moving that it would be impossible for her not to relent.'

'No, no, no,' he shouted.

'Then why shouldn't I be with the two disciples when they go to Emmaus? I, being a woman, would know who the stranger was, and he, knowing that I had recognized him, would put his finger to his lips to bid me be silent.'

'I will tell you why you can't be with the two disciples when they go to Emmaus,' Alonso bellowed. 'Because you weren't, or it would have said so in the Gospel. And when I want you to write my plays for me I'll tell you.'

They parted that day with some heat. Catalina was much inclined to refuse to play the part, but she knew that Alonso would then give it to Rosalia, and in the first two acts it was so fat that she might very well make a success in it.

'If he had been writing the part for Rosalia he would never have dared give her so little to do in the last act,' she told Diego.

'There is no doubt about it,' said he, 'he is not treating you well. He doesn't appreciate you.'

'I have felt that ever since Rosalia joined the company.'

Catalina, full of her grievances, told her troubles to Domingo before he had even seen the play. He was properly sympathetic and asked to read it. The actors had only their parts and Alonso alone had a full manuscript which he kept jealously to himself in case one of them should copy it and sell it to another manager.

'Alonso is as vain as a peacock,' said Catalina. 'Go to him after rehearsal tomorrow and tell him his play is so wonderful you will never have a moment's peace till you read it. He won't be able to resist letting you have it.'

This accordingly Domingo did and Alonso, flattered, but taking no risks, gave him the manuscript on his promising to return it in two hours. When Domingo had read it he went for a walk and on his return made a suggestion to Catalina. She threw herself in his arms and kissed him.

'Uncle of my soul, you are a genius.'

'But like many another, unrecognized,' he grinned. 'Now listen, child, don't whisper to a living soul, not even to Diego, what I have in mind, and at rehearsal play with all the talent you have. Be as sweet and as friendly to Alonso as though you had never had a difference of opinion, and he will think you are willing to let bygones be bygones. You will rehearse so beautifully that he will be pleased with you.'

They were to have two rehearsals on the Saturday and a final one early on the morning of Easter Day. On the Saturday, after the first rehearsal, when the company were separating for dinner, Catalina detained Alonso. She addressed him in her most cajoling way.

'You have written a beautiful play, my Alonso. The more I know it, the more astonishing do I find your genius. Even the great Lope de Vega does not excel you. You are a great, a very great poet.'

Alonso beamed.

'I will admit that I am not entirely dissatisfied with it,' he said.

'There is only one little thing that I find amiss.'

Alonso started and frowned, for authors are such that a pennyweight of reservation put in the balance will far, far outweigh a pound of praise. But Catalina, at her most endearing, paid no attention.

'The longer I rehearse the more convinced I am that you have made a mistake in not letting me appear to more advantage in the third act.'

Alonso gave a gesture of irritation.

'We have gone into all that before. I have told you a dozen times that there is no place in the act where you can possibly be brought in.'

'And you were right, you were a thousand times right, but listen to me. I am an actress and I feel it from the bottom of my heart that when I stand at the sepulchre of our risen Lord I should have more to say than you have given me.'

'And what, pray?' he asked indignantly.

'Well, it has occurred to me that it would be wonderfully effective if I narrated the story of Our Lord's betrayal, trial, crucifixion and death. It would only need a hundred lines.'

'And who do you suppose will listen to a speech of a hundred lines at that stage of the play?'

'Everyone if I say them,' replied Catalina. 'I shall have the audience beating their breasts, crying out and weeping. The dramatist that you are must see how striking such a scene would be just at that moment.'

'It's out of the question,' he cried impatiently. 'We play tomorrow. How could I write a hundred lines and rehearse them in that time? How could you learn them?'

Catalina smiled sweetly.

'Well, it so happens that my uncle and I have talked it over and he was inspired by the beauty of your play to write the lines which he agreed with me the scene demanded. And I have learnt them by heart.'

'You?' cried the manager to Domingo.

'The eloquence of your play excited me,' said he, 'and I was as one possessed, so that it was as if you were holding my pen.'

Alonso looked from one to the other. Catalina saw that he was undecided and she took his hand.

'Won't you let me say the speech to you, and then if you don't like it, I promise to say no more about it. Oh, Alonso, do me this favour. I know how much I owe to you, but do not forget that I have never spared myself to please you.'

'Say this cursed speech then,' he cried angrily, 'and let me get to my dinner.'

He sat down and with a scowl on his face prepared to listen. Catalina began. In three years her voice had gained in richness and she had a wonderful command over its modulations. The emotions proper to the narrative chased one another across her mobile face and she expressed apprehension, dismay, fear, indignation, horror, pain, anguish, grief without exaggeration; but with a telling truth. Angry though he was Alonso was too competent a dramatist not to realize very soon that the lines were well written and that as she spoke them, with the eloquence of her gestures, with the touching quality of her voice, an audience would be held. He leant forward and clasped his hands. Presently he listened spell-bound. Then, such was her pathos, so moving her sincerity, he could no longer control himself, he began to sob and great heavy tears coursed down his cheeks. She finished and he wiped his eyes with his sleeve. He saw that Domingo was crying too.

'Well?' said Catalina with a smile of triumph.

With the last line she had stepped out of her part and

was as cool as if she had been reciting the alphabet. Alonso shrugged his shoulders. He tried to make his tone gruff and business-like.

'The lines are tolerable for an amateur. We will rehearse the scene this afternoon and if I am satisfied with it you shall play it tomorrow.'

'Soul of my heart, I adore you,' said Catalina.

'I shall have trouble with Rosalia,' he muttered gloomily.

The scene was rehearsed and played, with the effect on the Bishop of which the reader has been apprised. But this was not its only effect. Rosalia violently upbraided Alonso for his partiality to Catalina and he was obliged to make a great many promises to pacify her, some of which he knew he would have to keep; this irked him, but for another reason he was none too pleased with what had happened, since many persons, naturally thinking he had written them, singled out Domingo's hundred lines for special praise and told him that for language and versification they excelled anything else in the play. When Diego very indiscreetly let it be known by whom in fact they had been written Alonso was deeply mortified. In retaliation he told friends that Catalina was nothing like the actress she thought she was and without him to coach her would prove to have had very little talent. This was no sooner repeated to Catalina than she decided finally to take the step she had been contemplating. As she said to Diego, a woman has her self-respect to think of. She severed her connection with the ungrateful manager and with her husband and her children set out for Madrid.

36

Don Blasco, his resignation having been accepted, retired to a remote convent of his order with the intention of devoting the last of his years to the contemplation which

Aristotle declared was the end of life and which the mystics have thought precious in the eyes of God. He refused to accept favours or privileges which, owing to the exalted positions he had held, were offered him, and insisted on having a cell similar to those occupied by the other friars and being in every way treated as they were. After some years his strength failed, and though he appeared to suffer from no definite disease it was plain to those about him that it would be no long time before he was released from the burden of the flesh. Friar Antonio, who had accompanied him to the convent, and the Prior begged him to relinquish the more severe of his austerities, but he refused; he persisted in observing the rule of the order in its utmost rigour and only consented to abstain from attending matins in the sharp cold of night when the Prior, exercising his authority, owing to Friar Blasco's increasing frailty forbade him to do so. Gradually he became so weak that he was obliged to spend much of his day in bed, but he seemed to be in no imminent danger of death. His life was like a flickering candle that any breath of wind may extinguish, but, protected from it, still continues wanly to give light. The end was sudden.

One morning Friar Antonio, after he had performed his religious duties, went to his old master's cell to see how he was. It was winter and snow was on the ground. The cell was bitterly cold. He was surprised to find him flushed, with bright eyes, and he rejoiced because he looked more like himself than for many weeks. The hope arose in his heart that the sick man had taken a turn for the better and might even then be restored to health. He uttered a short mental prayer of thanksgiving.

'You have a good colour this morning, Señor,' he said, for Friar Blasco had long since desired him never again to address him, as though he were still a bishop. 'I haven't seen you look so well for days.'

'I am very well. I have just seen the Greek Demetrios.'

Friar Antonio repressed a start, for of course he knew

that Demetrios had years before, as was only fitting, perished at the stake.

'In a dream, Señor?'

'No, no. He came through that door and stood by the side of my bed and spoke to me. He was exactly as he had always been, in that same threadbare robe he wore, and with the same benignity in his expression. I recognized him at once.'

'It was a devil, my lord,' cried Friar Antonio, forgetting the injunction his master had laid upon him. 'You drove him from you?'

Friar Blasco smiled.

'That would have been discourteous, my son. I do not think it was a devil. It was Demetrios himself.'

'But he is in hell suffering the just punishment of his damnable heresy.'

'That is what I thought, but it is not so.'

Friar Antonio listened with increasing dismay. It was likely enough that Don Blasco had had an infernal vision. Pedro of Alcantara and Mother Teresa of Jesus had often had encounters with devils and Mother Teresa kept Holy Water by her for the express purpose of driving them away by throwing it at them. But his old master's attitude was so horrifying that he could only hope he was not in his right mind.

'I asked him how he fared and he said well. When I told him what cruel pain I had suffered because he was in hell he laughed lightly and told me that before ever the flames had consumed his body his soul flew to the meadow at the parting of the ways and thence, because he had lived in holiness and truth, Rhadamanthus sent him to the Islands of the Blest. And there he found Socrates, surrounded as always by young men of a comely aspect, asking and answering questions; and he saw Plato and Aristotle walking together in amicable converse as though there were no longer any difference of opinion between them; but Æschylus and Sophocles were gently chiding Euripides for having ruined the drama by his innovations. And many more, too numerous to mention.'

Friar Antonio listened with consternation. It was evident that his old and revered friend was delirious. That was the meaning of those flushed cheeks and shining eyes. He did not know what he was saying, but the poor honest creature was thankful that there was no one but himself to hear. He trembled when he considered what the other friars would think if they heard him whom they regarded as saint utter words that were almost blasphemous. He racked his brains for something to say, but in his agitation could think of nothing.

'And when he had talked for some time in the friendly way in which we used to talk long ago in Valencia the cock crew and he said that he must leave me.'

Friar Antonio thought it better to humour the invalid.

'And did he say why he had come to see you?' he faltered.

'I asked him. He said he had come to bid me farewell since after this we should never meet again. "For tomorrow," he said, "when it is no longer night and not yet day, when you can just see the shape of your hand, your soul will be released from your body." '

'That proves that it was an evil spirit that visited you, my lord,' cried Friar Antonio. 'The doctor says that you have no mortal illness and this morning you are better than you have been for many days. Let me give you the medicine he has sent and the barber shall bleed you.'

'I will take no more medicine and I will not be bled. Why are you so eager to detain me when my soul yearns to escape from the prison in which it has dwelt for so long? Go, tell the dear Prior that I wish to make my confession and receive the Blessed Sacrament. For tomorrow, I tell you, when I can just see the shape of my hand I shall depart this life.'

'It was a dream, Señor,' cried the poor friar distraught. 'I beseech you to believe it was a dream.'

Don Blasco made a sound which in anyone else you would have called a titter.

'Don't talk nonsense, son,' he said. 'It was no more a dream than it is a dream that I am talking to you now. It was no more a dream than that this life, with its sin and sorrow, its anguished questions and mysterious secrets, is a dream, a dream from which we shall awake to life eternal which alone is real. Now go and do what I tell you.'

Friar Antonio, with a sigh, turned and went. Don Blasco made his confession and received the Blessed Sacrament. After the last rites of the Church had been celebrated he bade farewell to the friars with whom he had lived for several years and gave them his blessing. By this time the day was far advanced. He desired then to be left alone, but Friar Antonio besought him so earnestly to be allowed to stay with him that with a gentle smile he consented on the condition that he should remain silent. Don Blasco lay on his back on the hard pallet with its thin mattress which the rule of the order required, covered, notwithstanding the piercing cold, by no more than one light blanket. Now and then he dozed. Friar Antonio was deeply distressed. The certainty that possessed Don Blasco had shaken him and he was by then more than half assured that death would come as his saintly master had said. The hours passed. The cell was dimly lit by a single taper and every now and then Friar Antonio snuffed it. The bell rang for matins. He was startled to hear Don Blasco break the long silence.

'Go, my son. You may not neglect your religious duties on my account.'

'I cannot leave you now, my lord,' the friar answered.

'Go. I shall still be here when you come back.'

The long habit of obedience was effectual and he did as he was told. When he returned Don Blasco had fallen asleep and for a moment Friar Antonio thought that he was dead. But he was breathing peacefully and a faint hope arose in the friar's breast that he might thus be strengthened and perhaps even recover. He knelt down by the bed and prayed. The taper spluttered and went out. It was black night. The hours passed. At last Don Blasco made a slight movement. Friar Antonio in the heavy darkness could not see, but he had the intuition that his dear friend was feeling for the crucifix which hung by a cord round his neck. He placed it in the old man's hands, but when he wanted to withdraw his own he felt it lightly held. A sob broke from his throat. In all those years this was the first time that Don Blasco had given him a sign of affection. He tried to look into the eyes that once had shone with so intense a light, and though he could not see, he knew that they were open. He looked down at the hand that gently clasped his over the crucifix and as he looked he was aware that the blackness of night was not so impenetrable; he looked, and was on a sudden terrifyingly aware of the shape of an emaciated hand. A faint sigh escaped Don Blasco's lips and something, he did not know what, told the friar that his beloved master was dead. He burst into passionate weeping.

Don Manuel had by this time been for some years living in Madrid. Doña Beatriz had refused to go on with the plan she had been the first to propose that he should marry her niece, the Marquesa de Caranera; and since it had not been found possible to find her a suitable husband this widowed lady entered religion and was now sub-prioress of the Carmelite convent at Castel Rodriguez. Don Manuel felt that Doña Beatriz had treated him very badly, for the plot they had hatched between them had miscarried through no fault of his, but he was not one to cry over spilt milk; he went to Madrid and when he allowed his matrimonial designs and the extent of his fortune to be known it was not long before he was able to make a very satisfactory match. He attached himself to the Duke of Lerma, the favourite of King Philip III, and by the exercise of subservience, flattery, duplicity, unscrupulousness and venality finally succeeded in becoming highly respected. But his ambition was great. Don Blasco left behind him a saintly reputation, and Don Manuel was shrewd enough to see that it would increase his consequence if his brother were beatified, and the repute of his family (for heaven had blessed his union with two fine sons) if he were eventually canonized. He set about collecting the necessary evidence. No one could deny that the one-time Bishop of Segovia had been a man of exemplary piety; there were many witnesses who were prepared to declare that fragments of his habit worn round the neck had prevented them from catching the pox (great and small), and the various miraculous happenings at Castel Rodriguez were well authenticated; but the examining body at Rome demanded proof of two major miracles performed by the candidate's remains after death and this could in no manner be provided. The lawyers Don Manuel had engaged were honest men, for though a rogue himself he was too astute to employ rogues, and they told him that though it might be possible to get his brother beatified the chance of having his name included in the roll of saints was small. He flew into a passion when they told him this and accused them of incompetence, but on consideration came to the conclusion that they were in all probability right. He had already spent a good deal on the preliminary inquiry and saw no object in throwing good money after bad. After thinking it over in cold blood therefore, he decided that the beatification of his brother would not be worth the expense, and so contented himself with having the Bishop's remains transferred to the Collegiate Church at Castel Rodriguez, where he built a sumptuous monument, if not to perpetuate his memory of his father's eldest son, at least to manifest his own munificence.

In passing it may possibly be of interest to mention that Martin de Valero, the third of Don Juan's sons, sank back into the obscurity from which the exciting visit of his two distinguished brothers had momentarily raised him. He continued to bake bread, and that is all that can said of him. It never even occurred to him, as indeed it never occurred to his fellow citizens, that on one occasion the Blessed Virgin had vouchsafed him the power to work a miracle.

Doña Beatriz lived to a great age in full possession of her faculties and might have lived longer but for an untoward accident. On hearing of the beatification of her old enemy Mother Teresa of Jesus she had taken to her bed for three days, but when in 1622 she received news of her canonization she was seized with such rage that she had a stroke. She recovered consciousness, but on one side was completely paralysed, and it was evident that her end was near. Fear was an emotion unknown to her and she remained calm and collected. She sent for her favourite friar to hear her confession, after which she gathered her nuns around her and gave them suitable counsel for their future conduct. A few hours later she asked for the Blessed Sacrament. The priest was again sent for. She asked pardon for her sins and begged the weeping nuns to pray for her. For some time she lay in silence. Suddenly in a loud voice she said:

'A woman of very humble origins.'

The nuns who heard her thought she referred to herself; and knowing that there flowed in her veins the royal blood of Castile and that her mother was of the illustrious house of Braganza, were deeply moved by this mark of humility. But her niece, the sub-prioress, knew better. She knew that the words referred to the rebellious nun who was become Saint Teresa of Avila. They were the last uttered by Doña Beatriz Henriquez y Braganza, in religion Beatriz de Santo Domingo. The Holy Oils were administered and shortly afterwards she died.

37

When Catalina arrived in Madrid she still had the gold
Doña Beatriz had given her and during the three years on
the road, being a thrifty young woman, she had saved
money, so that, notwithstanding Diego's somewhat
extravagant tastes, she could look forward to the immediate future without anxiety. They called upon the patrons
who had promised their influence and money to help
them to get started, and finding them prepared to fulfil
their promises were able to form a company. They were
successful even beyond their hopes and Catalina became
the rage of the town. Many fine gentlemen sought to
obtain her favours, but though she accepted their presents
with gratitude they received in return no more than a
smile of her beautiful eyes and a pretty speech. She
became then as greatly admired for her virtue as for her
beauty and genius. She sent for Domingo and he came
with a dozen plays in his wallet. She produced two of
them. They were hissed off the stage, and, as was the
way then, the audience showed its displeasure by shrill
whistles, cat-calls and scurrilous abuse. Domingo, angry
and humiliated, went home and shortly afterwards died,
but whether of drink or disappointment has never been
definitely settled. Some years later Catalina, by then
acknowledged to be the greatest actress in Spain, sure of
her hold on the public, determined, out of piety to his
memory, to put on yet another of Domingo's plays; but,
so that it should not suffer from the ill success of the
first two, anonymously. It pleased; and indeed was so
good that it was ascribed to the great Lope de Vega, and
though he denied its authorship no one believed him, and
in fact it has been printed among his works to this day;

so poor Domingo was robbed even of that will-o'-the-wisp which has consoled many an author for the neglect of his contemporaries, posthumous fame.

Diego, notwithstanding his comely presence and his assurance, never succeeded in being anything but an indifferent actor. Fortunately, however, he proved himself a good business man and an efficient manager, so that with the years they became rich. They had long before agreed that it would be indiscreet to speak of the supernatural occurrences of which Catalina had been the occasion, and so, neither when they were with the strolling players, nor later, did anyone discover that she was in any way connected with events that for a time had been much talked about. Though, as she suspected, no more miracles took place to disturb the course of their married life, Diego was never, as he thought right and proper, master in his own house; but since Catalina was clever enough to let him think he was, he remained satisfied and happy. He was somewhat unfaithful to her, but, knowing that this is what you must expect of men, and so long as his amours were transitory and did not cost too much money, she accepted his infidelities with composure. Indeed it was a very happy marriage. She had six children by him, and being an actress with a conscience, rather than disappoint her public, would keep on playing persecuted virgins and austerely chaste princesses to the last possible moment of her successive pregnancies. She continued to play such parts to an advanced age, and a Dutch traveller who went to Spain in the latter part of the reign of Philip IV has left it on record that though she had grown corpulent and was several times a grandmother, such was her grace, the melody of her lovely voice and the magic of her personality, that before she had been on the stage five minutes you forgot her age and figure and accepted her without question as the passionate girl of sixteen she was representing.

So, with Catalina as it began, ends this strange, almost incredible, but edifying narrative.

25th January, 1947